OUT of PLACE

OUT *of* PLACE

A NOVEL

Joseph Papaleo

BOSTON LITTLE, BROWN AND COMPANY TORONTO

Published simultaneously in Canada
by Little, Brown & Company (Canada) Limited

PRINTED IN THE UNITED STATES OF AMERICA

Acknowledgments

I wish to express my thanks to the following friends who helped particularly in the completion of this book: To Harry Sions and Don Congdon, for going over the manuscript beyond the call of duty. To Bill Kelley, Gene DeWitt, V. T. Thayer and Stan Thayer for talks and letters that helped me find the courage to take the time off. To George and Cathy Martens, who got me moving. To Ira Kapp for helping me get to Naples, and his laws of life. To Eduardo and Carla Caianiello for their loving help in Naples. And to Marion Kraft for letters that kept me going. To the Jordans, who gave me a place to write, with viands and laughter. To Cathy Manson, for help on the manuscript. To Lois and Doug Smiley, for years of great help. And to Lois, whose trust in the writing remained steady for twenty years. For all these I feel more gratitude than an acknowledgment can show.

PART ONE

THE CHILDREN were stolen at noon. Annie Santoro received a call from the headmistress at school and drove over to see her. A man had come to take the children home early; he had identified himself to the teacher as their father; the children had greeted him and kissed him. Only after they had gone did someone recall having heard that the father no longer lived at home.

"Yes, that's right," Annie said to the commanding dry face while she looked about, ready to run. "My husband left —"

"You see, that's why we like to hear about conditions in the family. Just to *know*."

Annie was not listening. "We didn't want it to get around too much, about being separated. My husband — well — he came from Italy, it's only a few years ago. It's so hard to explain about him."

The headmistress was unclear about the facts. "Is he all there?" Her eyes went up, and Annie understood the question.

"Oh yes, there's no trouble. He works steady. But we had a lot of disagreement." Annie left these words to explain it all. "And then he just said he was going back to Italy. What could *I* do? If a man talks like that."

3

The headmistress sighed and offered to call the police. "Oh no," Annie said. "I'll check home first. I have to see my father."

She left quickly; the school was intimidating to her, anyway. Her brother Eugene had arranged for the kids to go there because they were bright and the public school was boring and filling up with all kinds of garbage. But Annie was never comfortable with the stiff, smiling, whispering people of the new school, and Carlo resented the school because he had never been consulted about it.

At home she found a cable from Carlo: he had taken the children to Italy. Her hands began to shake; she fell across the couch. In a few minutes she jumped up and called her father, then her brothers. Within the hour they were all in her kitchen.

Since her brother Eugene was the most important and had friends in government, Annie appealed to him first. He called his law office and ordered them to file extradition papers.

"Will that get them back?" she asked. Annie had always been the sheltered one, the only Santoro who had not been to college and who had been educated at home on pieces of information relevant to Naples before the wars. Yet Annie lived in the suburbs, too, although a little closer to the old Italian neighborhood than Eugene, whose financial success allowed him to live farther north.

"I'll call Washington after we get the whole story clear," Eugene said. "Phil Di Maris is sitting in Congress this session, you know." Eugene was breathing power. He noticed his father, sitting silent. "What do you think, Pop?"

Frank Santoro had had five years of retirement, and it sat on him like mange on a lion. His large button factories belonged

4

to someone else now: he had only his three bank accounts, his house, securities, his wife, children and grandchildren. "That man was not crazy," he said. "Unless you want to say going back to live in that shit, over there. *That* is crazy. But what happened that he would do a thing like this *now?*"

"Oh, there was the *nut* in him," Anna said. "Why kid ourselves now. You all know the way I met him. There's no time for all that right now. And you all of you know how you treated him. You couldn't stand the sight of him —"

"What I thought about him and what I did for him does not make him rob children." Mr. Santoro was adamant already. "I brought him in my house from the boat, from nothing, like a son. Gave him rooms. I financed him a bakery. Is that punishment?"

Anna looked at them with the strength of her loss. "Maybe not so much *you*, Pop. But the others. He was the *cafon'*. The greenhorn with the wrong shirt on. Oh, come on, let's face it."

Mrs. Santoro shook her head at the word for vulgar and cheap and prepared to speak, but Eugene started first. "Now just wait a minute, Annie. At first he was a little square, but then —"

"All right, then how about your club. There's plenty of parties we didn't get invited. Like every single *one*." Annie's hands closed like claws on the rungs of a kitchen chair.

"That's a club I couldn't invite my whole family to. It's just not a family club. It's for golfers and tennis. Carlo didn't play any games like that. You know that —"

"Name *one* wedding, *one* birthday, Annie — one thing like that where you didn't get invited." Her sister-in-law Emma, whose hair was blonde and whose youth annoyed Annie any-

5

way, had interrupted Gene. She was the most guilty about Carlo Marinara and therefore she could not wait. She had called him "the dumb wop" in her own living room to her husband Angelo, who had lowered his head in acceptance. But she had never been cruel to Carlo, as Annie's face tried to tell her now, and she would not be exposed.

"All right. Then let's forget it. We're sisters and brothers here." Annie looked at them all, *her* army, at least for now, in the pleasure of emergencies. "Can I make you something?" She had coffee ready and served it; then she brought out cookies and a frozen Sara Lee cake for those who took pound cake, some hard biscuits for her mother and father, lemonade with artificial sweetener for Emma, and a small glass of whiskey for Angelo, her younger brother.

The activity was helpful, bringing them together for something graver than plans: now they would prepare the future, which always gives the feeling of strength.

The talk went on: men's voices. The sun started down, and they separated to go home for a while. Eugene would not have Annie stay alone. "You'll have to come with one of us," he said. "Go with Pop and Mom."

"How about the phone? There might be calls to here."

"I'll get them put through to my house. And from now on, we'll meet at Pop's house."

Next morning Annie heard it announced on the white radio in her father's kitchen and began to cry, as if hearing of a death; yet she felt strangely important. The calls started coming at nine, offering help and words, but the voices seemed really to be congratulating her at becoming a celebrity. *Some* bad news was like a celebration, especially if no one was hurt.

Annie's sewing club — she had not seen them in four months — had met and were making a quilt. Two local merchants sent food baskets. The school authorities phoned, offering to visit and discuss the scholastic future of the children, the various possibilities for making up the work, and the police arrived at noon, interrupting old Santoro's lunch.

They were detectives, dressed in Robert Hall suits, and they wanted to know about Marinara, the kidnapper, silly things no one had ever asked about Carlo: did he carry a gun; did he have other known *relationships,* meaning women on the side; did he have political friends (the man from the Federal police); and did he ever act strangely or require mental treatment? Finally, did he have rages of temper that were observed by others?

Santoro began to emit dry burps at this last question. He was particular about the lunch hour and filled up with air if his food was delayed, and he could barely have lived without frequent rages of temper. That these now could be contrary to American laws was a shock his stomach reacted to, breaking his polite silence. He held his waist while Annie answered the questions, never too honestly, thank God, because he already resented these men more than his stupid son-in-law.

Was he associated with anyone in Italy? Annie did not understand this properly and began to recall names of cousins, which the men wrote down in their books, asking two or three times about spellings.

Santoro said: "These people are the cousins in our family," and the men smiled and calmed him with disinterest: they were only getting information.

7

Was the separation legal? Santoro began to tighten his fists; a little sweat formed under his strong mat of gray hair. Annie said no strongly. *Was there a divorce contemplated?*

"No divorce!" Annie said. "I told him no divorce. *We* don't *get* divorced."

She looked at their police faces: they seemed Irish enough to understand. "He just wanted to go back to Italy and live. He couldn't take it here, or something. Like it was too cold. And he wanted the kids, too."

It wasn't enough, but it was all the police would get. They left, empty coffee cups where they had been, squatting on the table where Frank Santoro was about to be served.

Mrs. Santoro had sat behind Annie and rose to deliver the food, shaking her head at the swelling moments: now she believed that the men were saying her daughter's husband was a criminal. But worse than that, he was becoming a growing monster who would make them all public, and she remembered from Naples that when your affairs were known, everyone had the chance to penetrate all your secrets, resulting in the loss of your money and possessions.

A cable from Naples arrived that night; the next morning a phone call came, and Annie spoke to the children, who seemed fine, wanted to speak about the houses on the mountains and the water, but said they missed their mother. Annie became hysterical.

Since everyone else was present, the effect was quick. Santoro would not see his Anna go down this way and decided on action.

"All right!" He got silence. "Someone is going over *now*. Carlino and Joanna will be back here —" he pointed to the kitchen table top — "In five days!"

8

This pleased everyone. "Gene should go," Annie said, and Eugene's wife, Francine, spoke up. "Well, wait a minute. Gene's got a family, too. Even if our kids are away in school. He's got a business and a law practice. He's the least who can afford to go so quick."

"I can take off," Angelo said. As the youngest brother, he was always offering to do what he could not. He was a successful man, one of those who make money but never look important enough to suggest it. When they talk about their money, you suspect they earned it in devious ways, and after a while you forget they have it.

But Angelo's small firm could revolve without him; he was a button specialist, his business an offshoot of his father's large one. Angelo sat on his supply, knowing that he was the man to call for any unusual buttons needed right away.

"Eugene must go," old Santoro said. "He has the law with him."

It was done. Francine avoided their faces; she had borne the burden of Gene's importance, the larger house, the boys in prep school, Eugene in politics and away at meetings, making a mayor, then Phil Di Maris, now in Congress. She could not hold him back without saying that Gene was a little man like everyone else; it would mean that Gene had power only in his words and that the big names he knew were unaffected by his power. Now everyone would see how far his voice could call.

The passport came through in record time; someone had moved. Eugene visited Annie each day, like a doctor, was packed on the fourth, and came in the evening to say good-bye to Annie. "I want you to come to the airport with me," he told her. "We've got to have a few words alone."

9

Annie had been afraid of driving in the city, of the bridges and crowded roads on Long Island. But now she would go. "I'm ready," she said, and went out with him.

They waited at a TWA bar while lines of people passed below, walking to their planes. Annie kept looking around, afraid Gene would miss his plane and suspicious that in some way she might be taken aboard one, stolen away herself.

"I want to ask you one thing," Gene said. He drank down some scotch and looked at Annie's small vermouth, her worn kitchen hands like crust on the bar glass. "And it's this. Do you want Carlo back? Do you want to try again?"

Annie began to nod quickly. "Well, yes, I do. Sure I do. We can work it out. He's my husband, after all." Her hands came up in a gesture, close together, imploring what else in the world was there to do. "Unless —" she dropped her hands to the bar again — "he's gotten crazy or something like that. Unless something maybe snaps inside him when he's over there. You think that's possible?"

"Why do you say that? What is it, Annie? What can you tell me? Now is the time."

Annie looked at him, tall, looking more American than the rest of them. She began to understand Gene's tone; she had only been thinking of something inside Carlo that she had not seen or known, some secret Carlo had had because he was human. "Oh no, Gene. He was all right. In all the time we were married, he was all right. He never did bad things. He was a normal person. But we did have fights. Oh, how we had fights. We fought about Italy and a lot of things. Now don't tell. Even about Poppa. Carlo was a tough guy when the door was closed. And then I used to ask him, what's so wrong about living here? Just tell me what's so bad. Should we go live in some one-horse town where he left — he knew what it is — and you can't even make a living. We all know how it is over there. He told me himself."

"Where did he want to go?"

"Back to Amalfi. Every word out of his mouth was Amalfi this, Amalfi that. So it's pretty. All right, I told him, it's pretty. But here's where we have our house and our *money*. Imagine trying to start a bakery there. He even said you couldn't raise a penny over there; they have a loan plan for the south, but you have to *have* something before you get a loan, a place already. So they wouldn't even loan him money. Oh, they're *sweet* on the other side, I really mean it. Why are all the relatives lining up to get over here?"

Annie turned away, as if to blow out the disgust. Italy, without her having seen it, was the arch-traitor, and she had learned this from her mother and her father and all the others in the Bronx thirty years ago. Gene was drinking again, another scotch. "That's it, Annie? That's really all? What about the things you said at home? About how you said we treated him."

Annie shook her head. "He didn't know. Only *I* had that to chew. Only the school. He didn't like how the kids were changing, getting fresh and snobby. With no manners."

"All right." Gene put his glass down, heard the call for the Rome plane and kissed his sister. "I'll be back in a week. Don't worry."

Annie wiped her eyes; her tears had their own power, and they came to hurt her. She felt an appeal for her husband Carlo: though she must have her children back, she did not want Eugene to take anything from Carlo, to strike him down.

"Buck up, Anna. Come on. You have to drive home. I don't

want to worry about you when I'm up there." Gene took her arm and led her to the glass exit doors and said good-bye.

After he had gone down the silver corridor to his plane, Annie went to the observation roof and watched people climb on board and then the plane scream and start and bounce away. She followed it as it rolled into a line of other planes, all the shapes alike. She began to count: forty, fifty, all in a line, all facing away from her, and lost Gene's plane. Every few minutes one shot up, like a thing coming out of a cannon; after five or six the noise drove her away.

Gene fell asleep as soon as his plane took off; he had not had the time for sleep, had had to work nights, then return to a silent, avoiding Francine who, although she did not cry, acted as if her body had been beaten by him. She was his sacrifice, her silence the refusal he was unable to give them. He had lain on his bed like a sinner on a rough stone, exposed to her possible attack or the ringing of the phone.

He awoke as a stewardess fell against him. The plane was still climbing, had become hot, the tops of heads in front of him in a stiff line, as if locked in. Through the dish-sized window he saw the night close in and fell asleep again, awaking to a rim of dawn: it was the next day over Ireland, though only three hours had passed on his wristwatch, and the stewardesses were dropping aluminum trays on the collapsible tables before the passengers, rushing like busy farmers filling troughs for the animals.

He began to eat because the sight and odors were familiar but soon lost the taste of what went down: the food was hot and soft and seemed to have been sprayed with odor, but it was arranged in geometric portions sunk in its tray cells, and the shapes, once cooled, were not like food.

After they had taken his tray, he watched the sky opening with light and color, and the wings of the plane rising up and down. A voice through static began to call the cities below and passengers jumped up to watch the squares of color that meant the land. Gene looked but could not picture Carlo in that toy picture passing slowly underneath. He looked down at the Alps rising above white clouds and then felt the plane fall away from its calm line, pulling his resistant groin down while he held the seat handles tightly. The plane fell through white streaks of clouds and leaned over the land, showing the wrinkled ocean. Then he was in Rome, on the sunny strip, in a bus, through customs in a line of staring passengers and on a smaller plane to Naples.

There he found a taxi that took him to his hotel room, rented from New York, passing crowded neighborhoods so dense with people that they spilled over onto the streets, were crowded in tiny cars, rushing across from one side to the other, throbbing like a wave that could overrun the taxi. The faces were curious, staring eyes in a brown darkness upon the dusty, crumbling streets or posed against stained houses, once white or yellow. Naples was a poison that would kill him: he had read some State Department advice on diseases, polluted water, waiting hepatitic shellfish, unwashed vegetables and fruits, undulant milk, and now they were all real in the puddles of garbage and the brown, marked people who ignored it all and stared like well-treated prisoners.

In his room he removed his jacket and went to the terrace to look. He saw a square below, with thick brown palm trees he did not expect and quickly moving people he did. The bay was blue and round, like an amplification of the postcards, and Vesuvius was still and purple; on the slopes he saw clusters of white buildings he did not understand and turned away, thinking of himself here, like an expedited package, now finding in the postcard view the machine grinding slower, the pictures for his eyes alone.

It was nostalgia sticking in his throat, but not his own. This was the place of childhood for his parents (almost humiliating to face during the ride through the streets); it had been invoked in kitchens until it was both unreal and real, his mother's thoughts and the excuse for her dissatisfactions. It had been in his child conceptions, heaven at Sunday Mass, seen beyond the window of the *Last Supper* hung on the wall, the azure and unpeopled land.

He went inside and looked at his image in the floor-length mirror. His black moustache was right, pleasing. The darkness around his eyes was Italian, too, and his black, curly hair, touched with gray, and the somber expression made by the long line of his thin lips.

The telephone rang and frightened him. He lifted the receiver and heard the voice of the lawyer Phil Di Maris had contacted from Washington. The man spoke in Italian, which Gene understood, yet he could answer only with English. "Schpeak, schpeak," the man urged him to continue in English. They arranged to meet at supper in the hotel.

Gene let the phone go down, then lay back on the bed. He had never decided for himself about Carlo, had flown on a wing of justice: it was all very clear when they were together back there. Now he was trying to summon the words, to tell Carlo the children were rightfully Annie's. But at home his assertion was automatic with his presence: assemblyman, Knight of Columbus, Chamber of Commerce, member of two clubs, a creature of parts that stretched his length.

His eyes caught the sky again, insistently blue, pink low clouds now along the edge of the city, others white and gray-blue suddenly rising. It called him, and he went to the terrace again. He would go down and try out the town, armed inside his jacket with his passport. Only the words of Francine, like a storm, rose up to say, "I am alone. Remember that. *Your sister's* troubles, but I am the one who will be left alone."

He went in to bathe and came out to dress, finding the shirts Francine had packed. He was smiling; he was just as alone as she, not even in his own home. He walked downstairs absolved of her, as if she were back in the green suitcase among the handkerchiefs, the box of Kleenex for emergencies, the shaving soap can, the new leather scissor kit, the wash and wear shorts, the hills of socks.

In the restaurant he was practically alone. The waiter asked if he were American, then told him of his own twenty years in America. "Why did you come back?" Gene asked, and the man simply stared at him.

After the soup he looked up at the waiter to explain that the taste was like his mother's cooking. The man smiled, nodded a brief bow and returned to the back of the room until called.

The lawyer came in and introduced himself, dismissing the waiter who had led him in. "Tubino, Vincenzo. I am the Napoli representor of the company of Rome you have taken."

Gene offered him a chair, smiling at his bow, the man's discomfort protected by the false respect. "Have some of this soup," Gene said. "It's very very good."

Tubino looked around. "Oh no. For me, nothing. It is early."

Gene saw him looking at the food. "You must have some or I cannot go on."

"Then I understand," Tubino said. "It does no good to the stomach to eat alone. Producing the condition of acid."

The waiter brought him a cloth napkin and took his order. The two men ate together, casting a few words at the food. Towards the end Gene asked about the case, and Tubino nodded but held up his hand while he ate.

"Acid," Gene said, and Tubino nodded.

Gene waited until the table was cleared; with the two small coffee cups and the half-finished green bottle of mineral water, they began. Gene took a large envelope from his pocket. "This is the money for your firm."

Tubino smiled, then lowered his head as if not to stare at the money, but he was waiting for the flush to leave his face, thinking that its color would tell Gene his thought: the madness of paying before the start!

"I want to know where he is, where the children are, and what he's doing. And then, how fast we can get the extradition going. Has your firm been active in Rome?" Gene put the envelope on the tablecloth, and Tubino placed a hand gently into the envelope, as if going under a skirt, counting with his fingers. Then he raised his eyebrows in approval and chewed back the sick, magnanimous desire to suggest that Gene pay later because they trusted him.

Instead, Tubino tried something else. "And tell me, signor Santoro, do you want to *fix* this man?"

"No, no." Gene felt a shock inside him, his own weapons touching himself. "Only get the children back. They go back to the mother. That's all I came for."

"Certainly." Tubino placed the envelope in his pocket.

"And this, too." Gene leaned forward and Tubino looked

steadily at him. "If there is a delay. In extradition. In the proc-
ess." Tubino thought of the corridors of Rome: *If there is a
delay. Blessed Mother, help them.* "I want to know this."
Gene's voice was coming to the end. "How much. How much
to get the children — now — and go back."

"Oh oh oh oh." Tubino shook his right hand. "It will never
go that way. *Mai, mai.* We will conquer with the brain.
Friends of Rome. All in helping of us."

"I'm very serious," Gene said. "I want those children back
home in a week."

"A week." Tubino said it as *wick.* His eyes tried to follow
Gene's tone. "Yes. A week. It must be done." Tubino paused.
"But here, you know, there are papers to get, and papers.
Many officials who must examine the case and read your
papers."

"I understand that machine. The wheels need oil."

"Exactly. Oil. Yes, oils for the wheel of Italy." Tubino was
caught between telling a bit of the truth and being correct.
"Even with the oil, sometimes, more time is taken." He saw
Gene's face, unsatisfied. "But for the infants, we must. Infants
to their mother's bosom must fly, as it is written."

The words were hollow; now Gene began to catch it: the
giant lie he had launched: it was there in Tubino's two-color
eyes, yellow streaks inside the blue. It had been in his tone all
the time, already saying that the children were not as important as that much money, that the large sum had placed
Tubino and his firm on galloping horses to ride down and club
the justice upon the unwaiting Carlo.

"Now let me speak." Tubino sipped half his coffee, pursed
his lips and removed a notebook. "Here. Marinara, Carlo Al-

fonso. Age, thirty-seven. Weight, seventy-six kilograms. Height, one hundred seventy-one centimeters. Service, artillery, the war, Africa. Mother, Eleanora, born Avellino. Married Anna Maria Santoro —" Tubino looked up. "Your sister?"

Gene nodded.

"Married, nineteen hundred fifty-nine. Emigrated to United States. Returned twenty-seven April, with children, Carlo, eleven years, Joanna, nine years. Now residing Amalfi, Via Calvino, seven bis. Living with father, Guglielmo Cosimo, baker. Has applied to Banco di Napoli for a loan, intending to operate a bakery in that city." Tubino closed the book. "Is this our man?"

Gene nodded.

"Did you notice the bank loan?"

"Yes," Gene said. "He is a baker."

"Here then we may begin. We arrange to have certain friends inform this signore that he cannot receive a loan until his records are, shall we say, washed. He will ask, *but what?* And knowledge of his theft will be given him on the spot — if you agree, of course — and this week, when he is at the bank speaking for his loan. We know that he has told everyone his wife died and he is returned with the children. We are ready."

Tubino finished his coffee, and Gene began. "Then I should go down there right away. Tomorrow. Or wait until he has seen the bank?"

Tubino first wiped his mouth. "That is difficult to say. My friend is in the bank. Should you perhaps go down in the morning, prepare with him." He rubbed his right thumb and index finger together. "When the loan is refused, this man is a poor man. He needs the means of life, as we say. Now there is no money for him."

"I'll go down tomorrow morning. I have a car ordered from Hertz —"

"But. If I may offer a word, and this — personal — from Tubino the man. I would tell this. It is impossible to ask a man to give up his flesh and blood."

Gene was nervous, anxious to move. "Then we have to wait for extradition."

Tubino shook his hands. "Wait. Yes, wait. And back to Rome, and then to Consolato and back to Questura and back again to Rome —"

"All right, then what else do we do?"

Tubino smiled, made a quick snatching gesture with his right hand, saw Gene's comprehension, and looked away.

Later, in his room, Gene lay in darkness and remembered the sudden gesture of Tubino. It had startled him, his chest feeling the surge, like a skipped heartbeat. He had wanted to scream, but felt chained into his chair, hearing a sentence given by the judge he had appointed, Tubino, who was now Italy.

In the middle of the night he awoke and found tears on his face, but he could not remember his dream. He went to the terrace and saw that the city was still alive, clusters of young men making noises in the piazza, cars going round the island of palm trees.

Asleep again, he saw a beast, like a wild boar, standing and snorting, with spittle on his lips, and Gene began to run. There was no chase, but when he opened his eyes in the morning, he felt his neck and body wet, as if he had fought. While shaving he noticed that the left sleeve of his pajama jacket was torn, a long tear from the shoulder to the elbow. It frightened him: the impossibility. He returned to the bedroom and saw his suitcase untouched, his jacket and trousers as he had hung them.

He dressed, went downstairs to pay his bill, and met the man from the car rental agency. He drove out of the square, following the green signs to the autostrada, and once past the toll station began to feel relieved at the opening sights of fields and groves of vines and trees and mountains close by.

His mother had always made an occasion of the first mushrooms of the season, cooked with spaghetti, which she called the specialty of Amalfi; and he remembered days in the Bronx, his father's business growing surprisingly large and the family beginning to believe that they were going to have luck, that they would be among the first to leave Lorin Place for a better house, and WESTCHESTER, a word everyone pronounced as if it meant a thorough whitewash, skin and hair becoming lighter.

The sign for the Vesuvius exit came up on the right. Gene thought of going off, to drive to the crater, but he did not have time because of Carlo, stupid, damn Carlo.

GENE KEPT the radio playing loud to fill the empty car and cover the coming of thoughts which were rising as pains, his neck and shoulders stiff in the attitude of driving. The signs led him off the straight highway, down to the town of Vietri. He hesitated on the streets, hit his brake again and again: walkers suddenly stepping into the streets, curves where the road disappeared, little Fiat 500's running close at his side, then in front of him. He was climbing, the road cut into the stone, black, winding, hanging on the green mountains. The water was deeper down, the Gulf sunk into a hole, its mist like smoke of the sun.

At a summit he finally saw a town, stopped the car at a lookout and went to the wall. The surface of the earth was water; he looked back at the cars passing, as if to escape the murderous road: it shrank you or made you feel anxious to increase the danger with speed and prove yourself better than its dangers. He walked back to the car and drove down into the town, parking near the water. An old man in a white captain's cap came to the car and placed a small slip of paper under one of the windshield wipers.

Gene went to the shore and removed his shoes and socks,

walking along holding them in his hands. A woman sitting with a child stared at him and smiled. He looked back at the mountain behind her, then turned to the water. It seemed cool, wanting to be touched, but he was unable to step into it. He stood for a while at the edge. A boat motor broke his reverie, and he looked up to see an outboard reeling by: a blonde girl on the deck turned to him and raised an arm slowly. He waved, then turned back to the main street.

The wind had been disturbing his hair; he brushed it back with his hands, but the sea air had shaken it loose, softened it; he caught his reflection in a shop window and saw curls at the top of his head and at the sides, upon his ears.

He walked along, looking for a barbershop. On a back street he found one, dark and cool, and went through the hanging beads of the entrance.

The barber was alone: he did not comment on the shoes, but stared at Gene's face and greeted him. "Foreigner?" he said in Italian. "French?"

"American," Gene said.

"Rio, Santos, Buenos Aires," the barber said, and walked to his chair.

Gene sat down. "United States," he said, and smiled. "The north of America."

"*Piacere*," the man said, and made the suggestion of a bow with his head stiff.

While the man adjusted the striped sheet Gene saw himself in the mirror. It was a face in shock: something was being done to him, without the touch of a hand.

The barber began to cut his hair. "An early vacation?" the man asked.

"I'm on the way to Amalfi — to see a relative."

22

"Do you have cousins in Maiori? Your face is now familiar."

"My brother-in-law is in Amalfi." Gene watched the barber in the mirror.

"Amalfi, Amalfi. It is all the same here. One is good, the other is good. Whatever your taste. What is your taste —"

Through the window, Gene could see the blue again, coming up from behind a wall. The morning sun had not come round, and though it could not be seen, its light moved like a liquid in the air, throwing scents into the shop.

"I have never been so happy." Gene felt his face flush.

The barber looked down discreetly and paused, dropping his hands. He sensed the embarrassment, the escaped emotion. "It is a sweet day," he said, using the word *dolce*. "One feels perfect on days like this. *If* things have occurred."

"What things?" Gene smiled into the mirror.

The barber returned the smile. "*If* the liver is working. If a woman has been good the last night. Don't you agree, signore?"

"Is there fishing here?" Gene said.

"If you want fish to eat, I will advise a restaurant near this door. There, ask for Lionello. And tell him — tell him you are my brother-in-law. Say Nardone the barber."

Gene stood up and studied his hair, brushing at the sides with his hands.

"I see you are a man who values the beauty of hair," the barber said, and Gene stopped, stepped down to pay and then walked to the door.

"Your shoes."

Gene saw them on the floor and came to get them. "Is there a shop here? To buy sandals."

"Look." The barber went through the beads and Gene followed. "Down there. Sandals, shirts, trousers."

Gene went to the store and bought the sandals, which did not fit his suit. The young woman waiting on him showed it in her look and suggested trousers and a shirt. Gene bought a light blue polo shirt and tight tan slacks. The girl packed his suit and shoes in a large bag and he went to the restaurant, where Lionello believed the lie.

"Sit outside," he said. "And if you permit, I will sit. You are the first — you are actually very early, like an American. They say he eats breakfast at six, with eggs, lard and dried fish. Then lunch before noon, and supper at five. Correct?"

"Some arise late," Gene said, and Lionello smiled: he *knew*. "We have those in every country. God bless them. With their fat pockets full."

Still, Lionello wanted to hear about money, the money that meant dog food in cans, two cars, television in every room, two pairs of luxury shoes for a dollar. Finally, Gene told him the story of the growth of his father's button factories.

"Now," Lionello said. "Here I comprehend. We have a great population, pockets full, or almost full, let us say, according to the color of the skin." He nodded with the wisdom. "Then one has to create a small object, like a button, something that is needed by everyone — yet not excessively necessary so that the government must control it — and make this in great quantity. And one is made."

Gene stopped eating and looked directly at the man: Lionello sat hunched, permanently bent from years of the servile bow, his stomach the only badge of ownership of himself. Gene felt mocked by the tone, but the smooth face was serious. "Then may God bless it." Lionello had caught the irritation in Gene's face.

He left Gene at the table. Gene finished the wine, though he was getting sleepy. Along the street, the Fiats ran to eat, the old man in the parking lot rested on a box and chewed on a loaf of bread. The water was behind him and it set Gene staring: he had lost the day. Wednesday. The Knights would be meeting. Thursday the Chamber of Commerce. Two weeks ago he had been given a Good Citizen plaque by Father Bontempi for twenty year's service to the Boys' Club, but Francine had not said a word when he brought it home. The week before he had been in Greenwich with Tom Regenshaft, whose garden homes were being opposed in court by the old biddies who lived alone and owned more land than they needed.

Lionello came back with a tray of coffee and yellow liqueur. "Sit down," Gene said. "You tell me. How do you get rich in Italy?"

"By being born," Lionello said. "In the right house. That gives you everything." He was smiling.

"Nothing else?"

"I read my newspaper. It comes from Naples to tell me about the miracles. We have had the Economic Miracle here. But until my tourists come down, I have this crowd you see here."

Gene looked back at the room of empty tables and then stood: "I am sorry —" Lionello was still forming words in his head, but he stopped for Gene's guilt.

He shook his head and did not speak; Gene asked for the bill, which was ready in Lionello's hand, paid and was escorted to the street. "Return again after you have seen Amalfi."

Gene walked to the car, found the old man in the cap smiling, paid him, then drove along the main street out of the town and up into hills again, pushing the car's speed until the tires squealed on the curves. Down in Amalfi he stopped in a piazza for directions and found the house on a street too narrow for parking. Beyond it was a small piazza where he parked.

He walked back to the door and pulled a long wire that rang a bell inside. A young woman opened the large red door, greeted him but held back in the shadow of the hallway inside.

"May I speak with Carlo Marinara?" Gene saw her eyes study him, and he looked down at his new Italian clothes. "I have come from America," he said.

"America? Come in." She led him inside and up steps to a sitting room.

"Are the children here?" Gene heard his voice from somewhere.

"Are you related to signor Marinara?"

"His wife's brother."

"Oh. *Piacere. Piacere.* Please sit down." She ran to the door, opened it and called for the children, then came back and stood before him. "I am Elena. I take care of the children for him. He works at the bakery."

"*His* bakery?"

She shook her head. "The bakery where his father makes the bread. Signor Carlo makes the *dolci.*"

"And you live here?" Gene stood up and stepped about the room, circling the large center table. "Is this the dining room?"

"No. This is the sitting room, for after meals." She walked to the door and motioned for him to follow. "Through here, dining room and kitchen." She opened the door for him to look, then shut it. "At the back, the bedrooms."

He noticed her legs as she leaned into the hallway to point. He understood the need of Marinara as a man from the powerful attraction of the legs, tan and yet shining, taut and yet round at the calf. And the rest of her, the breasts too large for innocence already, the face without a line cut in the skin.

He felt also the sour taste for the thief, Carlo, who now had new pleasures Annie could no longer have. This girl, though she was like trading clouds for sun, could not be: no one man could deny the dark, overcast days: they were men's lives, too, and they had to be accepted.

The girl was looking at him. "I will go downstairs to send someone for signor Carlo," she said. "If you will permit."

She left him alone, and he sat down to look at the room. He had already seen it, in films and in life: the high dark carved table covered with lace cloth; brown, tall, stained cabinets; stiff, upright chairs with carved wooden backs, a sideboard with two or three ceramic plates painted with flowers or chickens or nobody's coat of arms. It was the ancestor of the parlor in the Bronx house, the first wealth for Italians, a composite of memory, something the lords had before they had left. Rarely used, it served as ritual, stuffed chairs and couches which could have been replaced by price tags for all the inner proof they served. Westchester had finally dispelled it, there where the parlor became the living-dining-television room, with movable leather hassocks, iron and plastic chairs, foldaway serving tables and thin couches that somersaulted into beds.

The door opened and the children rushed in shouting for Elena. Seeing Gene, they stopped. Some recent, hidden past, which they had succeeded in erasing, came up. They stared at

Gene and became silent. Joanna took a few steps back. "Where have you come from?" she said.

"Why don't you say hello and give your uncle a little kiss first. Come on."

Gene held out his arms and Joanna came first, detecting the offer of love and losing her suspicions. "Hello, Uncle Gene." She kissed his cheek. "How is Aunt Francine? How is Granma and Granpa?"

"Fine, fine." Gene was looking at Carlino. "And how is it here? How's it going?"

"How's Momma?" the boy said.

"She's all right. She's only worried about you and wants to know if you're all getting along OK."

"Oh, we're having a good time," Carlino said, and came close to Gene. "You see, she shouldn't worry. We'll see her soon."

"Yes, why don't we go back to see her soon." Gene watched their faces. "I can take you on a nice jet ride back home."

Carlino smiled. "Poppa got us little blue suitcases, we thought they were clothes or something. But they were full of chocolate bars, from Barton's. The kind with silver paper — guns and cars and little men —"

"And I had a makeup kit in mine. And the lady on the plane gave us blue slippers to wear and after we ate she gave us the fork, knife and spoon." Joanna went towards the door. "I'll go get them, Uncle Gene."

"Not now," Gene said. "Let's just talk until Poppa comes. Carlino? Does everybody call you Carlino?"

"They call us in Italian," the boy said. "I like it better than Carl; they used to call me that in school."

"It's nice to be Italian," Joanna said. "Everybody here is

Italian, and so are we, so we're the whole place. It's nice, Uncle Gene."

"Yes," Gene said. "That's a very true thing. You're a smart little girl, Jo. Tell me about here. Where do you kids sleep?"

"We're at the back." It was Carlino, who now took his hand. "Come on and see it. The ceiling is round. I said it was like the sky and Poppa's going to put up stars. You know, like the real ones, in the same shapes as the sky has."

Joanna took his other hand. "Downstairs is Nonna and Nonno, and Elena is in front."

They started to leave, but Elena came into the room. "Uncle Gene, this is our Elena." Joanna ran away from Gene to embrace Elena, whose loose housedress pressed against her hips. Gene's eyes caught the lines, the features one by one: they moved into his head and began to block his mind, like a curtain.

He watched Elena touch Joanna's face, then respond to Carlino, who came up and hugged her. But again his feelings that enjoyed the love he saw, set off suspicion and anger, now at the mother this young girl had become, painlessly, without the form and the work.

"They were going to show me the bedroom," Gene said.

Carlino ran, but Elena called, and he came back to stand politely at her side. She spoke to him, and he went to the door, opened it for Joanna and then waited for Gene and Elena. "Go," Elena said.

Gene held the door and Elena came through, touching his arm. He smiled at her as she paused, and she went through quickly. "Thank you." She made a half curtsy, and looked at Gene, who stared as he had before.

In the bedroom the children were at the terrace, looking

down at a courtyard, lines of wash above, a few old women seated against the walls, some doing needlework, all of them grandmothers watching children.

"That's your play yard," Gene said.

"But sometimes we go down to the water," Joanna said. "And Peppino takes us in the boat. He's the older brother of Sergio." The child looked up at Elena, who turned away.

Just as they heard footsteps and reacted to them, Marinara was in the doorway. Elena had been standing behind Carlino, and Gene was leaning over the stone rail next to Joanna.

Marinara was still wearing his light white trousers, smock and cap, his baker's uniform. His hands were dusty with flour: there was flour in his moustache. He stared at them and his eyes bulged as he swallowed words he would spit at Gene, who had come to steal.

He wiped his forehead with his arms and pressed his lips together. Then he slowly wiped his right hand on his trousers and reached inside his smock. "Get out of my house," he shouted at Gene. "Or I must take blood."

He was holding a long, thick knife over his head.

Elena screamed; it made Carlo more active: he stepped into the room, looked around at what had already happened to his family. "Go outside," he said to the children, and they ran out.

"Signor Carlo." Elena had spoken to distract him. "Attention!" Marinara relaxed; he turned to notice her.

"This man; you don't understand. This man must go now, and not come back. Or I must kill him. If it means a hundred years."

Elena walked towards Gene. "Go. Please go." She walked closer to Marinara, who lowered his knife.

30

"But you must understand why he is here!" Carlo said to her.

With his knife down, like a dust mop at his side, he was weaker. The whining was starting within him, the sound of loss, someone else's voice assuming Carlo's own.

"You must not commit a crime," Elena said.

"He will take the children, the children. Let him go home — to Westchester!"

Gene had been moving off the terrace and was now in the room. "I only want to talk to you," he said slowly. His fear lessened; he saw Carlo down, yet not in control. "But I can go now, if you like."

"Yes, yes," Elena said. "Go for now." She stepped in front of Marinara and shook Gene's hand formally. To use the knife, Marinara would have to push her aside. He sat down on the bed while Elena escorted Gene down the steps to the outside door. "I'm sorry," Gene said to her, and she took his hand. "None of this is mine," he said. "My doing. Understand that. Please understand that."

Her face had accepted him; what else she thought and where she was with Marinara, he did not know. He stepped through the entrance and shut the door himself. Above him, Marinara's sounds were going, a confusion of screams, as if two men with the same voice were fighting through the rooms of the house.

3

In his hotel room, Gene was alone above the noisy street, the sound of wooden clog footsteps, car horns, buses arriving in the piazza, shouts of walkers as they passed. He lay on his bed unable to go out: it was either fear of Carlo and his knife and the loyal Amalfitani who would watch Gene bleed to death: the crowds along the white streets walled with houses had followed him with stares. Or it was the feeling in himself and the fear of its breaking out: having been threatened and shrunk to silence in front of that lovely girl was enough to make him ready to kill Carlo.

He was held in by the conflict all afternoon, locked and impatient while the town screamed and ran, boat motors started up, as close as his window, and ran out to sea.

When it was dark he came down to the restaurant. Italy was going, as it had been since he landed, like a force that expected no opposing reaction: no one gave thoughts to the payment for hours of eating and sitting until late, or what opportunities missed. And here it was worse than Naples, with the coolness of the water and the warm air, the streets too narrow for work. Gene left after he had eaten and walked into the interior of the town.

He was in step behind a child eating a sandwich, then went through the main square and stopped to see the striped cathedral rising up in its lights. He walked on, looking at windows of plates, bowls, coral necklaces: during each trip Francine went through her list of relatives, checking each name off after paying for each plate or vase or ashtray.

He had been walking towards the Marinara house and was about to pass it. A small terrace on the second floor was lit, and he saw Elena sitting on a wooden chair, alone and still, her face and legs catching the luminosity from reddish lamplight behind her.

She was more than a girl: her face had been open and questioning, but he had seen the expression on this street even on the old women in black. Her body was full, yet seemed light.

She was staring at something on a table, and there was none of the sourness of a woman in her face. He detested this as long as she was locked in Marinara's house.

But if she were a woman, as her body told him, then Francine and his sister had become beasts, whose only face was dissatisfaction and the dying of desires: they were beefy but they did not suggest flesh; they ate and slept yet they whined like those denied nourishment.

Elena's arms were moving; she was at the railing, calling to him. "Come on up here now."

"You want me?" Gene looked along the street. "Up there?"

"Yes, yes." She pointed to the door. "He is home. And you may talk to him now."

Gene stepped into the doorway and waited until she came down. "Speak to him now. About the children. Their mother and their home."

"Thank you." The words he had used since arriving were

33

either grateful or apologetic, but Elena did not let him stand in the beggar loneliness: she smiled, took his hand, changing the mood. "I can talk to you later." She started up the steps. "Come, come."

Gene followed her to the sitting room and waited while she announced him. Carlo came to the door, smiling. "Oh, *buona sera, 'Genio.*" He was greeting an old friend.

Gene followed him to the table. "I am so nervous from this afternoon. My hands still shake. Gene? Will you excuse me? My feelings —"

Gene shook hands and sat down. "Carlo, I want to say something." Marinara nodded his willingness. Gene paused, hearing the noises echoing in the narrow streets, radios getting louder, a TV show with shots. "I want to explain." Gene was in the degrading tone again. "Don't think I came over here to make life miserable for you. I hope you realize that. I did not ask to come here. This is not my business — really — but Anna was helpless. Do you understand what I mean?"

Marinara nodded, then called for Elena. When she appeared, he ordered a bottle of vermouth and watched her go. "You were always fair to me. You helped me, in the shop, the legal work. I always thank you for that. If you were only a lawyer here to help me —"

Marinara covered his face with his hands. "But what did I do? I hated it. *That* you don't know. To do it. I was afraid for the children. The plane. Danger of the plane. Of a crash caused by me!" He looked out and stopped himself with Gene's face. "But not for Anna. No! I did not care."

"That is not my business. I told you that. What happened between you and what you conceived to be your rights." Gene leaned across the table and touched Marinara's arm, and Carlo

34

smiled as man to man. "But let me tell you Carlo. Why I finally agreed to come here."

"You are here for one thing." Pleased by the faith of Gene, Marinara was ready to argue his side. "Let us say, for a legal matter, you are here. To get a thing, as we might say."

"Yes. Not between you and me." Gene had to finish his own words, without the syrup of Carlo's friendship. "I came because I saw those children, that they were from the States. That was their home, their *ambience*. As simple as that. And their mother exists, if you understand. What else was there beyond that? Their mother is over there."

Marinara left his chair, pushed by nervous anger again. Mother! Mother. This was a charge that pushed the sin through all of his body.

Gene watched him and saw the night blue beyond him at the window. Marinara faced the bay and placed his hands on his hips, his pose the proper expression of defiance. "Amalfi is pretty," he said with control. "Quiet before the high season begins. I have spent nights thinking about it all here. What you said. Once — one day, coming back from the ovens, I began to pack their little clothes. To take them back. But I had no more money."

"Don't worry about money anymore," Gene said.

Marinara turned and walked back to the table but did not sit. His undershirt shone with a lustrous white and his shoulders were bony and dark. "But they will never go back. Do you know that? Never."

Gene shook his head.

"No. Don't disagree. It is poor here. Yes. It is a bundle of rags here. The bank looks at me and sees a ragpicker. Italy does not — sustain us." He slapped the table. "When the foreigners go, we eat less. Yes." He stared at Gene. "But we can live here. I am the father. My family is here. I *feed* them."

Gene looked at the room. "I can see it. But I'm not telling you about life there or here, or what the future might be. I said *this*: their mother is *there*."

"No! No one is a mother *there*." Marinara pointed his finger. "Women who drive around. Drivers. Bus drivers. Bus mothers. Taking children like packages. Are they children over there, driven to stores, walking through stores? Objects! Did they live? Did they see anything like this? Here something enters you. There, you are hollow."

Marinara walked to the window but looked at Gene. "Those mothers who are not real. They hold a soap box with white false teeth and they spray wax from a can and smoke and smile at their cigarette — as if it were a man! They have no —" Marinara touched his trousers between his legs.

"That's your opinion." Gene heard himself saying it: it sounded like something he would say to a client in litigation.

"No, Gene. *No* and *no*. They are not real and you know it. A woman is flesh. She lives under the voice, the plans and the smell of a man. She becomes a woman and grows — grows as a woman. She gets flesh; slowly she makes her house like herself, something of herself, not an office room."

Gene had turned his face away, but looked up abruptly when Carlo paused: there was saliva on his lips, and he was staring at the table. Elena was standing at the door with a bottle and glasses. Gene watched her enter and come to the table, then back out of the room without speaking.

"Yes," Gene said. "I see a *woman* here. I see what you mean. Isn't it clear to the eyes?"

36

"What are you saying?" Marinara looked around. "Who? Who is it? Her? The servant girl?"

"Let us say this. You are not an old man, Carlo. You can begin having children right here. Unlike Annie, who cannot start again."

Carlo spoke calmly now. "This girl is a child from the countryside. Who works in my service, paid for by my father and myself. And friend of our cousins. I would not touch her." He poured the wine abruptly and passed a glass to Gene. "This is not the type of substance a man seeks in Italy." He began to smile. "If you want to discuss the proper material. Gene. Some night we can go —"

"Carlo. Look. I am a man and you are a man. If I had this beautiful girl in my house, it would not take long. You can have a future, with children. So let me have Joanna and Carlino for Annie."

Carlo held his glass forward, offended by Gene's ignorance of Elena. He raised his glass in a toast. Gene felt uncomfortable but joined him.

Carlo raised his chin and drank the glass completely. He smiled in satisfaction. "Let Anna have more children," he said.

Gene shook his head again and placed his unfinished glass at the center of the table. "She does not have the opportunity. As you do here."

"*Porco!* That girl is a child I told you. And you may go to the devil with your prick in your hand!" Carlo slapped the table, striking his glass on the wood, and strode out of the room.

Alone, Gene looked at the door that led to the bedrooms. He had not wished to take the children and run, but it was becoming the only way. First he would telephone Tubino and have the bank stop Carlo.

The door opened and Elena walked in. "Have you understood each other?" she said.

"Did you hear him? He refuses to let the children go."

"And what will you do?" She came close to him and leaned down for the bottle.

"What can I do? I will have to use the law and I don't want that. It means the newspapers and a bad name for him. I don't want to do that."

Elena was smiling. "Tomorrow he goes to the bank after work and will not be home."

"And the bank will have a bad surprise for him."

"I will have the children ready to leave at ten. His mother is shopping then, and he and the father are in the bakery."

Gene looked into her face: "You want me to come and take them?"

"It is *you* who want them."

"Yes. Then you will have a clean house here. And him."

Gene had been forced into the statement: jealousy now, some dumber emotion, made the words as he looked at her.

She stamped a foot and moved to pick up the glasses. "Have *him*? That one! Who works like a donkey tied to a wheel. That old man."

Gene looked at the door, embarrassed for Carlo, feeling himself included. "He isn't an old man yet."

"Then old ass. An old *asino*." Her anger made her smile.

"But you like the children. Why are you helping me?"

"You stupid fool." She let out a groan of trapped anger and walked to the door.

"Wait." Gene came up behind her and touched her shoulder. "I'm sorry. What have I said? I couldn't do anything dangerous to you." She turned and faced him, and he knew that it was himself she acted for. "Because I want them," he said to her.

He felt his hands shake with the recognition of her willing body. He took the bottle and glasses from her and placed them on the floor, and she embraced him. It was almost new: she pushed herself towards him with desire as strong as his own: it was what he dreamed the secretaries in the office would do.

Elena walked to the corner of the room. The overhead light reached little of its mild yellow there, and he watched her lie back on a couch he had not noticed before, a stiff, black leathery chaise.

His legs ached and the throbbing inside vibrated against his chest like the blows of a club. Screams erupted in his mind. The voices of women and smirking old men ran inside him silent as the screams. Yet his eyes could not stop telling him of Elena in the corner of the room: she lay silent, like a patient on a bed, like the body of Aunt Grace he had seen in the Zaccardo funeral home.

The association tightened the muscles of his chest. He would have to run, or die of a disease. But if he ran, he would have to leave Amalfi and then Naples and go back empty-handed. All that would show, then, was failure, some money lost. He cursed women, the things that opened and opened until you were in the chains of their helplessness.

Now the words in his head came loud towards Elena, cursing her. They could summon the house if he stood there. He went towards her quickly, almost as if to strike her but stopped when he stood above her: she was speaking — his name, other words — he did not understand the Italian now.

He could barely see her; he reached his hands down and took hers and she brought his hands to her breasts: he began to unfasten the buttons of her gray housedress, his body shaking uncontrolled.

Then the movement stopped as he eased down upon her, and as her lips began to kiss his neck, there was silence inside him.

He was aware of the coolness of her skin; its freshness had not been affected by the stuffy room. Part by part he became attached to her; she fought and pushed and took him down with her; her voice was the only sound, and when they had finished, the outside noises began again — the vibration of the tour buses off in the piazza, voices talking very loud, awake as day, the cars and motorcycles accelerating up the hill roads.

She said to him, "Go now." He was aware of Carlo again, his house, and stood up, but did not rush, knowing what they had both done to him.

GENE HAD gone along the stone quay and was looking back at the lights of town against the hills. The moon had risen to his left, lower than the peak nearest Positano. Couples had come by him on the streets, bringing the feelings that had come up earlier and now seemed about to start again.

The escape to the wharf was no good. The town was like a cruise ship full of party lights, the streets lighted and rushing with the noises of pleasure. The girls walking alone looked at him, his face, his body. He ran, from the affront to Francine, the departure from the mood of his mission, which was to be stern and silent, showing his place high among the councils of Westchester, Knight of Columbus, past president of trade organizations, the rest.

If Elena had been some hired girl, the action would have ended with the empty loss that is the payment of bordellos. But she was the warmth of home and a shape like love. She touched him like a younger sister, worked for him, found her tenderness with him.

This followed him down the wharf and was confused in the lights, the restaurants on the rocks and their music, their lights like toys in the air, the sound of the dream town.

Twice he had decided to run back to Carlo's, take Elena with him and tell her, with some words he had never spoken aloud, about being in love. His feelings would revive words, like phrases from remembered poems. And he became embarrassed, like a schoolchild being called on to sing a love song before the assembled class.

After walking to Piazza Duomo the second time, he had sat down at a caffè for coffee and there realized that the best move would be to pack and rush home, telling them he had been unable to get the children legally in a short time and was repelled at the thought of doing it Tubino's way.

Now Elena, her body and hips, her skin, had made that impossible. He would not be an old man. He went back to the house, which had become dark, called her name. When she came downstairs, he had lost the words for her, but she understood something of the halted feelings. "I am going to leave the children here with you," he said. "They will be better off with you."

But she had answered, "But no. I can't live my life here." She was angry, and it surprised him. "My life is my life. I must act for myself soon. And you, you must risk something," she said. "You must take your chance. Why did you come so far?"

She had shut the door, and Gene had walked back to the stone wharf. *Without risk:* it was what he had hoped for, the only way he cared to try. But she had spoken some stupid heroic lines, and the idea stuck. He would try to do the thing she would like.

Next morning, after Carlo had left home in his suit, Gene crossed the street, already pleased at having seen Carlo and not been seen, and entered the house. Upstairs he heard the children's voices singing with Elena. When he saw them, they were dressed for a trip. Elena asked about the car.

"Yes, I have it ready," Gene said.

"Did you hear that? The *car*." She turned and smiled at the two, who did not seem to understand.

Although Elena went on, describing the trip, the mountain roads past Praiano and Positano, the coast road down to Sorrento, Naples — still her emotions confused them. There was too much excitement inside Elena; her tone may have been describing a fear she would not mention with Gene present. "Aren't you coming, Elena?" Joanna asked.

"No," Elena said, and saw Joanna's eyes. "I am coming later. We will see each other in a little while."

Gene did not understand. "Can you come as far as Rome with us? For a few days."

Elena turned abruptly away, went to get the little suitcases, which were made of white leather. She carried them as they went downstairs and outside, down to the piazza where the car stood.

Gene placed the bags in the trunk and came round to the front. Elena was standing at the door, holding the children by the hands. "Remember Elena," she was saying. "Will you remember Elena and say my name sometime? Our walks in the hills — Joanna, the emerald grotto, remember that day in the boat?" She saw that the children did not have a response, too young for nostalgia, unaware of the love we construct for departures. She kissed them quickly and walked off, before Gene could speak.

While he watched her, he heard Carlino's dull voice. "Uncle is taking us back."

Gene called after Elena, but as she heard him she ran; in

her sudden spurt of movement, Gene saw the threat of Carlo and rushed the children into the car, then drove up the ascending road out of town. The children were caught by the views quickly, up in the mountains, seeing Positano ahead and the water larger from the height. When they finally came down near the autostrada, the children were hungry.

He stopped at a restaurant on the water and sat while they ate, watching their faces. Carlino looked at him from time to time and Gene saw Annie's eyes, the Santoro eyes.

"We're starting to have a good time," he said. "I like fried fish this way, but Elena says it's too heavy for us." Carlino was officious, like his grandfather.

"And you know what, Uncle." Joanna wanted Gene's attention. "We never got anything for Elena. Not one little thing."

"What do you mean?" Gene felt a trap in the child's thought.

"Buy! We didn't buy her anything yet."

"All right." Gene stood up. "You finish up while I get my cigarettes and then we'll get her something in Naples."

He went to the counter for cigarettes, and looked back at the children under the colored awning. They were eating too much, stuffing themselves with a desperation he did not expect. He came back to ease them. "Well, here goes my first Italian cigarette," he said, and watched them stare at him as if he had not spoken.

He sat and waited until they finished a dessert. "Come on. Now some shopping in Naples. Right?"

They followed him silently and watched as he drove to the autostrada and into Naples. "It stinks here," Carlino said. "That stink is killing me."

"It's only these oil plants at the end of town. Like New Jersey. You remember the smell just when you start on the turnpike. Remember that?"

"I hate this." Carlino's voice was shaking. "Get me out of this stink, Uncle. You want to kill us." Joanna was getting the fear: "You can feel it on your tongue. Like it sticks on you."

Gene did not answer but drove into the traffic of Piazza Ferrovia, where the smell disappeared, but the cars were stopped. Carlino spoke from behind him. "Oh, I hate this place. It's all rotten."

"See those stores." Gene pointed ahead to the Corso Umberto. "We'll only do our shopping and go."

He finally reached the parking places in the piazza and they walked along the Corso. There were outdoor stands hung with toys.

"Now here we go," Gene said. "Let's get things."

"But I need sneakers," Carlino said.

"All right, we'll get them, too. Now get a toy."

Carlino placed his hands on the toys, and the old peddler began to lure him, taking toys down and placing them in the child's hands. "I want all these three," he said, and Gene began to pay, but Carlino went on: "The plane *and* the tennis set *and* the models."

Joanna took a peasant doll, which had an American face, and they walked further. "Are we looking for Elena?" Joanna said.

"Yes." Gene did not like her comprehension. They found a shop of women's clothes and went inside. "I *know* she needs a bathing suit," Joanna said. "Because she never goes in when she comes with us to the beach."

45

But none of them knew Elena's size. Joanna placed her hand next to Gene's shoulder, to guess her height. But the salesgirl smiled and said she needed other measurements. Gene turned to other items, purses of leather, scarves, nylon stockings (which he had heard were scarce in Italy), sweaters, silver necklaces inlaid with red plastic, the new mode from England. Gene bought it all and as he watched it being wrapped, looked at the children. "Now we have to give it to her. Right?"

The children were silent. Carlino watched him, then followed him to the car. When they were inside, he leaned forward: "Uncle, aren't we going back home?"

"Not yet," Gene said. "You don't want to go yet, do you? Don't we all get a few trips first?"

Carlino sat back — in disgust, it seemed, but he was only giving up his belief in the logical pattern he had thought was the life of adults. He put his toy plane on his lap and waited.

Joanna had caught the change earlier, perhaps in the store. She sat next to her doll, readjusting its clothes, lifting its arms and legs in a silent game of life, no longer curious about the direction.

They drove back to the autostrada and reached Amalfi just before dark. Gene walked to the door with them, and Elena answered their ring. After her surprise, she embraced the children; the confusion brought tears to her eyes. Gene gave her the large package for herself, and she took it and turned away.

Joanna looked up at Gene and smiled: the courtship her sex always understood was good wherever it happened. "Say thank you to Uncle Gene," she said. "Why don't you give him a kiss."

46

Elena turned to her. "Carry your bags. Up. Quick. Change
your clothes and come back."

She watched them leave the sitting room before she spoke
to Gene. "What have you done?"

Gene shook his head. "I couldn't leave yet. And leave you
here to face him alone. Did you tell him?"

"He came home with his head down and went out again.
He asked nothing and I said nothing. But the bank has said
no. I heard them downstairs. He cannot get money."

"I will give him that money."

"No, *caro*, no." She was protecting him, unable to conceive
the Santoro button money in Gene's face reacting with confusion, too modest for wealth, too often as humble as a peasant or
a worker. Elena tried to stop his desperation.

"I can do just what I want," he said. "And even more than
that."

She thought his smile was his facade, like the Italian face
that was used every day to hide empty pockets and the weakness of owning nothing. "Yes, do what you will. But not to
empty yourself and whatever you have."

"I know what I'm doing —" His memory stopped his voice:
it was the seed of the marital fight, with always the same
words. "Don't worry," he said. "Begin to trust me."

She embraced him quickly and placed her head against his
chest. Gene felt her attaching herself, as she had done on the
couch: this time he had done it, ending the flow of words with
his own few, instead of releasing Francine's dam which drove
him away.

Elena stepped back. "Attention! He is here."

Gene had not heard, but Marinara was at the door and en-

47

tered slowly, nodding to them. His face changed as he saw Gene, his lips twisting tightly.

"What is it?" Gene said. "Am I not welcome?"

"Welcome. *Benvenuto.* Welcome." Marinara walked by him and sat down. He did not speak, staring at the window away from them. "The silence when I came home." His voice came out dull and hollow, reminding Gene of Carlino on the trip. "I knew you had taken them. Finished. *All* finished now. Even that. Everything taken."

"Not finished. Carlo. Listen." Gene came and stood over him. "You *will* get the money."

"No, no, they gave me *no.*" Marinara looked up. "The bank knows everything. The Americans have told them. I might be arrested — they say it is possible. And in *jail* I could never repay a loan —" His head was nodding with exaggeration. "In *jail. Jail!*"

"Listen." Gene touched Carlo's shoulder, felt love, saw his face turn. "I can go to the bank, the authorities. And say I just came over to pick up the children after their brief vacation. The rest is an error. If *I* say it. And then you get your money."

"Did you ever talk to the Banco di Napoli? They roost on money like chickens. Chained to the egg."

"Carlo. I am talking about my money. This is my money, and you get it."

Carlo took his hands and clasped them. "Gene? Will you do it again?"

"Yes, yes." Gene's control had gone: he had done it for all of them, made a short wall around Carlo, steps to Elena. "Get some paper," he said. "A sheet of paper."

Elena began to leave. "Stop," Carlo said. "There is paper here. In the cabinet. And my pen is there."

48

She came back to the corner chest of drawers and found the paper and pen. Gene met her and took them: but she was no longer enjoying what he had done. He went to the table, still flushed by his running thoughts, sat down and wrote.

Finished, he held up the paper and read it slowly: "I, Carlo Marinara, hereby promise to offer no resistance against the return of my children, Carlino and Joanna, to their mother in the United States of America. I will assist my brother-in-law Eugene Santoro in every way to effect their immediate return. I also accept, as a necessary reciprocal condition of this decision and assistance in expediting the children, sufficient financial help from my brother-in-law, the said Santoro, to enable me to purchase all the property and equipment for the establishment and maintenance of a bakery in the town of Amalfi."

Carlo was smiling; he reached gently for the paper, took it and read it for himself: the semilegal phrases Gene's lawyer mind had created in Italian, even with his limited vocabulary, were like a piece of power itself. "And Gene? This means that you will give me the money *first*."

"We'll do it all legally. Together. At the bank, most likely. The money is in Italy. It's here."

"Slave!" Elena had screamed at Marinara. "Whore! Wash your hands." She had snatched the paper from Carlo's hand and thrown it to the floor with all her strength, but after a first rush, the thin sheet began to glide slowly towards the floor, on a pleasure flight of its own.

Both men watched her leave the room, even before the paper reached the red floor tiles. Carlo looked after her, stood up. "Odious. I hate her. That odious girl. She breaks my teeth. I should —" Carlo swung his arms around, spun a little, came round to Gene's eyes. "Gene. Please, let me think a night about this. One night." He walked to the door.

"What is it?" Gene asked. "What went wrong in this minute?"

"Nothing. I am going to sleep. And think about it." He saw Gene's expression changing. "I must ask myself, for example, why you are doing this for me. To say the truth."

Gene stood up. "Wait. I told you already. They sent me over here to help you out. And then take the children home." Gene took up the paper and placed it on the table under the pen. "I think we should both sign this. I have signed my name, and you can sign yours next to mine." Gene held his feelings tight, his voice for clients coming out. "I'm here to help you, Carlo. Don't you see that? You are part of the family so you get help. It's *that* simple. And I think you deserve this help for what you're doing, this exchange. And because you're *family*. Anyone in the family. Just call Gene." He walked towards Carlo, then turned away. "Call Gene and you get help. That's all there is. That's my mission in life. I *help*. I help everybody. I work for everybody, and you too. Isn't that good, Carlo? And don't worry, you will be satisfied. Like everybody else. You will have your own little nest."

He walked to the door, stopped, then silently went down the dark hall to the street. He walked along, looking back where the reddish light shone in thin stripes through Elena's closed blinds. The blinds never opened as he stared, unable to go anywhere. He had checked out of the hotel, had only the rented car for a home. He went to it and drove back to the hotel and rented the same room. He had lost the moment.

When he was inside, the luggage near the bureau, the doors

closed, he heard the street crowds again and remembered his hunger. The restaurant was almost empty when he arrived and he sat and watched the lamp fishing while he ate, the boats sliding by on the transparent water. Slowly the unfinished people came back, and he knew he must call home and report the success.

In his room, waiting for the call, he thought of how he might mention Elena, a cook and maid who could create the home atmosphere of Italy for his mother and father in their last years.

But the conversation was finally the strict form of a telephone dialogue: Annie had recovered from greatest pain; Francine asked when he was coming back, and his father had questions about the size of the loan before agreeing to the plan. Though it was risky and against his instincts, Santoro understood that his son was among foreigners and that only money would render Carlo theirs, at the tip of their grasp.

In the silence after the call, Elena was gone. She would even be an old lady before the quota reached her, an undesirable Latin in Washington. Gene remembered the hundreds of cousins and unseen brothers he had worked to push across from Italy, year after year, telling the same story of delay to clients who showed him the latest photographs, new children, new moustaches on the waiter cousins, until he began to refuse fees until the people arrived, and then refused immigration cases altogether.

The sounds outside were increasing, and he went to the terrace to look down at the street. It was getting familiar: he began to pick out the shapelier women, all the bodies moving under thin dresses, wondering if any were streetwalkers. He turned away in disgust, not knowing why the touch of new love inside him could also help form these other thoughts, a desire for all the women on the street. He stepped back and closed the wood blinds and the glass doors before going to sleep.

For two days Gene was alone in his room, waiting for Carlo's final answer. He walked up the hill road towards Atrani, leaned on the wall and watched the sea far below until a fear inside him, almost a pleasure, of dying and flying, being smashed against rocks and hovering in air, drew him away. He bought a bathing suit in town and swam on his back, looking at the Amalfi houses stuck on the sharp, rising hills. He came back and felt ill in the shower, brushed his teeth to clear out the salt taste of the water, suggesting poison because it would not leave his tongue. Sitting later at supper, he felt the food would come up, tainted fish, a knifey bone in the red sauce: he was ill from the whole adventure. Its minutes were bursting without control, falling, collecting upon him like a hill of stones. If he did not leave, his inside moods would come out and assume shapes, imprison him. He held on to his silence, walking home, falling asleep, waking in the night with his jaw in pain from some action of his teeth, clenching and grinding, the fight continuing with his eyes shut.

In the morning he awoke, like a boy again, with an erection, shutting his eyes quickly in the embarrassment, then keeping his eyelids shut to continue at the edge of the excitement that still hid in dreams.

The bed sheets were wound about his legs, twisted, torn loose from their hold around the mattress. He looked down at himself in sadness: he thought he would cry, some chunk of pity torn loose in his throat.

The excitement was also entwined with anger, locked together, one impossible without the other. If a woman came in now, he would have to beat her before making love.

If it was love that kept him here, it had become unexplainable in its contradictions. Elena had acted to bring him together, but he was in pieces. He had fallen down and come up with a discovery, but it was more like a disease, one he would take with him even if he ran.

The knocking at the door was real and he ran to it. It was the voice of a messenger from the bank. He dressed quickly and ran down to the bank in the morning sunlight.

Two officials were waiting, one who spoke with him, the other who collated the many sheets of official papers.

"We have nine millions of lira," the speaking official said, and raised his eyebrows, reminding Gene of the lawyer, Tubino.

"That's a good start," Gene said, but the man did not smile. "Isn't that about fifteen thousand dollars?"

"Yes." The man thought about it, looked down at the papers. "About fifteen thousand and some, American."

Gene explained that he would lend the money to Carlo for a bakery, passing the money to him as soon as possible. "This will be sufficient," the man said.

"Then make an estimate of his costs." Gene stood up to go. "I'll give him what he needs."

"These things take time." The man held him. "To speak to the suppliers of equipment. The owner of the building. Licenses —"

Gene looked back: the face wanted payment. "Do it. Do everything you have to. And pay them all. Charge me for the work. Put some oil on the wheels. Understand?"

The man smiled at the vulgarity of overt statement. "Yes, yes," he said. He bowed, and came to offer a handshake, but Gene rushed out, up along the main street to Carlo's house.

Elena met him at the door. "He is at the bakery. Will you come in?"

"No. I cannot now. I must see him. I have his money. At the bank."

"Eugenio. Will you come inside?"

Gene stepped into the shadow of the doorway and kissed her. "I'll come back here after the business."

"Did you understand me?" Elena held his arms.

"Not really. You don't make sense — which team you're on." Gene was smiling. "But I don't need to understand you." He opened the door again. "You could be a fool like me. You want to help everybody."

"*Cretino.* Yes, like you!" She was smiling and came to touch him again. "Go run, then. Go."

Gene walked to the bakery, where Carlo was working at a long wood table. "The money is here." Gene was excited. "Let's get it. Do you have the location, the store you want?"

"Yes. I have all the information. I worked on it every day —" he was smiling. "I should have something." Carlo called his father, a small man with curved shoulders from years hunched over the oven doors.

"Eugenio has my money. It is here, in Amalfi. In the bank!"

55

Old Marinara bowed, the shoulders going down to accent for Gene the weight of his money. "We are all thankful, signor Santoro. Carlo —" he pointed at his son — "he had a real madness for this. But we have always worked for others. Until now." The old man spoke from far below, but Gene accepted it as he had the banker's bow.

"We must all help Carlo get started," Gene said to the old man, and abruptly touched his shoulder: the flesh was warm, pleasant to feel. "You should have seen his shop in America."

"Oh yes. But here we would have sat and waited. Now you have come with more than good feelings —"

"Good. Then let's take Carlo to the bank. We have to sign papers."

"The bank! No!" Carlo looked at himself. "I must go home and change."

"This is a short visit. Just give them your costs and the location. They will make up a budget."

"Oh no!" Carlo was angry. "I must get a suit."

"All right. Get it, get it." Gene had recognized the shame.

He walked back with Carlo, who babbled about the future. At the house Carlo ran to change while Gene went to the back terrace to watch the children and Elena below. She was playing a game with them and he saw her tan legs when her skirt flew up in the running. His head felt it and his hands, gripping the terrace rail.

When she caught his eyes, he took a step backwards. Elena stopped and nodded her head and the children noticed the greeting and shouted his name. He waved and stepped back inside to find Carlo staring at him.

They walked to the bank in silence. The official had another tone for Carlo, treating him like an incompetent, and he responded by forgetting his facts, the street address of his new shop, even stating his father's first name wrong, then correcting it.

When they came out, Carlo rubbed his hands. "Now we begin. Look at the day. The sun shines on me. Look. Gene? I am in the sun today."

Gene was silent; he remembered the children, who made him think of Elena. "Carlo. Now I have to take them home."

Marinara lost his expression. He walked with Gene to the house before speaking. "Gene. Listen to me. As soon as I receive the money, and no sooner." He opened the door with his key and shut it on Gene.

Gene walked back to the hotel to wait. He could not go to the house and ring the bell now that he was victor. He sat down on his bed, then lay back and fell asleep until the phone awoke him; it was morning. The bank messenger had come for him: he was to witness the check signing. He washed his face and went down to find Carlo in the office, waiting. They sat and signed papers and at last Carlo received the check and left alone.

Gene went back, changed his clothes and washed, then packed his suitcase again. He walked downstairs, bought ceramic cups and plates for all and had them shipped home. He ate his last meal, went to the desk to pay his bill and fell asleep before dark.

Early in the morning he went to Marinara's house but no one answered the bell. He tried again an hour later and then again, just before noon. Finally, he went to old Marinara at the bakery.

Marinara seemed honestly confused by the disappearance. "They would not leave now," he said a few times, and then, slowly, "There is really no cause now," and smiled with some embarrassment.

Gene returned to the house, and Carlo answered his ring. His mad eyes, the stare that some of the family had noticed, were fixed on Gene. "They are not here." His voice was a false monotone. "They are not here. Do you hear? Look. Look and look for them. And you shall never find them. Go home now, Gene. Go back. And your money will be paid you. On my honor. I will pay back everything."

"*Your* honor?" Gene looked over Carlo's shoulder into the dark hallway. "Your honor was to let those children go."

Carlo did not answer. "Then listen to me," Gene said. "And don't be deaf. Now I will use another way. And you will end up not liking it at all. You will be more hurt than before."

Gene started away, but Carlo followed him along the street, talking up near his face. "Never! Never! Never, do you hear *never*. Hear it! Hear it! You can never steal mine."

Gene walked steadily to the hotel and there called Tubino, who promised to drive down immediately.

At night, Tubino appeared in Gene's room with a uniformed man and one of the bankers. "This is a *Maresciallo*, Spadaro, my friend of many years; and Parenti of the bank. Together we are going now to speak with that baker."

Tubino and the *Maresciallo* walked in front, Gene and the young banker behind them. Elena came to the door and held her hand across her mouth as they came in. The *Maresciallo* spoke to her softly and she led them to the sitting room where Carlo was reading a newspaper. As she called his name, he turned and jumped at the sight.

58

The *Maresciallo* came forward and held out his hand. Carlo shook it obediently as he heard the names.

"What do you want with me?" Carlo looked at Gene, who stood back.

"If we may be permitted." The *Maresciallo* looked at the chairs.

"Sit. Sit. Make yourselves comfortable." Carlo watched them take chairs. "Are you ready? Do you arrest me now? I give you the charge. Keeping my own children near me."

The *Maresciallo* held his temper with twitches, pursing his lips tightly. He looked, with trained patience, at Carlo's vulgar face, dirty with its anger. "Please, signore. Think of yourself. We must speak to you —"

"Yes, yes. Please speak to me. Then tie me up with ropes. Saying please, please." Carlo held them at bay with his arms; his lips were edging with saliva.

"It is not a question of an arrest, Carlo." Gene spoke, and there was a waiting silence. Carlo saw the three men looking at him, their heads inclined like domestics, and he was afraid now.

"It is a question of our agreement. Which you accepted, and you know what it was. We only want to help a mother see her children again."

"Oh, go to the devil, Gene, with your mothers." Carlo's nerves were breaking his control: the emergency was calling up hate too fast. Somewhere inside he knew he should listen to their attack first, then make his response.

Tubino put his leather briefcase on the table. "Let me remind you, Marinara —" he tapped the case. "— that firstly, the government expects to produce documents that will extradite these children. And second, if it wishes, the law can speak harshly to those *who —*" Tubino, with his voice of lists, paused to make his quick, snatching gesture.

"And let me add this." The young banker spoke without dialect, and the lack of accent made Carlo think him a foreigner. "It is possible to stop payment of your money if signor Santoro rescinds the credit. The payment simply stops."

"No! Stop it!" Carlo jumped, with both feet stamping the floor. He searched his mouth for the worst words. "Capitalists! Capitalists!" His associations began. "Feudalists! Revisionists!" He found the last. "Imperialist dogs! Drop your bombs on me."

He pointed at each man, a thrust of index and last finger, the curse of horns. The *Maresciallo* moved quickly out of pointing range, but Tubino and Parenti stuck their faces in the path of the dead magic.

Carlo turned around. "Look. Look for them." He opened his shirt. "Are they here?" Then he held out his arms, like Jesus on the cross. "Are they under me? The table? Here, let's look under the table? No babies." He unbuttoned his trousers and stuck a hand inside. "No, no. Not here, either."

The *Maresciallo* stood up and took a step towards him.

Carlo stepped back and sat down, facing them with his eyes open but blank. Gene coughed, and the others turned to him.

"Carlo, you can see the situation here." Gene's voice was warm with the spent guilt from striking Carlo down. "We want you to keep the money. Start again and build a good business here in your hometown. Only be sensible about these children. They must go home. They need their country."

The others were nodding as Carlo looked at them. His head fell into his hands: they had made his children foreigners, another species.

60

The *Maresciallo* came and stood over Carlo, calling him away from an emotion that would embarrass them all.

Tubino raised his eyes and looked at Gene: it had been done: the humped, shaking body was proof.

The banker turned away, as if Carlo's tears might stain him. Gene was uncomfortable, looking for a way to avoid Carlo. He stood up and walked to the door, then stepped into the hallway, almost hitting Elena. "Beast," she said, and struck his chest with her fists. Gene held her wrists tight, confused again because even this touch gave him pleasure.

"Oh, *caro*." Elena had been subdued and her words changed, as if love came out of hate. Gene kissed her face and brought her body against his. "I had to do this," he said.

"No," she said, but Gene did not listen. "Now I want to take *you*," he said, and she began to cry, stepping back. "Don't talk like that," she said. "I don't make dreams."

Gene looked at the door: there was no sound of others coming. Elena had taken his hands and was leading him along the hall, to her room.

Inside, he began quickly. "I came back because of you. I could have gone on that day —"

"You should have gone." She walked to her bed and sat down. "That was the natural way, the way it was to be. Now you are with this army."

"That's something else." Gene sat beside her. "You know I'm a married man. And I'm getting old. I thought I was old. But now I don't think so. I'm not tired —"

"To me, you are love." She took his hands again. "Listen. From the first time I saw you. You were lost, a man concerned with these things, and yet you talked to me without these other matters of your mind. Italian men are never like that:

they are wrapped in their own pride, like men with mirrors — covered only by themselves. You had respect and care; you want to know about me, what I did, where I will go."

She had stopped, it seemed, in the middle of a formal charge to Gene, and again he did not understand. He kissed her and pressed her back on the bed. She was quiet, holding the moment with him, not able to tell him it was dead.

She was the first to hear the sounds. "It is your men. They will look for you." Gene stood up and went out, finding the men in the dark hall, without Carlo.

"He will have the children ready in a day," the *Maresciallo* said. "And I believe him."

"And we may assume the credit continues," the young banker said.

"As soon as I leave with the children," Gene said. "I'll have the girl who works here tell you in the morning."

Tubino shook hands silently, using the right hand that made the snatching gesture. "I return to Naples now, via Hertz. All is finished here, and tomorrow is business." He looked back at the sitting room door. "But call at once if there is any change." Tubino unclasped and stepped away.

"I know these southern types." The *Maresciallo* touched his chest. He nodded for Gene and started down the steps quickly, followed by the others. He held the door for them, then shut it and stepped into the lighted street. "Would you gentlemen please me with a cup of coffee?" Tubino said, when Gene did not take the proper role of host. The banker and the *Maresciallo* smiled, but Gene simply shook hands and said goodnight, leaving them alone and startled on the street.

62

6

A CHILD had come with a note. Gene held the half-opened door, looked at the expectant eyes, and instinctively gave the boy a hundred lira coin. He brought the envelope inside, found it to be the same kind of paper he had written on in Carlo's sitting room. Someone had written: THE CHILDREN ARE READY.

He had been ready except for his tie, and now folded it into a tight knot, brushed his hair again, and went down to the desk. The clerk was smiling. "So you are leaving again, signore," he said.

"I will come back for my bags," Gene said, and did not join in the emotion.

"Any way you prefer," the man said. "Did you enjoy yourself?" He saw Gene's angry stare. "In Amalfi? Your vacation. Did you enjoy it here with us? Was the food to your taste?"

"Yes, yes." Gene could not get up the words, and he walked out into the sun, stopping as he entered the light and crossing over to the walk along the water. A few fishermen were out beyond the main wharf, almost silhouettes standing in their boats against the white morning mist. He had not thought of the pleasures of the morning before this, the boats pulling away from the shore in lines of bubbling wake, the day starting with the ever present houses on the cliffs set for celebrations.

Each day the people seemed to do a single job; nothing cut their day into odd pieces, running their duties like too many beads on a long string, falling over and over to the same point. He thought of the fragments that had seemed fulfilling and thick with necessity at home: the phone messages on slips of yellow paper when he came into his office at eight, exciting him with the prospect of a big day. The luck they had had buying property and building houses, he and the DiMarco brothers: once they had started — it was first only four attached red brick homes in Mount Vernon — it seemed that everybody in the North Bronx had saved enough money to buy in Westchester. And the bits of politics at night, the meetings, running down to Washington for a few days and latching on to the beginning of some new things through Phil or whoever was in Congress that session, something which stuck in your mind, a tin deal, cement houses in Guatemala, can openers for Africa.

They were sticky lumps in Amalfi, banners of hope to fill up a vault, not a man. But they were good: let any Wop try doing it. They lost their life here only because they were temporarily not present: what was far away lost its existence for a time, especially if one had the headache of Carlo's aching face, and Elena.

But Elena changed nothing: she had pressed herself against him only in a moment when he himself was free, helping him out of the beetle crust he wore. There were no secret loves at forty-five, nor even illicit moments of sin that made men more masculine and able to be forgiven by wives.

There was merely Elena, who had unbuttoned her dress and let herself be seen and taken, acting as if nothing had been taken from her.

He decided to walk to the house before getting his bags at the hotel. Passing it he saw the front door ajar: it was unusual. In his mood, he decided to go up to Elena's room and insist upon making love again.

As he climbed the steps, he heard Carlo talking. "Stupid open mouth! Let me finish, let me finish first. So much good you have done me with your advice on everything. And I am here in this mess and your mouth cannot shut even now."

"Sì, signor Carlo." Elena gave him her echoes, without the strength Gene knew she had, with a subservience towards Carlo that made Gene angry and excited.

"And don't be stupid again about *him*. Lock the doors. Keep them inside. If I get the money, in my *hands,* I will come back myself and give them to that pig. I will stare in his eyes when he takes them. But listen! If there is no money, I will come and take them to Ravello again."

Gene hid himself in the hall darkness as Carlo came rushing forth from the sitting room, wearing a suit jacket over his white baker's clothes.

When the downstairs door had shut, Elena came out and went quickly to bolt the door. Coming back, she saw Gene and was not surprised. He held out his hands to her, but she stepped away. "Come to the back."

Gene had believed his thoughts would show to her like words; he watched her go along the hallway, her wooden clogs clicking against the red tiles. She opened a bedroom door and a square of light fell into the hallway. "Hurry. Come on." She was calling orders.

Gene came quickly, stepped into the room and was about to take her arms when he heard Joanna. "Hello, Uncle Gene." She spoke from the terrace. "We're all ready to go."

"That's nice," Gene said, but looked at Elena, who smiled and shook her head. Passion was funny with the children around. "Don't we have to get something in your room?" Gene said to Elena.

"We *have* our suitcases and flight bags right here." Joanna would not stop, and Elena picked up her blue canvas airline bag. "That's my model case," the child said. "Someday I'm getting one of those round ones. You know them, Uncle?"

"Yes. If we see one, we'll get it." Gene saw that Elena had planned it for him. "Where is Carlino?"

"He's crying like a baby," Joanna said. "Because Poppa talked to him."

Gene was angry. "What did Poppa say?"

"I don't know." Joanna was playing with a red hairbrush she had forgotten to pack or was leaving: she began to brush her hair, counting. She saw Gene staring at her: "Oh, *you know*, Uncle Gene. Like, be nice to Mommy. And be a good boy. And come back and see Poppa soon, and all that stuff."

"And that made Carlino cry?"

"He doesn't want to take a trip. He wants to go back to Ravello with the cousins. See, that's what Poppa said we were going to do. In time for the fireworks. And go down and see the abbey in Cava, with bones. And the temples."

"The temples. What temples?"

"Where all the people were melted by the Vesuvio."

"Well, *we* can see that. Come on, let's tell Carlino we'll go see things."

Elena moved first and came back with a slow, pained Car-

66

lino. He had lost himself in his tears and was staring and limp, pushed along in Elena's hands.

"Come on," Gene said. "I've got the convertible and we'll eat at a great restaurant and see temples."

Carlino smiled at him, but stood, uncomprehending and small; he sucked in some breath and a little groan came out of him, annoying to Gene, who would not be the cause of this. Gene came to Carlino and patted his back, but the boy remained lost in his fears.

"I'm going to buy you a temple," Gene said. "We'll bring it back to the States. How about that?" He removed a pack of thousand lira notes from his pocket. "See all this. They're no good back home so we've got to spend it all now. How many are you taking for yourself, Carlino? Here."

Carlino took some money in his left hand and began to walk, holding Elena's arm with his right hand. They moved downstairs to the big doors and stopped while Elena released the locks.

When they were in the street, Elena retreated inside again. Gene went back. "Please. Take this." He held a white envelope, but she did not take it.

"Is this the silver?" she said. "The thirty of silver. Don't do that to me."

"There is no money here." Gene held the white envelope. "Only something I wrote to you. Words you can't say."

She took the envelope and held his hand. "Then I might say at last *thank you.*"

"I will never forget you," he said. Elena looked away and walked towards the steps. "Wherever I go." He heard his voice rising, and stopped. They were words out of some TV love story.

Elena ran up the steps and Gene heard the children behind him: their voices were like the morning talk in the street: it did not know him or wait for what he had to say, even shout now to Elena up in her room.

He came out into the light, to the children. "Elena wants us to go," he said, and they followed him along the street to the car.

The children stood and watched while he packed their bags in the trunk. "Well, let's go," he had to say, then opened the car doors.

Joanna tried to keep in contact with him, as though she had to appease him. "Carlino likes the back seat, Uncle. Then he can lie down and see the sky. He likes convertibles for that. And I'll sit with you."

Gene helped the boy, carrying him part of the way. Then Joanna sat next to Gene and smiled.

He drove along the road out of town again. At the sharp turn where the sight of the town disappears, he saw the high rocky mountains and raced the car faster. "Look at all this," he said, and Joanna touched his hand on the shift lever.

They soon came in sight of Positano, white and yellow in its fjord, and Gene called out again, reaching to touch Joanna's hand. Then he heard a cry. "What is it?" He touched the brake.

"I want Poppa!" Carlino had been saving it or been trying to swallow it.

Gene looked back and saw the boy with his face down on the black leather of the seat. He began to drive as if he were being pursued, through the curled mountain roads, until they were on the straight descending road beyond Sorrento.

Carlino had whimpered all the way but was now asleep.

68

Gene saw the hands on the seat, as if they had been clawing.

He stopped the car at a restaurant before taking the autostrada into Naples. Carlino awoke, and Gene felt the headache that had been building. He left the car and looked at the children before helping them out: they were passive again, and he could take them into cities.

After the lunch, they drove into Naples and left the highway to buy toys in the market piazza near the terminal. The children did not ask him or look for approval: they bought, they grasped at the objects — radios, large dolls, record players, finally candy in awkward, over-large boxes.

Then they drove to the Rome highway and the children became drowsy and fell asleep, Joanna against Gene's hip. As the miles went quietly, Gene's thoughts were stilled as his eyes took in glimpses of castles, monasteries, broken towers among trees that made the hills.

The children awoke and after a bit of staring turned to their toys. Gene called attention to sights, but soon gave up: they were not looking: their faces were on the toys, as if on a family ride along the Bronx River Parkway.

But as the ride became tiresome, Gene looked at them to see if they were affected by anything outside. It was all the same to them, but perhaps they were more at home in it than he.

He was trying to catalogue the shapes that passed his eyes, to relate them to names, to something he should remember having seen. The half-known things made him tense: he had to suppress his wish to scold the children for their disinterest. Their concern for themselves disturbed his own half-aching wish to let it all go, to race crazily like the Italians, his left arm hanging on the door, with no more thought than a boy's on his way to a beach.

69

But at last Carlino had stopped crying and looked like a child on a trip; they could check into the hotel in Rome without embarrassment. At dusk, after being lost in the streets on the outskirts, they found the hotel entrance: Joanna had loved the city lights going on and asked to ride around more: Gene did not answer, but went up the steps to the glass doors ahead of them.

Two porters had come out for the bags, but the children had not followed yet. Gene watched them smiling at the shine of the entrance. Then Carlino took his sister's hand and followed the porters.

Seeing them coming up in their own pleasure, Gene knew he had them: he had done it. The effect of it was a rush of love for the children. Perhaps the feeling came so strongly because he and Francine had not had babies around for so long, their house as quiet as a dentist's waiting room, Francine asking about services and purchases in the morning — painting the rooms, installing a freezer chest in the basement, building a patio surrounded by a bamboo fence.

But here were the two kids, walking hand in hand, alone and yet not alone under him. They stood like little lovers, but they were pure. The elements of his feeling were diverse, but they were strong, and he would give anything he had to Carlino and Joanna.

They had rented adjoining rooms, with twin beds for the children. Gene sat down on one bed in their room and took Joanna's hand. "Now let's call up Mommy and tell her we're OK. We're coming home on the plane."

"Can you do that?" Joanna's voice had no feeling.

"It costs a lot, but they have wires under the ocean."

Carlino had been looking at the city from a window but had heard.

"Want to talk to Mommy?" Gene said. "And hear her voice?"

"No," the boy said, and walked out of the room, into Gene's larger room.

Gene followed him, calling. "What is it? What do you want to do? See the temples first? Carlino?"

Carlino was face down on Gene's bed, and he had begun to cry again. "Oh, now, please." Gene knew his tone was artificial. "Be a brave boy a little while. You'll be home very soon."

Carlino cried louder; home was not home: it was mother or father, each one meaning absence of the other.

"What did your daddy tell you?" Gene asked. "Did he say something bad about your mother?" Gene looked at the boy's shirt, wrinkled, showing part of his tan back. "Look. You'll be taking trips. You'll be seeing him again. Planes, they make it here to there in seven hours." Carlino had not turned yet. "Now, how about those temples? Aren't we going to see them and buy some postcards for your collection?"

The child raised his head and nodded.

"Then we'll see hundreds of temples," Gene said. "You heard about Rome and all its temples."

Carlino now looked at Gene. "And the catacombs, Uncle."

"The catacombs!" Gene took a hand. "Bright and early tomorrow morning. Into the catacombs we go." He stroked Carlino's hair, then leaned down in the flush of the feeling that had filled him at the entrance, and kissed Carlino's face.

The child jumped off the bed and ran to his room, then called back: "Hey, Uncle. Look what she's doing."

Gene rushed in and saw Joanna talking on the telephone. He took the phone and explained that the child was trying to call America. "Shall I ask this operator to put in our call?" Gene said.

"Let's call tomorrow, after we take our trip," Carlino said.

Gene was uncomfortable. He needed the family's words, to detach him a bit and take some of it on themselves. But he could not disrupt Carlino again.

"All right," Gene said. "Maybe you want to talk tomorrow." Carlino's face was victorious, but Gene did not see the boy's wish to hold his mother unreal and away a little longer. "But maybe Joanna wants to talk *tonight*," Gene said. "We'll make a little call from my room, and then Carlino can make *his* call in the morning."

"No, she doesn't want to call," Carlino said.

"Just a minute. Let's ask her for herself."

Joanna had taken up her large doll. "No, I don't want to call," she said, and leaned back on her bed.

Gene spoke to the operator and placed the phone in its cradle. "Joanna. Now, listen. Wouldn't it be nice to talk to Mommy before going to bed. It's very nice when you hear the voice, the sounds under the ocean, like echoes."

The child had been undressing the doll and did not answer. Gene watched the slow, careful movements, sensing the silent words of mind-play with each gesture.

"Do you want your mother to worry?" he said.

The child stopped and smiled at him. "Is Mommy all right?"

"Yes, Mommy's all right. But she's waiting to hear your voice right this minute. Don't you understand that simple fact?"

72

"All right," Joanna said. "If Carlino talks to Mommy, too."

"But *he* doesn't want to."

Joanna returned to the doll, watching her own fingers: the doll was undressed now, but it did not seem nude. Instead it was a reddish painted statue, stiff and lifeless without the clothes that gave it life. "I'll call right now," Gene said. "And you just say a few words to your mother."

"I'm tired, Uncle." As she spoke, Carlino looked at the doll and moved his fingertips over the smooth body. "Leave it alone!" Joanna had said it so suddenly that Carlino was startled; he slapped the doll in revenge, but Joanna held on.

She picked up one of its shoes and threw it at Carlino's face, and he spit on the doll, the bubbly white saliva rolling easily along the shining body.

"*Porco, porchino!*" Joanna spit back and turned to Gene, who stood staring. "Uncle, get him!"

Gene was unable to stop them, though he knew they would fight. When they did, and Carlino hit his sister repeatedly, Gene stepped between them and held the boy's hands. "That's enough," he said.

The child tried to break loose but could not. He looked at Gene's stronger hands. "I hate you, Uncle. You're a bad man and you took me away from my place."

Gene let go. "You know your place. It's back home, your place. With Mommy and Granpa and Granma. And all your friends back home. That's your place."

Carlino smiled and remained silent. He walked to his own bed, sat down and began to untie his shoes. Gene watched his back, leaning over twice, then sitting up and placing his feet on the bed. "Can we have melons and toast for breakfast?" the boy said.

73

"Why not? Have anything," Gene said. "Even lollypops."

"Let's call Mommy." Carlino held his legs in the air and bicycled.

Gene picked up the phone and tried to get an overseas line, then went to his room to undress while he waited for the connection to be made. But there was no luggage in his room; he had forgotten it in Amalfi.

He called Amalfi, spoke to the hotel owner, who promised to send the suitcases to Rome. Gene asked if Tubino might pick them up for shipment. "Perhaps you know someone in Amalfi?" the owner asked, and Gene thought of Elena but did not know her last name. "Send the bags to Rome," he said. "And I'll arrange for this hotel to ship them to me."

He lay back on his bed when the call was done and tried to remember what he had left. His electric shaver seemed important, but the clothes were not: they were shirts, socks, another suit and perhaps a third: he could not remember. He damned the children as he heard their voices come up, then took off his shoes, his socks and trousers and slid into his bed to wait.

Soon he was asleep, awakened after a few restless hours by his own room light. The lights were shining in the next room, but there was no sound. He thought the children might be gone but did not get up. In the morning he would surely find them, but if by some chance they had started back to Amalfi, like lost dogs, he would have had a measure of revenge.

7

But **they** were there the next morning, changed, like new children minted in Rome. They ran into his room; Joanna held her new doll: "Kiss Uncle good morning," she said, and placed the pink face near him.

"Let's go, Uncle." Carlino sat close to him on the bed. "When is the plane?"

"The plane already. I thought you wanted temples." Gene was suspicious of Carlino, too satisfied with the present, contradicting yesterday, which Gene could not forget.

"OK," the boy said. "But when do we leave here?"

"Tonight." Gene could not understand it. "About seven tonight."

Joanna made the doll dance, and Gene rubbed its yellow curls: he was relieved by the children's change, their softness: it became his forgiveness in some way. "Go get dressed," he said, "and we'll go downstairs."

When they left, he dressed in the same cramped clothes, the wrinkles making them an escape uniform, and went downstairs for a shave, leaving the children in the hotel dining room. He ordered melon for them, and when he came back found Carlino with a menu in English, having found toast, scrambled eggs, and peanut butter.

They spent the morning in the ruins and stopped at the steps of a cathedral on the way back, where Joanna saw necklaces of Mary to buy. The old man selling them placed blue rosary beads about her neck, once he had seen Gene's eyes on the child. Joanna said that they must buy one for each of the women at home.

At the hotel it was time for lunch, which they ate in a quiet shade, as if no one else were in Rome. Back in their rooms, the children tried to sleep but could not. Gene fell back on his bed, with heavy legs, listening to their tired voices ready to break into argument.

His eyes shut against his will and sleep took him quickly down; sleeping, he fought to awake and when he finally did, the children were gone. He ran from his bed and found their room empty. At the window he saw only the Roman traffic below.

He walked to the door and heard their voices in the hall. They were lying on the red rug near the door of his room, looking at their postcards and a large map; Joanna had the doll sitting next to her.

Gene watched them: surrounded by gifts, they responded to everything around them as a sign of a future event. No Carlo, Elena, Amalfi seemed present near them. Carlino, who had cried so long, who had struck his fists against the force that drove him away from his father, now was living in the maps, postcards, plastic things, content to be lost inside.

Gene turned away from them and went to dress. The wrinkled suit reminded him of Marinara, as if he had Carlo's body for a moment, squat and stunted from work that loses the self.

He remembered his suitcases in Amalfi, traded for the children. They would probably never come, but he had taken out insurance.

It was still afternoon, but he called for a taxi, then packed the children's bags. They walked downstairs, following the porters again; at the desk he sent a brief cable; the taxi reached the airport at five.

Joanna wanted a snack after they had walked through the terminal. They ate in silence: the engine noises from outside were changing the world. Gene took out his last lira and the children went out, faster now, for some final shopping. Still walking the corridors, they heard their flight announced and ran to the gate with the crowd.

Seated, they were made silent by the movement of the passengers, throwing bags up on the racks, removing jackets, reaching for the pillows. Carlino stood in the aisle but a passing stewardess sat him down. The engines started and pushed them all back as the plane moved quickly out to the runway. In the air, the movie began and took the children's attention. Gene watched the last sunlight and the quick change to darkness, which made him draw his shade and turn to the children again.

Something was happening inside him: he wished the two were his own. He remembered Dr. Monachino telling them to start another family (*You've still got the juice left, Gene.*) when he had gone in for pills to help his depressions.

But they had never succeeded. Francine had cried because she was unable to have more children, and Gene turned away from the hope of a new child quickly; he could not find the dream of being a father, a mood that made you wait for something to serve: the pride of it was gone; he saw no pleasure in bestowing his name again on something that would demand his work for more years, make him unable to *retire,* although he had told Francine that he got his pleasures from his office and the way it ran.

For a long while Francine had lost her feelings at night, did not look at him, would go to the bathroom to undress. She was protecting herself, as if the new fact were only a sexual fact, that making love was not right if no children could be imagined.

She began to have headaches when the weather was wet and humid, and parts of her became swollen, swellings that the doctor could not explain. Some nights Gene had shaken with expectation as she began to undress, waiting for some sign that he might touch her; finally, always seeing her turn away to remove her final clothes, go into the bathroom to wash and apply creams, he would fall asleep as he waited, with unsaid words in his mouth, like old food.

He had gone back to dreaming about the girls in the office, his mind forcing it on him continuously, though it became an insult, making him a day-peeker at crossed legs. He had even gone to stag movies with the men of his bowling club (who called him *the Boss*) and had each time felt a dry, nervous feeling, as if a burning rock shook in his stomach.

Every month or so, relaxed by a party, forgetting herself after four or five scotches, forgetting relatives who talked about her because she drove a Thunderbird and played golf three times a week at the club where they had been the first Italians admitted, she began to make love like the young girl he once had, in the days when they stayed in bed and laughed at their exhaustion, and ate steaks afterwards.

Finally, Gene fell asleep and let the movement take him.

He awoke for a tray of food and looked at it until it was taken away, the stewardess dividing it between the children. Quickly the stewardess cleared the tables, folded them back, placed an Italian newspaper in his hands. Gene looked up and saw her hunched, holding on as the letdown began, the plane pitching and leveling over and over before landing.

He led the children through customs, not looking up to find the family yet in the crowd waiting outside. But they were finally let through the barriers, and Anna came running to the children. Joanna ran to her, but Carlino stayed back, holding Gene's hand.

An immigration officer followed, walking with old Santoro and Angelo. "Well, are these our little children?" the man said to Gene, and smiled at them. "How did you get them out?"

"Nobody asked a thing," Gene said. "We just got on board."

Anna came to him and embraced him quickly because the official was near. "Are they all checked out?" the official said.

Anna went for her purse. "I have the papers from my doctor," she said. "Here. They had their smallpox, polio, measles, allergy, lockjaw —"

"Tetanus." The man said it and smiled.

"And the boosters." Anna held the yellow booklets near his face. "It's signed by my doctor and the Board of Health." She turned to Gene. "They have to make sure the children are safe."

"That's fine," the official said. "How did you find them?" he asked Gene.

"Well, I just drove down to Amalfi —"

"No, no. I mean, were they healthy all the time? Did they seem to be living in sanitary conditions? What kind of water source, for example?"

"It's a sizable place." Gene thought of mentioning Phil Di Maris, in Congress. "With running water and all the facilities. There's a lot of Americans there every year. The kids were in a nice big room, very clean."

The official was nodding. "Well, good work. We've got our little kidnaps back. Do you want to call the newspapers?"

"No," Santoro said. "Say nothing!"

The children had moved close to their mother: the man frightened them, a new kind of thief. "Did you eat a lot of pizza?" he said, and reached to pat them before walking away, escorting them to his office.

The Santoros went in a line behind him to a windowless room, awaiting the next obstacle, a fine, some new trick to keep them apart from each other.

The man sat at an almost blank desk and wrote out forms, writing facts about the children and Gene. Old Santoro saw an Irish or German face, the ones ahead of him who had always managed to embarrass him and with sarcasm ruin his tenuous use of the new language. This man did not see Joanna and Carlino as perfections of the Santoros, free of taint. Rather he listed them as creatures who were exposed to strangeness, the other thing that is not America.

They left him at last, silent, hurrying from the terminal into the Buick.

"Where's Francine?" Gene asked.

"Home with Momma and my Emma," Angelo said. "They're getting some food ready."

He put the bags into the trunk. "Did you get anything else besides toys?" Anna said. "Look at all this."

"Yes, we had some good times, too." Gene sat in front next to his brother, impatient now, riding with guilt, as if Francine had stayed away because she sensed his time with Elena and the feelings he had left there with her.

By the time they crossed the Whitestone bridge, he was aware of his father's silence, thinking it was a reproach towards Francine. The car went to Anna's house first, where Francine was waiting, excited to see him, hugging him like a girl. "I thought you were mad at me for staying away so long," he said, but she did not answer.

The meal was served by Mrs. Santoro and Emma, and though the children were asked many questions and did most of the talking, Gene knew his father had something waiting, a new heavy secret.

When the children had finished, they were taken upstairs to bed, and Frank Santoro began quickly. "Gene, I got something to show you."

"Can't you even wait five minutes?" Francine had come and stood behind her husband, holding the rungs of his chair. "Poppa, can't you leave him out of it for once. He did enough. Now let him get back to his business in peace, will you?"

"Anna, get the note." Santoro had looked up at Francine, then lowered his eyes as if to bury her; he lit a Tuscan cigar and stared at the table while Anna came with a yellow cable and gave it to Gene.

It was from Carlo, a rush of words saying he would return. Gene looked at them. "It's only a gesture. To keep up his pride. He'll never do it."

"He did it once already," his father said. "And very easy, too."

Anna was annoyed at Gene's estimate of Carlo. "He's a stubborn man. Tell him, Poppa."

Mr. Santoro nodded. "This man will fight for his children.

Once he told me — I never spoke about it, but I told Anna now. He said to me to have good children grow up in this *mescuglia*, this *porcheria*, this American shit. Was a crime to children. He said America hates babies."

Gene had been looking at Anna, who was changing. Someone had given her a new hairdo, colored reddish blonde; her brows were thinner and the lipstick she wore made her lips a short, heart-shaped orange — she was all the colors she had never been and seemed at first glance twenty years younger, except when her face moved in irritation or anger and the old darkness came through her eyes. "Carlo wants to live over there," he said to her. "It's nothing personal." Gene's instinct was to protect her, as if her new face were a mask covering bones.

"Well, what's so damn good about Italy, I'd like to know." Francine had started from behind him, but stopped as she saw her father-in-law's flushed face. Her remark was sudden, and she regretted it already because it would make them draw Gene further in. "Oh, let Marinara blab on," she said. "It's all over now, and we know it."

"No it is not!" Santoro's face shut them up. "When the plane is on your door in seven hours. When a man can hire agents to do anything — rob, kill, take what you have. When the richest are shot in their own hotel. Oh no! Now we need a whole family to protect. Each the other."

Gene saw his father spreading over the table, the Santoro who had grown out of the peasant shell little by little, a swelling ego that finally looked down at hundreds of machines and a thousand workers as if they could fit in the palm of his hand. "What do you propose?" Gene said.

Santoro turned to him, pleased. "I have my eye on a house

near White Plains. Something very big. We all will live there."

"Gene, did you hear him?" Francine said. "We're not the keepers of those kids."

Santoro raised his right hand, the bishop's palm. "Now is no time for fights." He removed an envelope from his shirt pocket, then unfolded a photograph of a large stone house surrounded by a high black steel fence. "The iron," he said, "is all electric. Anyone touches gets the shock and the lights go on and the alarms, all automatic."

"Where did you find this fort?" Gene was trying to lighten the thrust, the determination of the old man.

"It belonged to a racketeer. You know him, too. Tranto, who moved to Washington. I will buy it —"

"No!" Francine had screamed. "I will not live in that house."

Angelo was smiling; he would agree to it to cast Francine, the snob, in a worse position.

"There is plenty privacy," the old man was saying. "Three apartments, all separate, like a house each one. No feet will be stepped on." Santoro had it all done.

"What do you say, Angelo?" Gene asked.

"I'm ready to go. It's a beautiful place, and I was thinking the whole bunch of us could get together more. We never get together anymore. It's always, *we want to,* but this one's busy and that one's got a kid sick. And when it gets cold out, forget it. You know what I'm trying to say."

"Then you would have enough without me, I think," Gene said. "I'm always nearby, on call."

"No, no." Old Santoro's voice was becoming harsh at the thought of losing Gene, having a weak flank before he began.

"Carlo should not be able to trace our homes. He knows where you live, Gene. When we go up there, it's all secret."

"I don't care, I don't care, I don't care." Francine's hands went into the air, her curse in her gestures and her lack of control. Still she knew that her protests would bring them further together; insulted, they would press their stupid plan until its *raison* was only honor and what they would call love, her refusal exposing all the unspoken resentments usually kept within: they would attack her openly, until she would be like the sounds of Marinara's plotting.

Santoro turned to Gene for his response to the detestable rebellion by the woman who had already destroyed most of the principles of the past by playing golf and riding a Thunderbird too frequently, far beyond the necessity of shopping and visiting relatives. He would press his son now: would Gene defer to the bird shriek of the unmanned creature trying to wear testicles or would he remember the actions that passed only from father to son, the shields carved with words made by men for men: HONOR, ALLEGIANCE, DUTY, BLOOD, LOYALTY, PATRIA: they waved in Santoro's head as he waited.

Gene knew the old thoughts and felt the questions as if they were being written on his skin. Like the celebrant at Mass who looks at the wafer and knows it is God, Gene saw the square chin, the hooded black eyes, the short-cut silver hair, the thin lips.

"We all have to chip in until this thing blows over. That's clear." Gene was speaking softly. "Until you people look around and see that Carlo is never coming. But I can't sell my house — that's my pride and joy, that house. I might sublet for a while."

Francine released a sound like a moan and stood in place. She allowed her pretty face to take the sourness of acceptance, tightening, becoming heavier. No one saw the change or could know it would be permanent, that Francine was the first casualty in the war against Marinara. And had she seen her face she would have attacked them, struck out at one of them, taken a knife from the table without control.

Anna sat down as if she had been running. Having lost and won, she was still a hostage, but a changing one, and her role was less a human one: she was the face of their cause, like a relic kept in a vault, old bones or dried blood. She would be kept at the center but never asked anything.

A secret part of her wished for Carlo to come, burst into the house, even beat her. Then he would stay, and they would be together again, and he, like the conqueror, would become fat and mild.

Carlo had loved her, brought things to her, remembering each day, until his mind began to hate the changes in the children and the wasteful thing he thought she had become. And the greatest mistake in her mind, the fact that his being a baker was unimportant to her, hurt him as a man; but she could make up for that now that she knew that all he had to be was present near her, a husband in any way he chose.

And he hated the days of their lives, with no festas, Christmas like a trade fair, people who drank but did not eat, no one who sat and talked about human things, men who did not see other men, children who jumped up from table after five minutes of eating, debts greater while money increased. He had called Annie the Countess of Korvette and begun to hate old Santoro, who spoke only stocks and gastric juices; and finally he detested even Gene, his expert's voice, his foghorn of knowledge, blaming all evils on the Communists, though Carlo's favorite nephew was an official in the Italian Party.

But Carlo claimed to have a wisdom the Santoros no longer had, brought from Italy inside his head: how one should live, travel, act towards neighbors and relatives, a flood of words that stopped actions. They did not listen to him; he was a whine of complaints, arriving too late, in 1950, smelling of defeat, which meant he was stupid and probably amoral.

The Santoros had an Italy in a sealed compartment, a boxed memory with old stunted kings, horse carriages, even highwaymen; they were Italians who had not changed a child-Italy, knew Italian ways locked in their heads, filled also with frozen peas, powdered soups, and thick beef; their government was their house, next door a foreign country began. Their children were their art, and their science was success.

And Carlo screamed against it all, yet followed the Santoros all the way. Then he stopped; one day he leased his shop, exchanging the sixteen-hour baking day for eight with Giacinto Lo Pinto, an eighty-year-old friend who had silently plodded Westchester gardens for years.

Being outside helped Carlo; he could come home for lunch and sit down in daylight. Anna had not liked it: it had stopped her day, first for a meal, then for his wish to go to bed; then in the evening she would have to cook a meal for the children.

She could not convince him that the bed was impossible in the middle of the day, when phones rang, deliveries came, the A & P was least crowded, her noonday shows were on TV. But she had given in plenty of times and then lost three hours unable to think after he left.

"In Italy we sleep after lunch and we eat," Carlo would say.

86

"And we lie down and we know our wives before dark. Not like your stupid brother, who must chase his wife in a car to get her."

Anna looked now at Gene, touched with embarrassment for him. Then she was aware that Francine had left the kitchen and was slamming closet doors, had come back with her coat on, looking down at them for a moment before walking out.

Gene remained silent, sitting with his father. Angelo had joined them for a while, then slipped away to watch TV with his mother while Gene and his father finished the decisions.

"If she makes trouble." Santoro held up the flat hand of the threatened blow. Gene nodded and smiled, to turn the gesture into a joke, but he knew that his father was serious and understood that all men longed to feel free to place their hands on reluctant women and children.

The feeling lay inside Gene and yet the acts were antique, crude, illiterate. His father looked cheap doing it, not weak or strong, and that was the worst of it: it embarrassed the world of clubs, societies, schools Gene lived in.

It was a disgust he knew, when as a school board member he had watched the debate on a proposal for the return of corporal punishment. Some bitch of a woman in a corset had explained what had been already done in Delaware, describing the campaign to hit children in schools as if it were a charity drive to enrich heart research. And he had noticed his good friends Tony Di Maris and then Terry Cerone and Walter O'Neill approving, men who never touched their own children, whose wives would not permit hitting, who would look upon spanking as the act of a savage.

"Poppa," he said. "I just got back. You hit me with all this. I need a little time to think." He stood up. "I'm not sure the threat is real. Because I *saw* Carlo. I saw him over there. And we've got to sit down and talk about it some more."

"All right. That's enough now." The old man shook his hands as he spoke. "But I will show you. And will you come if I show proof?"

"Yes. Proof." Gene left silently, stopping only to kiss his mother, who was dozing in her green armchair that faced the TV screen. "What do you think of all this?" she said softly to her son.

"Marinara will never come," Gene said.

"No? Are you sure?"

"Once he gets going in that bakery. No. He will never come back here. He doesn't like it —"

"Maybe next year —"

"Momma. I saw him. I talked to him. I saw what was there. And why he let the kids go, finally."

"You don't know the hearts of men," she said. "When it is their blood."

"Yes, I know. Blood is thicker than water." Gene was saddened to see his mother nod automatically. He kissed her face again and stood over her chair. "But money is thicker than blood," he said.

Mrs. Santoro smiled and squeezed her son's hand. She would believe him, though never disobey her husband, whose power, though touched with ignorance, was like her own signature.

"Gene?" she said, coming suddenly to a new thought. "Did you like Italy?"

"Very much, very much." Gene held his voice down as Angelo looked away from the set to his face. "I want to go back soon. And spend more time there, all along the coast. You know, I didn't even get to Capri."

"Amalfi, Sorrento, Positano. Now you know what I had."

"Yes."

Mrs. Santoro smiled, vindicated — she was no longer sure for what, yet vindicated by Gene's excitement. No one had even spoken against her Italy, but it had never been mentioned, recognized, no school had taught the children a word about it, and it lay invisible, like a lie.

She saw Gene turn and leave, a saddened man who had Francine to face. But what could they do: only the fort lay ahead for protection.

PART TWO

8

GENE ENTERED his own door, forgetting Francine and the family. He had driven through the adjoining towns, stopping at an all-night diner in Pelham, and had had coffee alone, watching the crowds coming in for eggs and coffee like people from a wake.

He had not realized that the house itself would affect him on return, like a friend — the shapes of windows, the stones in the path up to the back door, the silent collection of tools and hoses at the back of the open garage, and their odor — whatever it was. In the house his lamps, the color of the light, curtains and tables and rugs. He sat in the living room until Francine came in, wearing a robe.

"You don't know how good it is to step into your own house." His quiet voice, the affection in it, seemed to Francine emotions for herself. She did not catch the exile's tone, the loneliness of killed pride.

Francine stood before him. "Gene, I've been thinking about what happened today." Her tone was calm, as if her suffering had stopped, and Gene was relieved.

"I've been driving around alone," he said. "Trying to piece it together. And I forgot the house. I mean, I forgot it was here

93

for me. And then the feeling that just came out of me — I don't know how to say it — the welcome the *things* gave me, the dead things —"

He looked at Francine, but could not invite her to sit with him; the feeling inside him coincided with Elena in some way, yet he did not want her here — she would have been a stranger and was already unclear.

"I'm glad, Gene. This is your home. That's one of the things that got me. Why do you think I was screaming tonight?" She sat across the room from him. "Would you like a drink, or some coffee?"

"No, no. Thanks." Gene wanted to go to her, but sat back, embarrassed by the memory of Elena, as if it were an odor on him that Francine would recognize. "You were going to say something, Fran."

"Yes, yes. How crazy, I was forgetting it. And seeing you. As if you'd been gone for ten years. You look so handsome, Gene. Italy must have been good for you. Whatever it was — I mean, the mess — at least you left this rat race for a while. You had a *kind* of vacation."

"You look delicious." Gene felt his mood as he said it, as if Francine were new. He stared at her body.

"I was thinking about us, about all of us," she said. "The picture of us around the table today. I got home and my mind went back. What I was as a kid. My father was Sicilian, with all the old ways. And he was a rock. He was the boss of everything and what he said went. We lived when he talked. All us kids were polite, obedient, never restless or pesty. And I remember feeling like a failure when our boys went over to see him because they were never good in that way. I blamed myself every time. I even blamed you for not putting your hands

94

on them, knocking sense into them. I saw our kids as pests, the American crap they always called me. And they never acted polite to Pop and Mom — I was always telling them on the way over, say hello, kiss Granpa and Granma. How they hated it all, and me too. I saw it in their eyes. Frankie said once that Granma stank — my own mother. And then *I* noticed it, too. He was right. She had that musty smell of all the skirts and aprons and long underwear and days and nights inside. You smell it at the early morning Masses in the pews when all the old ladies are hunched over the rosaries.

"Tonight I found out something. And it's horrible. The fathers, they *are* dead. The kids were right — the way they acted, I mean. All the old ways are gone; they don't mean anything. The pesty kids are impatient kids; they've got things to do and they can't wait orders from King Victor Emmanuel. Gene, could that be true? Could there be a time, could we have an age when the fathers are dead?"

Gene did not answer because he saw that she had more of the weight of it to give out.

"I mean a time when we don't have to live with the *dead* orders from the past. Why am I talking this way? You and I had it injected into us from childhood — we can listen and try to obey. But maybe even *we* can't act on it. We really can't. I don't understand if you know what I mean. You, with your position, what you do, the way you live. You can't really go along with Poppa in the old way, even if you wanted to. You can't go up to some fort and live like old Sicily. And all that made me scream. I can't do it; I'll run away first and go live and work in an A & P in Buffalo before I'll live like that."

Gene was smiling, and Francine stopped. "Do you agree?" she said.

"That's the way it is," he said. "But we run like turtles all the time. I did some thinking in Italy — I did it even when I didn't know I was doing it. And another kind, which I'll tell you about someday. But all of it — it only meant this: that I got to find out about myself and how much time for obedience and how much time for work and how much time for other things. We only live in what we do. And this — what do I like? What do I *really like*?"

He did not mention Elena, say that she was "other things" because she was only a clue. "Naples was a bad shock," he said. "Everything there was rotten. The machines fell apart. You ask for a room with a bath and they tell you yes they have it even when they don't have it. You get the smile and agreement but not the truth. Nothing gets done, and you see they're interested more that you smile and tell them how good they are, how nice the place is, how nice the sun shines — then everything can go to pieces. Rotten. And yet you like it more than here. Not that everybody's so great — that lawyer I met would sell his mother, I'm sure of it. But life is going on outside; they're all so different from each other; everybody you meet has a little crack to make, his eyes are open, nothing's locked up, nothing's locked up — even when they're sitting still, they're sitting in the sun, it's all moving, the thing is moving. A day's got color, the people are feeling everything, looking at you, staring at everything. I hate to say this — it makes me feel like a spy. What a stupid thing to say." Gene leaned forward to shift his position and change associations. "There was this man I had a little talk with. From Milan, who was sent down to Naples, a factory there, just on the outskirts. To find out why this place had such low production. This guy gets there — a college man, a liberal from up

north. So the first thing he does is raise salaries. The workers
were being paid too little and that was true enough. So production went up again for a while. Then about five or six
months and down again, this time more down than before, and
he found out that people weren't coming to work. So he
started talking to the people again — what was the matter, did
they have grievances and all that. No, they were very satisfied,
they said, but now they had a little extra money to live on,
which means get along a few weeks, so they went fishing, they
went to see uncles up in Benevento, the mountains — whenever it was nice weather. Their first thought was doing something like that as soon as the sun came out. They just forgot
about work.

"So don't you see, Francine. We never want to take off anymore. Even if we fly to a hotel and fly back on the twenty-one
day tour. We really love to put the bit in our mouths. Every
day. I know it, I know it. Don't think I'm any example of the
opposite. Like that horse I read about in the Plymouth
Colony. I couldn't forget it. The one the kids wrote poems
about; he was the idol of what to be, the horse that was tied up
and went around and around the damn well or whatever the
hell it was every day and never asked for anything else. I know
it! I can't wait to get to the office, why deny it. Even on days
I'm feeling sick. I go to get pepped up. So here's these Wops.
You know, they're very far from us. They are not like you and
me. And if your father and my father stayed over there, you'd
look like a black sack of dough and I would be working on
some rotten farm until my back was crooked. I might be one of
them. Beaten down from not enough money, knowing every
day I'm in a country passed by progress, pissing on the damn
Roman cities the rich foreigners come to and take pictures of,

hating those goddamn dirty pieces of rock and marble the rich people can go ooh and ah about with their pockets so full of power they can do anything they want. Sitting in the second-rate place. And yet!"

Gene began to walk back and forth and raised his hands to the ceiling, unusual for him after spending years acting like the formal lawyer, training himself to big shot stillness. "Doing more and laughing at the damn thing too. And eating! Oh the eating. The taste of things. You could forget everything eating there. Just treating your mouth and your — making love more —"

He stopped, again because the exaltation was not enough to cover his guilt about Elena; he had also wanted to say making love with more people, which you could not say here.

He sat down and looked at his wife, whose face was respectful; but her attention was unfixed by her own thoughts, whose strength held her. "And yet I can never feel right," she said when she thought he had finished. "I must go my own way, and I know I'll always feel horrible that I'm going against them. I'm always going to be a failure in front of them. We'll never be free of that. Either of us." She tried to get Gene's eye. "That's why I need you so much."

Gene stood up and walked to the bar; he had suddenly wanted to run out: her statement unlocked another piece of feeling that had exploded in Italy. He did not want her if he was the only reference she would have, as if his blood were needed to keep her alive.

"We all need each other," he said, and took the scotch and poured. "But we need ourselves. I learned that."

"With who?" Francine had understood part of the tone but not the stupid way that men thought: she was certain that all philosophical statements were hidden personal attacks.

"That's not the point," Gene said. "If I had a hundred women in Naples, I wouldn't learn that between a woman's legs."

"Let's not talk about what you *learned* yet, if you don't mind. Your father's trying to change my life, and I won't do it. That's where we start." Certain now that Gene had been unfaithful, Francine backed into survival, a way that would also serve as an insult to Gene, who had left her unguarded.

"One thing I promise you." Gene brought her a tumbler of whiskey. "We don't go to that castle. Under any circumstances. He can just shove it, as they say." Gene was smiling at his anger, finally escaping. "Right up his old Italian ass, *if you don't mind.*"

Francine drank the scotch and gave the glass quickly to Gene for another. She watched him walk to the bar, stand over it confidently, mix the drinks like someone she could not let go. "And what do we do?" She had almost added, *"Boss,"* but remembered that this was what old Santoro was often called.

"*Time.* Give it time. Day after day they'll see a little reason. Marinara is trying to exist. Plant his crops and feed himself." Gene brought the second drink and sat next to her. "The last thing a man in Amalfi wants is to invade New York."

Francine smiled, catching some knowledge Gene had, though unaware of what it was. "We are getting so damned scared," he said. "Scared of our own shadows here. Do you know that?"

Francine did not; she embraced Gene because his certainty seemed like a return of love for her, as if he were dropping off the other encounter she guessed at.

Gene thought she believed in his judgment about Marinara. He placed his glass quickly on the coffee table and began to kiss her.

Now he was embarrassed that making love to her was as exciting as it had been to another in Amalfi; as if all female flesh, soft, sweet-smelling, were exciting and permissible — the thought he had turned away from on his hotel terrace in Amalfi. Yet an energy came from Francine that could accept no refusal from his body; she had once waited for him to create it, as if by marriage he purchased ownership of the switch that ignited her.

But now he lost his thoughts in her stored passion, in the extra intimacy of the living room couch, sudden and spontaneous, a moment without plan or preparation and therefore more exciting.

In the morning Francine was pleased as she dressed, strong and anxious to start the day. Gene looked at her from his bed, still dizzy from the flight; her movements were too aggressive, and he felt the wish to get up and stop her: his sleepy mind was certain she was off to his father to deliver their refusal.

"What is it?" he said.

"Nothing. What do you mean?"

"I mean where are you going so damn early."

"It's nine-thirty. I have to get Sylvia and buy a gift."

Gene reached his hand to the bedtable at his side: there were no cigarettes, Kleenex — his radio had been removed. "Where's my stuff?"

"We were cleaning. The girl must have moved it."

"Well, make her move it back. I'm here now and I want my radio and a pack of cigarettes here in front of me."

"I know that. I'll get it. I'm getting stocked up today. That's why I want to get going."

Gene could not control his head or his words, saying what he did not wish, his voice parrying for a fight that was stronger than he felt. He watched his wife dressing, was eased as she lifted her skirt to adjust her stockings, the intimacy some dim assuagement. "I'm not going anywhere today," he said. He turned to his left side, facing the wall: "And why don't you just come right back in here?"

"I'm dressed." Francine was confused, not wishing to disobey.

"You're always dressed."

"What do you want me to do? Take off all my clothes, *now?* I'm trying to get this house set up for you."

"You're trying to take off like a rocket again. As usual." Gene's anger was like blindness, thrown wildly about, striking Francine, but the emotions were not for her, disappearing, or the others, waiting, with typewriters, appointment slips, messages. It was the day starting, time, like a cripple or a filthy beggar always at the same place, the same hand out, reminder of the dark contrasts between the destroyed and the successful, telling those with money their reward is to keep working.

"Gene, please don't get mad." Francine came to his bed and leaned close. "Let's not start again. Last night we sounded like different people. Like different people. You got a new spark getting away. It's good for you." Gene did not answer. "I don't want to talk the same way we used to." She was leaning closer and she kissed him, her hands on his shoulders.

"No!" He threw the covers off and jumped up, standing in his shorts.

"What is it?" Francine forgot her shock, thinking Gene had become ill.

"Nothing, nothing." He sat down at the edge of his bed and covered his face with his shaking hands. "I'm sick of everybody. I don't even want a hug. It only means somebody's going to ask me for something by tomorrow —"

"Not me, Gene —"

"Please. Please don't make it an argument against you. I'm not here to hurt you." Gene did not speak for a while, then looked up at her face, twisted and frightened, old again, the lines in it like cuts that showed her damages. "Just break the telephone," he said.

Gene's thoughts were covered by a picture of the Bronx river, a wooden bridge in snow, the first picture he had taken, his first camera, a Christmas Kodak.

When he looked up, Francine was at the door. "Why don't you sleep as late as you can," she said, catching his eyes. "I'll bring you back something you like and we'll make lunch."

She had had the grace to be silent; perhaps, with all her ruin, she was the only one who sided with him, whatever his past choices were and what his future ones might be. He suppressed the words of thanks, clichés of affection, to avoid returning to the repetitions of their lives: after arguments, apologies in code words. He looked at her and smiled, and Francine waved, a reminder of an old game they played, and walked silently out.

Gene got into bed and shut his eyes; his body was ready for sleep, but his head had one more reminder: he would see the children, but not the others, as if Joanna and Carlino had also suffered something of this return.

As HE opened the door to Anna's house, an alarm went off. The door stopped after a few inches, held by a thick chain from within.

Anna came, running. "Who left the lock open?" She stopped the alarm bell, then unlatched the door. "I'm sorry, Gene. Somebody keeps leaving the lock open."

"What the hell *is* all this? You got a guard, too?" Gene looked at the box behind the door, topped with a red blinker warning light.

"You can only get guard service at night, unless you take one for the whole twenty-four hours." Anna was resetting the alarm system. "They have the night patrol, though. They drive around and check the houses for all kinds of strangers. It's worth it —"

"Two for the price of one. Niggers and Carlo." Gene found a smile: it was insane enough for a little laughter. "How about the day? Can't you get a squad car from the cops? Like the Chinese Republic embassy? I think you only have to prove a bomb danger."

"Big jokes to you." Anna turned away and walked to the

kitchen, and Gene followed. "Where's my Italian friends?" he said.

"Poppa's downtown," Anna said. "And Momma's still upstairs. She doesn't come down until about twelve. Did you know her hip's been killing her?"

"I mean where's the kids."

"Oh, the kids." Anna was pleased. "They're upstairs and screaming to go out. All they want to do is go out, and Poppa's having a fit —"

"Well, you trust them with me, don't you?"

Anna's response came after a slight pause, enough for Gene to catch. But he would not mention it and start the madness of last night. "All right," he said, "we'll just drive around. How about the police station — we'll drive around the station house."

"Please don't be funny, Gene." Anna turned away from him. "I'm just a nervous wreck here. I can't take jokes like this — it's *not* a joke."

Anna had the only justification for the delusion of Carlo's coming; if she hadn't, it would have meant she married a fool, an inferior creature that made her even less than she thought of herself. "Don't worry," Gene said. "Those kids are like my own. Why do you think I'm here the first day, instead of the office?"

"Yes, Gene. Yes. I'll go get them." Anna remembered her brother's job and what he had done that she would not have dared, the plane, the strange hotels, another country. "As a matter of fact they've been talking about you ever since they woke up."

She left before he could answer, and returned with the children, both dressed in slacks, with heavy shoes, sweaters buttoned up over their shirts.

Joanna ran to him and embraced him and Carlino came shouting his name. They were his in some way, like messengers in this time of indecision. "Let's go," Gene said, and took them to the door.

Anna called after. "What time you coming back?" She came to the door. "I just want to set the alarm right so I don't have to do the whole damn thing over again. This timing is a pain —"

"Who knows?" Gene looked at the children, who were already in his resistance and smiled with him. "Maybe we'll even take another plane ride," Gene said to Carlino.

Anna looked down at the alarm box and did not answer: everything was possible for those who had escaped the house once: she was helpless near them.

"He's only kidding, Mommy." It was Joanna, who had caught her mother's sadness. "We'll be home soon."

"Not me," Carlino said. "I'm staying out all night —"

Gene slapped the back of his head playfully. "I got to," Carlino said. "Because when I get back they'll keep me in for all the time."

"Don't you understand we are trying to protect you?" His mother's voice had risen quickly out of her hurt moment. "Gene, please talk to them and explain it. Especially him."

Gene led the children to his car, and Anna locked the door on herself.

They sat in Gene's big car, Carlino in back as usual. Gene drove away from town and out to the shore road, then up to White Plains and across Westchester on the expressway.

The children did not speak; driving was like escaping. It was a sunny day and the car became hot, making them sleepy. As they slowed down for the exit, Gene said, "Now we're all getting hungry. I'm just getting my appetite again."

"Me too," Carlino said from behind. "The plane makes you full and empty the same time. I was so hungry and then I ate and felt so stuffed."

"Let's go to the Adventurer's Inn," Joanna said. "You know that place, Uncle?"

"Sure," Gene said. "Kosher hot dogs and french fries. But now they call it Nathan's."

"Nathan's! Nathan's!" Carlino shouted for the first time, a child shout he had never used before in Gene's presence.

"We're coming onto Central Avenue. There's Korvette. Remember we couldn't find model paints over there."

"Oh, that's OK," Carlino said.

"No. I need some stuff too. You know I left my suitcases in Amalfi. And Francine put most of my shorts in there — she thought I was going to change every hour."

"I heard her screaming last night," Joanna said. "Is Granpa mad at her, too?"

"He's mad at somebody else?"

"Us." Carlino's chin was on the seat back. "He wouldn't let us call my friend Frankie. He wouldn't let Joanna go out on her bike."

Gene drove off the highway and soon was in the parking lot of the shopping center. Inside the store, the children were excited: the filled shelves were a welcome Amalfi did not have, the swollen fullness that took away fear. They wandered in the aisles, laughed with Gene as he selected shorts of crazy colors, stripes, polka dots, two scotch plaid.

On the way out there was a special counter, a new electric fan from Japan, a little blue and white cylinder held in the hand, operated by a battery. Gene bought two, and Joanna and Carlino held them in the car while they sat, and later in the restaurant while Gene bought the food.

While they ate, Gene reminded them that they were becoming American again, trying to make a joke, comparing the greasy hot dogs with the Italian food, but the children had no comparisons. The noisy delicatessen was all of time and part of the pleasure of Gene, who was the substance of the country.

When they reached the house, the sun had just set but only the front blue warning light was lit. When Gene rang the bell, many lights went on, and Santoro opened the door. He stood while they passed him, shut the door and came quickly to Gene after the children had passed into the house. "You did not call. You did not tell your time. We had to call the police."

Gene stopped to stare at his father's face. "I told you this is no joke," the old man said. "I believe he can be in the street there. Remember, he did it. He already did it! *Schtupido!*"

Santoro walked away and up the steps to the room he shared with his wife, his emergency room next to Anna.

Gene walked into the kitchen where the children were talking to Anna. "Did you really call the cops?" Gene said.

"How did we know anything? You never came." Anna stepped back because of his silence.

Gene turned and left; at the door, he heard Joanna call him, but he went out to his car and drove off.

Francine was in the living room reading when he came in. Her new glasses, with wide brown rims, were resting on her hair above her head: it was a look, that and her white sweaters, that he enjoyed, an appearance that now stood against the black silk, the look of Anna he had just left.

She had not heard him, and he came in and kissed her. "I'm glad you have no alarm bells," he said, and told her about the day.

"That's the way they want it," she said, then stood up. "I have a casserole if you want supper."

"Yes." Gene walked to the kitchen with her. "I had some lousy hot dogs with the kids. But they had a good time." He sat down. "They loved it, that greasy delicatessen. They'll turn to shit in a month."

Francine prepared the meal but did not answer. When she had poured water and wine and placed the casserole on the hot plate, she sat down and looked at Gene. "Do you realize what's happening?" she said.

"Don't ask me that." Gene drank some wine. "Nobody knows what's happening."

"At least what they're doing. What's right in front of your eyes."

"Francine, I'm telling you. I don't know what's in front of our eyes. I can't tell you what's making them do this. Do you believe people can do things that are totally not themselves. Like they were possessed. You know the phenomenon. *Possessed.* But none of us can believe it can happen today."

Francine saw that Gene's emotions had caught something else, like a secret, a solving thread in a mystery. But after she ate a bit, she had to speak. "They're possessed, all right. By their own hardheaded stiffness. By being always in the right. And deaf."

"I know all that, I know all that." Gene was weak and put

down his fork. "But you got to understand. That's my family. I've got them inside me in some way."

"Oh, Gene." Francine had not understood time: Gene had been a young man, whose life began as her suitor. "I'm so sorry. I didn't mean to talk that way —"

"No. No. Talk that way. Say everything that comes into your mind. Maybe we'll know something. Maybe." Gene was dizzy. "I've been yelling too much. I ran around with the kids like we were still running away over there." He stood up. "I think I'll go to bed."

"Gene, shouldn't you eat?"

"I had enough today." He walked to the kitchen door, looked back at the lamps they had had installed because they liked to eat in the kitchen. "I'm all right," he said. "But it's those kids I think about. I hate to think what's going to happen to them."

"You mean Carlo coming again?"

"I mean us. *Us.* To keep them safe, we'll kill the whole world." He turned the knob but did not move. "Maybe we're so afraid of others coming for them, to do them some harm, that it's really *us*; it's really what we want to do inside us. To them." He shook his head and went quickly up to his room.

10

CARLO HAD not counted the nights he had spent sitting alone at his high table; thus he contented himself with feeling it was his lifetime, alone, abandoned and forgotten. But he was getting out the fury silently and changing within: the clocks of Amalfi were turning inside him, new rhythms. For the first weeks he had gone down to his mother and father and heard their screams and shouted himself, striking his fists against the doors like a young man, cursing Gene the *vigliacco*, wishing horns on his marriage. In that time he had come upstairs and struck Elena, having found her singing in the kitchen. Joy of any kind insulted his grief, the death of another Carlo, revered inside his head, dying like an overdressed general.

But then rage had ended, as it always does, abruptly, and he was limp and silent, like the corpse and its mourners together. He had only the copy of his cable to the Santoro family and the thunderbolts of his wishes, night after night, and loneliness.

He had gone to the children's room, and hung his head over the empty beds. Then he had dismissed Elena, who had gone somewhere, to a sister in Ravello or a mother somewhere in the province or Calabria — he was not sure, except that she might be coming back to do laundry.

Checks and money had come from the officials who hated him. He ordered machines and supplies and they all came. He had made his shop appeal to foreign tastes, advertising American pie, the crust made with a northern ingredient, lard.

The Germans and the Americans came, and then surprisingly Italians from the cities, who seemed to have abandoned the taste of vermouth and pastry for scotch, potato chips, Coca-Cola, pie — the long list of Westchester. In Naples, they were making hamburgers, smoking only Marlboro, chewing chocolate chip cookies, installing freezers in the stores for frozen foods. A man called from Naples, the Vomero, and asked about daily shipments of pie, and Carlo said he would think about how he could ship them.

He had come back at the right moment, and with the money that came in he was careful and frugal. What had worked so well was the idea of charging a high price, quite beyond reality, making the new also rare. People came anyway, and he had watched them from the back of the shop, like a thief, seeing them accept the prices as if they alone proved quality. Even the Italians.

He brought home the money to count in the evenings, and after paying his debts, he stored away the rest in an iron case. He had learned in America that business failure should mean the shop but not the man: bankruptcy was a tragedy of machines and equipment: you buried them in the hands of creditors and took a trip to the resorts.

The size of the money *made* new ideas, and one night he dressed in a suit and went out to Atrani, where Carla Gennatasio lived. Just before leaving for America to marry Anna, he had met Carla, a woman whose husband had died in a quarry accident. In telling him of the anguish of early loss, she had squeezed his hand, and he had never forgotten the pained, exciting face, its agony passing through him to create desire.

It was as if he had filed her away and that now she came up out of the box of money, her name and then her face and body. Or had he made her come up one afternoon in the caffè while the men were talking about women, single or married, fat and thin. His younger cousin Vincenzo conquered the conversation with his description of older women, thick with health and bulging with want, more untouched than virgins because they contained so much that was insufficiently used. "And particularly widows," he had said, "under the right conditions," and the words had struck Carlo.

One of the fishermen had interrupted to describe a woman in Sorrento, who awaited him in the morning after her children had gone to school, her bed like a cooling oven, the sheets with her taste of night in them.

Others mentioned tourists; there were always fables of foreign women, the Germans who once in bed with an Italian ignited like blast furnaces, the northern woman down to taste the rich southern men, even the Americans, whose only knowledge was acting like clams in the sand: they learned, too.

Carla's apartment was the upper part of a building, entered through an outside staircase with flower boxes along the wall.

She remembered him, had heard of the new shop, did not think he remembered her but was pleased he took the pains to stop while passing by.

"No," he had said. "I came to bring some of the new sweets I make. My secrets."

Without ceremony, not standing in the doorway with proper politeness and form, she brought him inside and served coffee. The next week he came again, this time with three pies. The house was more open, the living room had flowers — the conditions were a pleasing comment on him. They had coffee; Ninetta and Paola, the two young daughters, came in and spoke with him.

They were there on Sunday when he came to dinner and their conversation never mentioned a father, the gap pleasant to Carlo: there were, in fact, no shadows or presences in the atmosphere of the house, only a space where a man could fit.

Carla herself was like a late summer fruit, overripe with juice, all that said *now*. On that Sunday he had forgotten the ovens and the tired night walk home. He stopped in the languor of Carla's body and her house, prepared in modern furniture which must have come from Salerno or Naples. After the children had gone out, he sat in the front room, with rugs, and waited for coffee to come in. The sunlight cast a rim around the fabric form on which Carla modeled the dresses and blouses she made. Behind it, on a cypress table, were the bolts of cloth she used, colors that conjured women.

While they sat, she explained that she had been "discovered" by tourists from the hotels in Amalfi. Now she mailed her handsewn work to Germany, Denmark, England, and France. "I have the touch for design," she said. "I can invent a style, and quickly. Some say I am unique, and they have copied me in London."

Carlo nodded with a new admiration: to see a woman like

this and see also a success of this kind: it was a type of miracle. That she could be waiting here, untouched, was another sign of the good luck that was flashing up out of his own ashes. Fortune was having its way: it was asking Carlo to join with Carla (even their names!) in a partnership of styles.

"In such a short time," he said. "You were able to make all this." He jumped up to examine the cloth, the work table, rub his dry fingers on the mannequin and silky chairs around it. "Even with —" he stopped as he looked at her, but he had already begun to mention the unspoken, and she knew what he had thought. "With your personal tragedy," he said.

"You sit a month. Two months, maybe waiting to die yourself. Then the children need clothes. The time passes. I may have profaned his name changing so soon." She was working at the cups and saucers she brought in, filling glasses with Strega, setting out large blue paper napkins, and was speaking slowly. "But you must accept it. And then learn to succeed."

He nodded and came back to sit with her at the glass coffee table. Strange, but what she had said was the one part of America he had liked: that a single person, still in rags, with no training, could stand up and start a business and then succeed. Carla had done that, and though she was a quiet woman, the energy of it came from her, someone who would never bow again.

She was at the end of her dependence; as his sweets created customers, so her work was created first now, then some were allowed to knock. He had been thinking of objects that come once creditors are weaker than yourself, a brown motorboat like those that skim in from Naples and Capri, something with which he could burst away from shore, find the beaches of the coast accessible only by water.

Carla described her work, thinking he was following her and not playing with his own thoughts. She had stood up and gone to a garment, holding it up. It was white, a dress. "A German woman will buy this. Whose husband makes cars."

"Cars?" He thought of buying one at discount from the man.

His eyes left the garment in her hands and studied her blouse which caught some sunlight; her shapes were suggested, the breasts so large he lost the thoughts he had had of the practical future and was aware of the rudeness of his breathing.

He studied the lines of her face to calm himself, her short nose, unusual, foreign but childlike; round eyes, large and open, almost a replica of tiny moons — blue bubbles, hanging lights — his mind was entertaining a rush of pictures which made him laugh aloud.

"You laugh!"

He stopped. "No."

"You think this work is small. Like a tailor on a side street." She brought the white dress to the table and dropped it, then strode to a desk near the window and removed a ledger. "If you knew the numbers in here." She laughed herself. "And you don't know what there is waiting."

Carlo had jumped up. "No, no." He stared at the ledger. "Oh, please, no. I was laughing in my own good feelings." He ran to her, took her hands and made her drop the ledger. "I don't care what it says — to ask you to marry me." He had embraced her, and in his excitement, pulled at the white blouse, removing the bottom tucked into the skirt, sending his hands up along her back, finally touching the flesh.

His chest pressed hard against the cushions of her breasts as he heard her sounds, the melting sigh of women.

Her voice continued louder and one of his eyes opened to see her face, imitating pain. A small flash of disgust had run through him because she was so anxious; but he remembered she was no virgin and therefore could be a woman, making the sounds that come from knowledge, increasing the cry of want without insult to either of them.

As they fell down together on the couch, on silk covers he had not noticed before and which therefore felt strange, he was held in two parts: the person he was in his hands and face that was possessing her; and the other, made reluctant by the thoughts begun with her willing way: had she been a virgin, tight and frightened, he would be starting with honor as well as newness and could face all the faces of the town with the confidence that comes from first possession, the sacred one. Instead, he would have something not of his own — that had already cuckolded him in the dim past. He damned his country and friends, and the codes like glue, stuck on them all, as if they were cannibals.

Eventually her shyness helped him come back to her. In saying yes to him, the acceptance was greater because it had been said once before, and he felt his body shudder as they embraced and found each other. In saying yes she seemed to say all the words that yes implied, and she blushed and stammered and turned away from him. He walked to her bedroom and she followed.

When Marinara was satisfied, he touched her hair, a bit too dry, and leaned to kiss her. She had been thinking again of a husband, had known he was to be the one from the first time he came. It had taken longer to think of him as a father, but this love had done it: there were no longer veils between them.

"I would not wish to marry here," she said. "Might we go to Naples?"

"Naples? No." Carlo was suspicious and sat up. But when he watched her face, its embarrassment, he saw her feeling of disgrace in marrying here again. "In my house," he said. "In Amalfi, which is your home, then."

"Carlo? One matter." It was painful, but she could speak frankly now. "Is it true, as they say, that you had a wife or *have* a wife. In America?"

He raised his arms and laughed, but it was harsh, almost a scream. "There are no wives in America. Only drivers of cars, models for washing machines and cigarettes. No flesh and blood. Flesh, flesh —" He began to pinch her arms.

Carla tried to laugh, but he was threatening to her in the excitement he had stirred within himself.

"Machines that give orders," he said, stood up, then sat down. "You must stop making love if the machine needs repair. Take it out and answer the phone." The tone of his voice changed to speak directly to her. "They are unbelievable there. Such women; so able. At first I was impressed. Mechanics, it seemed, and dressed like countesses, actresses, yet modest like farm girls. In every house a Doris Day. Standing in the kitchen, and all the wheels going round — tick, tick, the washer, the dishes being sprayed, the air being cleaned out, pulled up, the food being frozen downstairs, the shirts drying in another room. Good. Until the day you see it. Machines are them; they are the machines; what were women are now handles, parts for the machine. And worse. Worse. They like it."

Carla covered herself with a robe, forgot the rest of her nudity as she followed him; he was serious now, sad and yet eloquent.

"The newspaper is a book of sales. Each night you prepare to buy for the next day or night. Buy it, buy it." He saw Carla's eyes go up with interest. "Oh yes, it is wonderful. But done *every* day, being the point of life. With nothing else." He leaned close to her, and pushed her shoulders down. "You should stop sometimes to enjoy what you are — in bed."

Carla laughed at the rudeness.

"The bed disturbs the hairdo." He laughed and threw her back on the bed. "The head must be kept clean. Clean. Clean. Soap. With soap. You must have no smell. Use soap, eat soap —"

He had kissed her and let his body fall against her breasts again. Only when the sound of the children came close, did they rise quickly and finish dressing.

The girls came in and Carlo went out to them, talking until Carla came out of the bedroom. "The girls prefer a car to a boat," Carlo said to her.

"I have wanted to own a 600," she said. "Do you drive?"

"I did," he said. "But I have no license here. I can take the lessons right away."

"I will buy the car now."

"No, no," Carlo had to be proud. "Let me handle that." He remembered the debts; the box was full, but he was not planning this yet, not willing to leave himself with too little.

"And this is no time to be sad," she said. "We will be happy."

"If God wishes," he said, standing up, letting the girls go. He walked to the window, disgusted with the fear that his boast about a car had brought up. The night was beginning, a

118

red dusk on the water. God was many things — bankers, storms, debts, even lost souls who might arise unexpectedly.

Carlo left soon after and walked up the dark curved black road, stopping when cars passed him. The moon had come up over Amalfi and he stopped at the turn before going down into the piazza.

He could not hope to ever keep his promises if he said too much, spoke what he hoped instead of what he could do. Carla was affecting him as Anna had, and women made him ready to give everything he had. With Anna it had resulted in his being forgotten in an American city, living with those who called themselves Italian but were neither one nor the other, but only laborers. With Anna he had promised and given as much as he could at first, all for *her,* until he found that he was working to avoid her whining, demanding voice, like a siren filling his ears.

Would he go down again, like a willing fool only because he loved Carla? But she was a woman surrounded by Atrani, the sea on one side, the silver cupolas above, sunlight for a few hours in the day, the whole presence — and Carla within it something that would never admit America. He could never know if he were right, but he must try it — it was beating inside him, the arms, the breasts, the eyes, the money — he must try it *here* where he might get the answer, with a woman in his bed, children in the house.

11

GENE HAD been going three times a week, had cut the visits to two when Francine was annoyed at the time given the children; afterwards, he had felt relieved but did not thank Francine. His visits were not a duty; there was always a pleasure in being with Carlino and Joanna, as if they were all immigrants from the same place who meet to share a lost past.

They had been to baseball games, movies, even *Swan Lake*, which Gene enjoyed more than the children; but when he suggested another concert, Carlino protested. Still, Gene found time for them, and often during the day, picking them up at school, driving to some new place, ending at some store.

One day he had cancelled an afternoon appointment — he was to show a house to buyers — and had gone out with them to Westchester airport to watch the planes. That was the first time he had said, "Do you ever think of taking off again," and Carlino had answered, "Could we go to Miami Beach sometime, like Uncle Angelo?"

Later Gene knew that, having meant Italy, he was the only one who still had it in mind. But he still believed that the children would accept the idea if he spoke about it seriously —

and if they did not yet accept it, they would once they were taken and placed in Amalfi again.

One Saturday, after Francine, still patient, suggested he go to the club for a little golf because he needed the exercise, he agreed and said he would take the children with him. "They always ask about the club," he said. "And I was thinking, they have all those children's activities and supervision — we pay for it every year."

Francine was smiling. "Might at least get your money's worth." She followed him to the door. "At least this way I'll see a little bit of you." She saw Gene's face harden. "I'm sorry, Gene. I know you want to give those kids a life, and I think that's a nice thing."

Gene left and drove to Anna's house, which was empty. Because it was early morning he could not believe that it could have been vacated; then, standing there, he realized that he had last visited on Tuesday: there had been time.

The alarm box was still behind the door, but its mechanisms had been removed. The rooms were dusty and white and clear; nothing had been left, not even a slip of paper on the floors. He locked the door again, drove to his office and called Angelo's house, but the phone had been disconnected.

He called Tommy Esposito, who was a captain at the police station. Tommy asked around the station house, but could get no information. "I'll have to call you back, Gene. But don't worry. We'll have to get it. There's just so many moving companies."

Gene waited at his desk, scratching designs on his pad, making elaborate sketches as he sat paralyzed with conflicting wishes: he would gladly move to another town, forget them all; it was a bad feeling because it was true; his memory met the emotions of last autumn when he had visited his sons at boarding school. It was Homecoming Day, Thanksgiving, they walked around; the boys were uncomfortable with him: when he said something about morals or music or people in the news he could feel their laughter — not in his face, but around him. His view was always different, a little strange: he knew it. Finally he had said something about the habit-forming nature of marijuana and saw their condescending faces — there were two other boys with them on the field. He knew that the stuff had no horror for them, and he became like the old men of fifty years screaming at cigarettes.

And as the weekend passed and the boys took him here and there, patiently and sometimes pleased, he was nothing but a guest of two boys in a boarding school. Two nice boys. He had come to admire their work, meet other boys, the teachers, sit in the stands at the game.

On Sunday when they had said good-bye there was some feeling in it, yet no other words with feeling had come out during the weekend. Their feeling at departure was loss, which happens whenever anyone leaves: at air terminals he had felt it while alone, as if departure was enacted inside him.

Finally through the school gates and on the highway again, he had known that if he never saw the boys again, nothing would be different. Either they had detached themselves from him or he had found a dead spot in his heart. Was he supposed to be happy feeding them, supplying them, making them proof of his virtue through good sports jackets, an MG, trips to the Caribbean? If so, he could add them to his list of charities, two more names to be remembered.

He had arrived home sweating, as if flu had struck him,

with pains in his thighs, his neck stiff and his head burning hot. In bed, he had received a cup of tea from Francine, unable to explain what had happened, the ugliness in it refusing confession.

It had passed as everything passes, but these last days *it* and every other piece of garbage from the past was coming up, so that when one event occurred, a hundred others came up, some he could hardly believe had happened to him. But sitting now, he slowly remembered that they all were true: they *had* happened, even if the person he had been at the time was now obscure.

Finally, Tommy called with the information. The new house was out in North White Plains, and Tommy had been able to get the address only by telling the moving men that it was a police case. Obviously, Santoro had stuffed their mouths with cash.

Gene drove out and finally found the outer gate, nameless but seemingly in the right place, and rang a bell planted in a stone pillar. He could see no house, only a grove of pine rising up, making a sizable hill. A car came around this grove, driving towards him: it was Angelo and a driver.

They stopped and opened the locks. "This is my brother," Angelo said to the driver, who was dressed in a gray shirt and matching trousers, with a small leather bow tie at the collar, a badge on one shirt pocket, all of it suggesting a uniform but none that could be taken too seriously. "He is OK to enter at all times," Angelo told the guard.

The man was silent, and Gene followed them in his car. Beyond the trees the house had been placed at the top of a hill, a square of light fieldstone, gray and clean, as if sprayed with wax, with windows sunk in, casement on the first floor, white frame above, as if two architects had raced each other, starting from either end and working towards the center.

From the front steps Gene could see the Cross Westchester Expressway where it releases cars to two other highways in a butterfly of roads. Busy as it looked, it was far off and silent. Gene walked to Angelo, waiting at the open front door. The guard drove away, his car noise disappearing and making Gene aware of the pretty silence where they stood: it was a place for the nesting of birds, the surrounding trees like walls against the winds.

Gene turned and walked into the house, along a hall of dark red rugs that went as far as a wide staircase, like a farmhouse. The walls were alternately panelled and papered, the darkness of it making the red flower print on the paper hold back. "It's like — what's the name of that place?" Gene said.

"The Hudson River Museum," Angelo said.

"No. A mansion I saw up near Albany. What was it, again; some famous family — the man who invented the safety pin or the can opener — something like that. This same kind of hollow hallway and the red rugs like an old Gran' Hotel, and rooms all over the place. How many rooms does this one have?"

Angelo thought of how he might explain the house. "There are whole sections of rooms, you can shut them off from the rest. The second floor can be closed off in three sections, with staircases from outside, private entrances. It's a great place."

"You got separate but equal."

"Gene. Listen. Are you mad about this?"

"Why should I be mad because of what you choose to do. Should I get mad if you buy a fort against a ghost?"

Angelo was smiling at the joke in the anger. "Even if nothing happens," he said. "This is a great deal. We were lucky. Tranto wanted to get out *fast*. He insisted cash, so Pop jewed him down. I think he got this whole place for something like sixty-eight, sixty-nine."

"Well, thank God something's worth it."

"And did you see where I live? There's even more." Angelo walked to a circular hall window that faced the trees. "Look through there. Can you see it? Down the hill. It's a little stone house that used to be for a gardener. It's like one of those Swiss Alp houses —"

Gene looked, then turned away and walked towards the interior of the house. "And where do the guards sleep?"

Angelo followed quickly. "The *guard* goes home. Come on now, Gene. Lay off. Wait, here's the door. Right in there. Poppa's here."

They had stopped at a closed door. "Angie, I don't know what to tell you," Gene said. "Poppa, I think I can understand from what he is. But please, *you,* don't follow everything blind. Please."

Angelo took Gene's arm in his hand; his big bulk of face, long jaw hanging even lower, was moved to tender emotions. "Brother," he said. Gene blushed. "Don't worry, because I'm keeping my freedom here. And I think about what's going on. I *think*. But I'll tell you this. In general, looking at the whole thing — Pop is right. He couldn't do anything else. You got to go along with that. Specially because he didn't start it. He didn't *start* it. And now he's only trying to end it. He said to me himself, as long as Marinara stays in his place and Anna is settled here and running her own affairs, then Pop steps out. He is done with it. And that is something. Do you know? Do you realize that this is a man who years ago would have got out the shotgun; or you or me would have to go shoot Marinara in the face. Remember that."

"All right. So he's only left with a fort and an armed guard who looks like he might be some kind of army. OK. And where does that leave Marinara? In Scarsdale? Heading north?"

Angelo placed a finger to his lips for Gene, who stopped speaking. Angelo pushed at the door, then held it while Gene walked into the room.

Santoro was sitting on a couch that made him small, like a stranger in someone's house, but not a poor guest. Small but strong, his silver hair was stiff and cared for, and it covered him like success.

And he seemed to be waiting to judge Gene instead of preparing to defend himself, as he actually was. "Hello Gene. I was waiting for you."

"Waiting? How long did you think it would take me to find this place? You didn't leave a trace. You sneaked away and didn't even leave a message."

Santoro swallowed the filth in the tone and placed a folder in his hands, then lifted it up. "Now look at this. Try this."

Gene stepped forward and took it: a private detective agency had typed a report on Marinara's activities. Gene read it, then spoke to his father. "All right, so what does this say? That he's making money. Even paying back his debts. That's what I told you would happen."

"A man who now has money is ready to move. And you forgot it says there he is seeing another woman in Atrani." Santoro felt annoyed to say it again and again; the thoughts and its feelings began to shake in his head, like a rattling screw that would knock too much and make him ill. To keep saying it made illness, and Gene was the cause.

"Ready to *move* his bowels," Gene said. "That's what he's ready to do."

"What! What! You shit on your father. Gene, are you the woman's slave?"

Gene saw the face corroding, the power going because Gene did not agree. "Poppa," he said with care for his tone. "We want to talk sensibly, don't we? We want to look at this report and say, where *is* Carlo now? *Here,* or in Amalfi? And which place is he likely to stay? Seeing a woman means he wants to start a new life."

"No, no. We don't want to talk. We have to *do.* Do the right." Santoro stood up and walked past Gene to the door. "I'm going to show you. I'm giving you this whole trouble for yourself; you'll see what the hell you say when *you* have it all." He had reached the door but could not turn the handle correctly to open it; he kicked at the heavy sides and pulled, and suddenly the door sprang open. "I won't do this all by myself. I won't be the whole thing all the time. You are a stupid, you always talk against me. You don't love —"

Gene was left in the silence as his father ran out. He stood up and moved towards the doorway, finding Angelo, who walked in. "Angelo, where are the kids? Is there a nice cell here for them?"

"Stop it, Gene. Will you please. I'll go call them for you." Angelo walked back to the doorway and stopped where his father had stopped. "Gene, don't you see. Carlo's got money. Money makes you move. A guy starts to go places he never thought of before."

"Like us," Gene said.

Angelo was hurt; he had spoken to make his brother agree.

His heavy jaw, that could take all insults, moved but did not continue with words.

"It comes out of your heads," Gene said, "and I'm sorry for you."

Angelo took it and went out. Gene waited, walking about the room, touching the furniture of the former owner. A tall wood cabinet opened at his touch and showed white shelves of a bar, a lighted bulb behind colored bottles of whiskey and liqueurs.

Behind the bar were wooden frame glass doors and a large library of leather books. Gene did not open the cabinets but thought of the house he had sold the past winter, where he had touched the books in an impressive library and found them all a false front for storage cabinets full of broken lamps, old toasters, battery radios that had gone dead, flashlights, and at least a hundred ball-point pens, shining like silver vials.

The whole room seemed conceived at the same moment, woods perfect in stain, red leather chairs, thick, cold, and unused, all the surrounding furniture large and unworn, and the rug stretched tight from wall to wall.

Angelo's steps came along the corridor. "Gene. Gene. The kids can't come down. They have to go for a lesson. Annie says they're due in White Plains in a few minutes."

Gene heard it as his brother came rushing in and immediately walked past him towards the outer door of the house. In the hallway he heard Anna calling to him, and stopped. "I'm awfully sorry, Gene. The kids are so mad they don't even want to go anymore." Her voice came from upstairs but Gene could not see her. "This is the first lesson, though. We have to go."

Gene saw Angelo at the study door. "Can you give me the number here? I'll call you."

Angelo went back into the study, then came out with a sheet of paper. "Don't lose it. It's an —"

"Unlisted number," Gene said. "I know that." He went out to his car and drove to the gate, where the guard ran up smiling and let him pass.

Instead of going home, Gene went to his empty office and sat at his desk trying to form words, answers, even an attack to clear the air of them for good. Each time the thoughts came back to himself: he became tired, the thoughts like tears inside him. He was reluctant to go home to Francine, who was still trying to look at everything in the new way but was wearing out again, whining and annoyed at his late hours, suspicious when he came home and went to bed, resentful that he spent more time reading. One night he had turned to her — she had been staring at him while he was reading in bed and asked, "But tell me, what do *you* like to do? Tell me. Whatever it is."

"Be with you," she had said. "Do things with you."

"We do things," he had answered.

"Only now and then." Her tone changed, knowing that he was attacking her. "And very little."

"But a man has to work," he said. "Just take a look at my day, sometime. I have things to do all day. Tell me what you like to do for *yourself,* to satisfy you inside. Is it reading? Driving in cars? Do you like to see shows, operas? Tell me."

"You have too many damn things to do," she had said with anger.

"Well, thank you very much. I think I know what you

think about my activities. Like the big noise you made when I got that plaque."

Gene had then dropped the book and turned to the wall, struck his pillow with his head and left her in silence. But soon his mind was echoing with her statements and his responses, a dialogue for the two of them within himself. He answered her arguments one after another, until he reached the position that he liked his work, preferred it to anything else, and defied her to offer a suggestion out of her own life. *Travel? Miami? Once in winter, once in spring?* The words were in his head like shouts. *Sure, sure, let's go find it there.* The weeks of noise, crowds like drying fish in the sun, the letdown on a day of rain after the feeling of importance and luxury wore off, when you saw the same fat, half-crippled people around the marble fountains that you sat next to in cafeterias and subways back home. And the highlight a seat in front of Sammy Davis and some comedian who told wife and mother-in-law jokes, as if the natural state of women was always to devour the man passed on from mother to wife. His own mother had been at him all the time, shadowing over him as he took to the streets, screaming, calling him back from the foreign, cold city. But then she had spent more of her time on her longing for Naples and all its sensual times and the dream of weather and a clear world, where men looked at women and women at men, not the daily trip to work in the icy subway, like a rehearsal for one's days as a corpse. She had railed through the kitchen and now he was thankful she had been lost in herself. It had let him go, that selfishness, and allowed him to look at her, loud, vigorous, and superstitious, who had gone quiet at last, but still had said, *Now you know what I had,* her tone catching what had happened to him in Italy, the only one. When had she gone quiet, watching them all, not speaking anymore? In the first big house. A Sunday. She had been remembering the Sunday afternoons in the Bronx, when they made pizza for Sunday night. She was alone with him, talking. She had said something about their having lost loving kindness, some kind of love he could not understand, something that made you accept everything, open and flowing. He understood only that she did not like them anymore. And after that she was silent.

Gene found that he had been sitting with his head down, facing the floor, a position he had been adopting of late; it kept his thoughts with him and helped him ignore for a while the notes on his desk, the pens, dossiers of cases, even the phone. The remembering hurt yet relieved him, but only briefly, for the thoughts they allowed never came out whole or complete, as if he had swallowed them once and was able to get up only sections, the rest hanging in his throat.

He was still waiting for words to express the orders of what he must do, but whether these were to come from within himself or from outside he did not know. He was aware of the sounds of Saturday afternoon and decided to go home for Francine and see what was doing at the club. Then early next week he would talk to the children again.

12

THEY WERE always waiting for him, since his arrival was now telephoned up from the gate, and he would come upon them like statues which stared at him for a long time and then spoke. When he finally made an insulting remark, about their spying or the fort, his father would simply walk away into one of the many rooms. Gene saw it as hatred of him, but as the weeks went by he knew that the condition of the house was in each of them, in addition to their waiting for a phantom.

This new house was larger, silent, the rooms separated from each other the way Americans were. In the spaces between, in the emptiness, they had their places to prepare for the assault a bit more every week: they had installed new lights along the outer gates and increased the alarm system to include the upper floors and the grove of trees.

Because his father was becoming more silent, Gene began to notice him more; his gray hair was not combed tight to his head anymore: it blew out at the sides, soft and dry, a sign of his forgetting himself. It made Gene feel an affection, as one reacts to an infant unaware of itself and the vanity the world eventually teaches; yet the very love was composed of watching the old man sink slowly down, like an animal seeking its last resting place: it ended in Gene's head with a crawling guilt.

If his father was losing something of himself, it was difficult to see it as more than reaction to the threat of Marinara. Gene sometimes thought that senility might be taking the old man, but he could never consider it seriously because the subject of the threat came into their faces and voices as soon as he arrived. He came to the house for the children, he told himself, but always the old man or the thought of his new presence filled the rooms, and Gene had to hurdle his feelings as he waited for the children, speaking as calmly as he could to their cold voices.

For a few weeks he had decided that he would talk to the children specifically about going back to Amalfi, but each decision threw him into a depression. He would get a cold, pains in his thighs, be forced to stay in bed for a day or so, falling behind at the office.

He did not tell Francine because the plan of return included himself; she was so certain that Gene wanted to have other women, to insult her by it, that he often believed his only motive in going back was to make love to Elena again.

When he denied this to himself, he felt like a liar, then started another dialogue in his head, finally proving that if it were only flesh he sought, his office was full of it waiting to ride out to a motel in his Toronado any afternoon.

When he spoke to Anna, she filled him with her own desolation. In her world, she was alone all the time, dying in loneliness, locked in the house of war.

She would get to Carlo, his picture changing. "He wasn't

right," she said over and over. "He never became American in any way. You couldn't trust him to have sense like the rest of us. They do crazy things. And I'm telling you he might do anything. There's no relief."

Angelo, in his small house, repeated the story of Marinara's coming over and over to Emma, his wife, who gave him the agreement he wished. "But I only wish," she said, "we could take just a few days some time, and go away. Up to the Giusti hotel and relax."

She knew that Angelo loved the Italian hotels in the New England mountains, eating lasagna among the trees, buying maple sugar in the towns, finding apples and peaches at the roadside stands. Angelo always answered that they would go, then became silent and depressed. He could not tell his father he was leaving, would not speak to Annie, like asking permission.

One day he had met Gene leaving with the children, and Gene had called him aside to ask his help in talking to their father about getting back to normal, selling the fort. "It can't be done," he had said.

"Is that your only answer?" Gene said. "That's all you ever say. You agree with me, but you can't do it. You're all up at the house chewing on it every night. It's becoming all you have. If Marinara died tomorrow, none of you would believe it. You'd have to go right on."

"I would be in New Hampshire in five minutes," Angelo said.

"Let's hope so," Gene said. "I really hope so."

The blankness in all of them affected Francine. She had hoped for a final argument, so that Gene might divest himself of the fort forever. But with no answers, with Gene coming home like a man who has just lost a business, her complaints began to get louder as Gene turned his back on her.

In the midst of all this, he opened a morning letter in his office to find Marinara's writing, his long list of thanks for the money, his report of success. *My life will change very soon. I have found a new woman.* Then he invited Gene to his wedding.

The letter was ultimately illicit, and Marinara must have known what he had done. If Gene dared now start another attack against Carlo as bigamist, it would involve Gene publicly in too many embarrassing ways. If Gene kept the secret, he was an ally of his own bad wishes.

It was a Friday in late June. Gene could not work anymore and went out to the castle. After the cold moments in the hallway, his father walking away, his mother coming by to kiss him, then going upstairs quickly to her sewing, he went outside to find the children on the lawn at the side of the house. "How about a little ride to cool off," he said, and they ran to him. "Sign out with the Commandant first," he said, and waited until they had told Annie. She did not come out to the porch, but sent sweaters with them, in case of sudden cold.

Gene drove south on the Bronx River Parkway, as if it were a random choice. But he was remembering the Bronx, as he did every June, the hot days reviving childhood time. He began to talk about the river as the highway rode along its edges. "Would you believe I used to play here every day. With our shoes off, catching crayfish. Did you ever see one? Like a dirty small lobster."

"I wish we could do that," Carlino said. "How could I get down here?"

"I don't see many kids anymore," Gene said. "I heard that

the river's dead now." Gene stopped the car and they looked over the fence down at the water. "They say everything's died in it. From the sewage."

Joanna turned to him. "Sewage?"

"People's waste. You know, Jo, *poo poo*, all kinds of garbage —"

"You know, Uncle, I never touched a fish." Joanna looked at the water again. "I wish I could catch one, just once, and feel it with my hands."

"You never touched animals? At the zoo? The Children's Zoo and the Farm?"

"No," Joanna said. "But we saw a monkey in Amalfi. One of the fishermen had it."

"Then why don't we go. It's right along the Parkway here." Gene turned to Carlino. "Should we go touch some animals?"

Carlino placed a hand on Gene's shoulder, the affection reserved for a father, but by now Gene accepted it as normal.

Gene started the engine and drove along the Parkway to one of the parking lots. They took a zoo train to the Children's Zoo, where Joanna was first afraid to touch anything. Slowly she came closer, hung over the animals in a circle, watched other children reaching out. Then she petted a lamb, which did not move. The feeling was like an initiation, something that had been waiting inside her.

Then she would not leave, even after Carlino became bored. She sat in the little ring, with the lamb, geese and rabbits, transfixed by their soft warm peace.

Carlino wandered off and Gene went to get him, then brought him back to Joanna and enticed both of them to a snack overlooking the elephants.

Sitting at table with them, Gene filled up again with the

emotion that had often seemed a mistake once he arrived home. "Tell me," he said. "Are you having a good time now?"

"It's still no fun," Carlino said. "Only when we go out with you. Then we do something."

"Did you know Momma still won't let me see my friend Rita over her house," Joanna said. "So Rita always has to come to us. So now her mother said we have to go over there once before Rita can come see us. But they all said no."

"But you know why, don't you?"

Carlino looked angry and stared at Gene. "Yes," he said, and Joanna lowered her head.

"What is it?" Gene placed a hand on Carlino's face. "What are you thinking?"

"They hate Poppa," the boy said.

"They hate him and they want to punish us." Joanna's words had an echo; they had been said before, learned from someone.

Gene sat back and tried to smile, but the children had a real line of feeling caught, hooked. They were uncomfortable having shown this anger, afraid of Gene now and what he might do with their confession.

"But this means you must hate me most of all," Gene said.

"Oh no, Uncle. You were good." Joanna's expression changed.

"But I also took you away."

"No, Uncle. You were with us." Joanna was desperate; either Gene was leaving them or planning a trick to remove his love.

"I still have all those cards you got me," Carlino said. "My postcard collection won the hobby prize."

Gene leaned over and kissed the boy. Joanna watched him,

then took his hands. "Oh, come on, Uncle Gene. Let's go *get* something."

They left the outdoor tables and found a souvenir stand on the way to the car. Then, as they walked in the sun, Gene looked at them. "Let me show you something," he said. "We'll see Amalfi right here."

Joanna smiled and took his hand. "Yes. It's where I grew up. Right over there. Bakeries. Pizza. *Calzone.* Fresh cheese in the stores. Homemade pasta. It's Arthur Avenue."

They reached the car and drove out of the zoo and into the close, crowded streets, quiet and old until they reached the market street of Arthur Avenue.

Joanna and Carlino had never seen an Italian neighborhood in their country. They watched as the car moved slowly along the street, passing the rows of hanging cheeses in the windows, baskets of shellfish on the sidewalks and the loud fish sellers, pastries and loaves of breads stacked in white windowed shelves.

"It's so filthy," Joanna said. "Are all these people very poor?"

"Very poor?" Gene glanced at the crowds, which were what he knew. "No, not real poor. These are working people, bricklayers, plumbing, things like that. The wives stay home and shop and cook. It's not like downtown, like *El Barrio,* East Harlem. If you ever heard of that."

"The *slums.*" Carlino had heard. "Isn't this a slum? Look at the people."

"I am looking." Gene saw the boy's face, but it was honestly annoyed. "I think you maybe get mixed up with the way they dress. Dark colors. You see the black dresses. But that's their way. You must have seen the black in Amalfi."

"No," Joanna said. "No! These people look so old and terrible. Everybody has black hair."

"Well, they're Italians!" Gene could not see what continued to disturb them. "We all have black hair."

The car was approaching the house where Gene was born and had first lived, before the move north. "Now. I am going to show you a special house. Then I want to hear what you have to say."

He heard Carlino's voice, a whine. "Please. Uncle. Can't we go home now? I'm so *tired*. I can't keep awake."

Gene pushed his right foot heavy on the gas, went by his house, and kept the speed until they reached the Parkway again. He could not speak to them again; a tight, almost desperate feeling came up into his throat, and he held his teeth clenched, unable to summon the right words for the children's betrayal. But they sat back and accepted the silence, unaware of his feelings because they had only said the truth about what they had seen.

Coming into his own house he found a note from Francine on the coffee table: she was with Sylvia, which meant shopping, and had left his supper in the oven.

He went to the bedroom after eating some of the casserole, a warm mixture of meat and sauce and rice. He had bought an evening paper and lay down on the bed.

Francine had changed the lamps, new oversized stands with statues of a Venus, and long hooded shades that confined the light. He lay back and smoked and held in the anger of the day, so that when she came in, holding three bags and happy, she was hurt as he spoke. "You call these lamps where a person is supposed to be able to *read*."

"*Now* what is it? Now it's the lamps. You want different ones?"

"I'm telling you the light is held down by this shape. I can't see a *damn thing.*"

"Well, we'll get new ones, then. I'll throw these out. Unless the money is needed for your niece and nephew."

"I am talking about lamps. These lamps which my wife bought." Gene rose from the bed and rested his newspaper on his lap. "I can't see to read my paper."

"Then don't read in bed."

"Where else would you ordain for me to go, oh great queen of Lord and Taylor."

Francine was not relieved. "I told you. Go get new lamps, if your niece and nephew say it's OK — it doesn't take away some new motorboat they were planning —"

"All right, all right. I know what I'm doing. You're not going hungry yet. I don't see you in rags. There's a new rug all over this house, I noticed. Mirrors on every door you could find. You still got nice blonde hair every week. What's the bad time here?"

Francine dropped the bags on the bed and walked towards the wall. "I hate it, I hate it." She grasped her hair in her hands, "I hate it all."

Gene stood up quickly, dropping the paper as he ran to her. The action was desperate, the worst confession she had ever made, the movement of pulling at her hair like some grief Gene moved quickly to prevent.

He embraced her from behind and she was still. Feeling the thickness of her hips, it was as if he had forgotten her again in this discovery. His hands moved to touch her breasts, the soft texture of the green sweater she wore.

Gene tried to lead her to the bed, but she continued staring at the wall. Part of her image was caught in the mirror of her dresser and behind it she saw Gene's face and lost her own embarrassment: his hair was flattened and unkempt from lying on his pillow, his face caught in tight, nervous lines. She lowered her head at what she saw: he looked old, and she had not seen it before. The dark lines in his skin, around his eyes and lips, were permanent: they had exposed themselves in these last months, while the family had been changing, dying, exploding, though some force still brought them together.

"Oh Gene." She turned and placed her arms on his shoulders. "It's me. I worry about everything. I worry about money." Her voice was soft for his tired face. "I know you must be spending so much on the kids. And you don't tell me — I don't even know why you have to do it anymore —"

Gene stepped back. "You know me when I get worried," she said. "How crazy it is. I feel so bad about myself —"

Gene walked back to his bed and sat down, looking away to the wall. Before he could speak, Francine came closer and sat on her bed. "I'm not a cook like Anna. I don't work like Emma with Angelo at the office. What am I good for?"

"You're better than all of them." He turned to her. "Don't you see yourself?"

"I wanted to work in your office." She was still in the thoughts of her weakness. "I can do something. Answer phones. Help around —"

"Stop it." Gene sat up. "You're better. Listen to that, for God's sake. I told you what pleasure I get when you go to the club, take off in your own car. You know all that. Why did I work for? To give you something. But let me tell you — something you don't know — that you're *known*. Your name. In charities. In town itself. They know your car. They know your clothes. You're not supposed to look like a cook in a kitchen. Do you know people come to me — *customers* — because they heard of you. Or they met you."

"Is that true, Gene? Are you serious?"

"Don't you know yet how it is here. They see you, they hear about you. It's *class*. So they think of me as solvent. I'm a good bet. It's the same way all over."

Francine reached across the bed and placed her hands in Gene's, who said, "So don't get confused. And don't think that my troubles are yours. What's happening in my family is not yours."

She kissed him and moved her body against his: what she understood she believed, but the rest, the part that was on the verge of running, had not been mentioned.

Gene was suddenly standing. "You know that I went over there and grabbed those kids. I'm the only one who took them."

"All right. You *went*. But Angelo could have. Anybody could have. Wouldn't the law have made them come back?"

"Yes, I know all that. But *I* brought them back with these hands." Gene stopped himself, looking at his hands thrust out, the dramatic gesture of mood that was Italian, practiced in his father's house as if they were all actors, yet now an embarrassment to him because the manner had become vulgar and hysterical, the mood that made forts.

He moved farther away from Francine and sat in her padded silk dressing table chair, holding the back with his hands. "I snatched them. I put them in that stupid prison."

Francine sat up. "No you didn't. Your father made that. He gave all the damn orders." She stood up and took a step

142

towards him. *"He's* the general. *He's* the big shot. *He's* going to change everybody — in Italy, too, to fit his orders. The new Uncle Sam!"

"I know that, I know that!" Gene rubbed his face with his hands and leaned over, as he did in his office. "He thinks they're all animals over there. They haven't really come out of the woods like himself. I acted just like that myself. I thought Naples was a jungle when I first saw it — old, the people filthy. I thought they were all trying to get me. You know what he said to me one night? All of them had become Communists. All of them. Even the Pope, I asked him. Even your cousins? And he gives me this how-little-you-know look." Gene's chest was throbbing. "But he's my father, Francine. That man's my father."

Francine took a few more steps towards Gene, her body leaning over, pointing at him. "And *you.* And *you.* You also have a loud voice now," she said. "And you can use it. When you want to."

Gene jumped up. "I know what to do. I've known it, I've known it." He was beginning to shout, but his thought brought his voice under control. "I'll do it. I'll end it once and for all." He turned and walked away as he spoke, reaching the bathroom door. "Gene? What are you saying? Don't be crazy."

He leaned on the door frame. "No. I know just what I'm going to do now. Once and for all. Fix it up just the way it was."

"One thing you *could* do is stay away from those kids a little. Stop worrying about them."

"I'm going to take them back. It's very simple." He walked into the bathroom, took his toothbrush from its holder, spread some paste on it and began to brush his teeth.

Francine came to the doorway and watched him; he was leaning over the sink, brushing rapidly, spitting out the paste, rinsing his mouth with water.

"You are going to start the whole damn thing again?" she said. "And then what? They'll have *you* to blame for everything. You idiot!" She struck the door with her hands, and Gene's head snapped erect.

"You just shut up," he said, and turned to wash his mouth again. "They can't touch me." His mouth was cold. "I got a business that goes by itself. Do you know that. I could live on the interest alone for ten years."

"Live? How? On two, three thousand a year? Is that how we'll live?"

"All right, it isn't a million, but I couldn't be touched. I got equity. I got some houses that are three quarters mine. I couldn't be touched."

Francine left the doorway and went to her chair; she saw her face in the mirror, but she could not work on it now. She wanted to undress but felt tired and reluctant. Gene had stopped speaking but she was held in the madness of his idea.

She stood up, waiting, then walked to the bed; again, there was nothing, no advice, no orders, and screaming at him was finished. She lay down, her arms over her face, and was soon asleep.

When she awoke it was morning. Gene had not touched her, nor awakened her to undress, and she was hurt by this. She walked downstairs and prepared coffee. While she sat, Gene came in, dressed, shaved, like someone very different from her: she felt an illogical embarrassment in her wrinkled clothes as he sat down. "Some people are coming to the office about a house. Larry can't be there, so I have to go in early."

His voice was peaceful; it was trying to say he felt no rancor. She followed his steps to the car after he left her. He was framed in the window of the door as she looked out, his heavy shoulders hunched, aging in some quick way, beginning to suggest his father, though the old man had become white and bony, his jackets all too loose, and really looked nothing like Gene.

The empty house was behind her; she could hear the sound of each room: the kitchen ticked with clocks, the electric coffeepot's metal sides crackled as it cooled, the living room drapes swayed and hissed in the thin wind that came from the partly opened door. She shut it and went into the living room to sit down.

The glass coffee table in front of her responded to passing cars and trucks, vibrating in their rhythm. She wished they had gone up to the castle, something she had not allowed herself to think before. What would have been avoided by that? Gene's wildness? Taking it all over by himself because he was far away? It was a stupid wish of her own: she wanted to be near the others, to confide in them because they were Gene's blood.

She went to the kitchen, looked at the cups and plates on the table and decided to leave them. She was very tired and felt that she had to sleep in her nightgown, at least for an hour or two.

After undressing, she walked by habit to her dressing table, but looked quickly into the mirror and left it for bed. Seeing herself made her forget Gene, but thinking of Gene produced nothing new: he had become strange; he was guilty about what he had done to the kids; he had a hunger to go back there for himself, fool around in some way she could not understand, but without her. She would have to be alone again; sometimes it was peaceful and pleasant having the house around herself, as though it were only hers; other times she could barely go into a room, pass through a door.

If he could get it out of his system and then come back and settle down. But if it wasn't journeys and battles with his father, then it could go on forever; he could become a tramp looking for blank answers, like drunks. One thought came to her before another was fully stated in her mind. It was a webwork; it was made by everything that happened, even her own mistakes.

She got into bed, the untouched sheets cool and new, and pulled them with the blanket and spread almost over her head, leaving only a small opening for breathing. The line of thoughts began again, but this time she lost even the few words, and this enabled her to find sleep.

13

GENE FINISHED some contracts while he waited for the couple who had called him about a house. They were coming up from the Bronx, and since both worked in Manhattan, they had made this early appointment. He heard them moving in the outer office and came to the door, reluctant to leave the silence.

The man was short and heavy, with the long jacket that clothing men wear. His wife sat down stiffly; she was taller, also fat, with a girdle that made breathing difficult if she bent over. Bending over made her groan; her left hand would catch at the wall jutting up under her silk dress, and she would hold it down while she sought a comfortable position.

They were telling Gene the usual story of the neighborhood filling up with Blacks and Puerto Ricans, talking in low voices, appealing to him like patients with a new disease.

"We'll take care of you," Gene said. "Don't worry anymore. We're going to take care of you." He was bored by it and began thinking of the time already, of taking the children to the club to ask them to leave with him.

The wife, who had been shy at first, only giving a description of their defenseless house, began to open up after her husband agreed that he could afford the prices Gene gave.

"Our streets are falling apart, too," she said. "All in pieces, and the city never sends a man anymore. They don't even try to patch it up. And the stores they are closing up, the good stores. They're going away. Last week I heard two more new ones opened up in White Plains. Even the same markets are different down there now — I don't know if you heard. All you have to do is come up here to Westchester and shop a little. The same A & P or the Finast and yet everything's better. And even cheaper. Those poor people, they don't know the difference. What they expect, I don't know. What they eat, the smells you smell, they're all different. You smell pig fat on the streets. It's no good for you. I told my husband, he's complaining a little about his liver: *that* smell gets in your system. You can't digest pig fat. And them! They scare you. They're not like *us*. I don't care what anybody says — they scare you. They don't know certain things. Little things. Oh, I try to be nice to them, neighbors, give a hand, tell them a little about how to cook a thing or get a good cut of meat. But the butchers take advantage of them — they give them rotten cuts and short weights. So pretty soon they're selling all cheap meats and you have to hunt up and down the blocks for a good butcher. That's what they caused. I'm sorry."

The woman was angry and contrite; it made no sense, but it was true to her feelings and Gene had heard it over and over; but living far away, it was not even real anymore; it was only the preamble to a sale, the whine of refugees who need to be told they had been treated badly before they can act selfishly.

"Yes, I feel sorry for them," the woman said. "I do. I made friends among them, and I like them. They're good people;

148

they love their kids, you can see that. But I can't just sit around while the whole thing falls apart. So what if they got out of Harlem and they still getting the dirty end of it from everybody. Is that my fault? I ask you. I mean, I help others. I even said I'll pay to send people to clean it up. And they should get educated. But I'm not going to live in the midst of it and get the lowest grade of everything right in my face when I know what they're doing to them."

"Some say they're like children." The husband interrupted to calm his wife.

Gene looked at the clock on his desk. "We're going to take care of you, and you'll be out of there in a week or two at the most. Is that all right?" He stood up and shook hands.

"They told me, see Gene Santoro —" The wife worked her way out of her chair. "And we came to you and nobody else because we heard of your name." She was being admitted to a private preserve, not sure it would happen.

"Tomorrow morning Larry Spina is picking you up, and he'll show you the best five listings we have right now." Gene was smiling at the woman. He went round to her and walked with her to the door. "I know you're going to help us," she said. "I put myself in your hands."

Gene had been at the door, in this moment, many times. "We'll get you a nice place. Just what you like. But tell me, what do we do when they come up here? Then what?"

He saw her face look up at him in shock, her eyes wide open, the red lips beginning to move. "Up here? Up *here?*" She went out the doorway and through the outer office.

Her husband held back. "We'll let the kids worry about that," he said, and shook Gene's hand before going.

Gene shut himself in and sat down at his desk. He saw the

couple's name on his pad and scratched it out with a pen. The intercom went on with a buzz and he switched it on. "Your father called while you were seeing those people. Call him right away. Urgent."

"Mary? When did you sneak in?" Gene said.

"About ten minutes ago. While you were in there with them."

Gene switched off, then dialed the fort. Anna answered. "I'm glad you called. He went downtown again. I don't know what he's been doing every day. But he wants us all here to-night. It's something big. He keeps coming home with luggage. New suitcases, but not very big ones. I don't know what it is now."

"Is he all right?" Gene could not explain. "Does he seem — normal?"

"He acts a little strange, if that's what you mean, but nothing special. I thought maybe he heard about Carlo, some-thing he's not telling us. But he's very excited about some-thing; but then sometimes he'll get very calm and smiles at everybody. I wish you were up here, Gene."

"I'll be there at lunchtime. You know I'm taking Joanna and Carlino to the Club. They have a puppet show."

"At your club?"

"Yes. It's from one to three."

"Gene, what you do for these children, I'll never forget it. No matter what Poppa says —"

"What does he say?"

"Nothing, nothing. Just bring them back when you say."

Anna hung up, and Gene went out to Mary's desk. She had not expected him and was typing with her tight skirt pulled up high against her upper thighs. He stopped and stared at the garter elastics sticking out of her skirt, pulling her stockings taut. "I'm going out for coffee now," he said. "Then I'm going away for lunch. If you need me, call my club."

Mary nodded while she stared at her typing; Gene kept his eyes on her thighs, shining in the desk light, the pleasure and disgust felt together. Then Mary looked up at him, and he left.

In the coffee shop he planned to set up the words for Joanna and Carlino, to give them understanding like a picture: what he had done to them, what they had lost. But he became distracted by pains in the head, muscles in his neck and shoulders stiff: he fell into a thoughtless time over the coffee, his awareness moving out, to the odors of cologne and powder and bubble bath, the musty air of the store; it suggested wealthy women, pale Bronxville women who still made him uncomfortable when they passed him.

Paying his bill at the cashier's counter, he saw a box of Japanese flashlights, bought two, and went to present them to the waiting children.

They drove to the club, which the children seemed to recognize, walking directly to the soda bar after the puppet show, ordering from the waiter (who called Joanna *Missy*) as if they had known him for years.

The blue breeze of the Sound flew across the tables; the glare on the white tabletops was like the shine of a boat deck. Gene saw the children caught by that excitement he had known his first few months as a member: in the white, painted stone, the stone rails above dark green gardens that went to the water, in the quiet where everyone's conversation was held in its own circle — the club gave him some new ownership, freedom from his customers, a shore far beyond the center of the town. Gene had once thought of the balcony as the deck of a large yacht, in which you sailed alone and saw the sight of miles of coastline you did not have to share with anyone. But then he had come to know the others, the various groups, the cardplayers, golfers, old families who never spoke to him except for polite words at entrances and exits. He learned that the club demanded your coming every week to give the secrets of your life: only then did you receive the island whiteness of the place for yourself.

Yet the children were new and saw only the surfaces, which were made for enjoyment. He watched them finish hamburgers, sodas, cakes. "I am merely waiting until you both get stuffed," Gene said. "Before I tell you something important. A serious thing, really. One of my thoughts, that never leaves. So I have to say it. And it's about you."

He saw their faces trying to come to him from the laziness of food. "You know your Uncle Gene loves you," he said.

They nodded for him. "I can't forget you two when I saw you there in Amalfi. How free you were. You were playing so happy in the back, in that loggia —"

"Piazza Modugno." Carlino remembered the name suddenly.

"Yes, you were having a good time. It was so nice there, don't you think. How do you remember it now?"

"You never met Niccolo," Joanna said. "He went out fishing with his father. He knew about the sea."

"That's it." Gene placed his right hand on Joanna's arm. "Yes, yes. People like that, who have the feeling for the sea inside them. Didn't you like that? And where is it here? I would think you miss it very much."

"Miss it?" Joanna was confused that what was gone could be made into an idea that felt as strong.

"Yes, it was very good there for you. And maybe it was really a bad thing to go away. Now, when somebody loves you. Like I do. He'll want you to be happy even if it means he can't see you anymore himself — for a long time —"

"Oh, no." Carlino dropped his plastic straw. "You want to take us back!"

"Not *take*. I wouldn't take you anywhere against your will. Not anymore. Because — you know it — I did that once. And you wanted to stay there. Remember."

"No, Uncle Gene. Do we have to go to Amalfi again?" Joanna looked from Gene's face to her brother's.

Gene saw Carlino's lips open, still in the surprise and fear. "Only if you kids say it," Gene said. "It's your decision. But I know you liked it better. You were having so much fun there. With Elena. Weren't you getting such a good training being with her?"

"Yes, we liked it," Joanna said.

"Uncle!" Carlino had focussed on Gene. "We want to stay here! With you."

"Yes, I know. But a child needs a parent near him, his own flesh and blood. You could choose. I know that. You could be there or here. But the way I saw it, you liked it better over there. And you said you *hate* it here."

Carlino did not answer; Gene was a threat like the others, though his aims were different. And perhaps he was worse because he was so much to be liked. "No!" the boy said. "I won't go back to that hellhole —"

"Hellhole? Amalfi is a hellhole?" It was as if the boy had meant him.

Carlino twisted his red straw and began to tear it open. "Where do you get a soda over there? Uncle. It was so boring."

"The TV was on for maybe an hour for kids. Stupid programs. There's nothing to do —" Joanna had joined her brother's feelings.

"You can't get anything *good*." Carlino was searching for the words to explain a world that had died for him, but he was caught in the fear of being stolen again.

"All right," Gene said. "Cokes you can get already. French fries I'm sure they'll have for you." Gene tried to fix his eyes on theirs, but they were avoiding him. "You know what I'm talking about," he said. "The feeling of things over there. Elena. And how nice everyone is. Kind and helpful. Gentle. Always interested in you."

Carlino was affected by this and lowered his head, as if he had heard the unanswerable, some bad news.

"Don't you remember how it was?" Gene said softly. "Those sweet days."

"No!" the boy said. "And I'm not going. I'm not going to the poorhouse."

"Where did you hear that? Who said that to you?"

"*I* said it." Carlino knew Gene had caught feelings not his own.

"I know you just said it. But who told you to say it?" Gene was ready to shout at the boy, but the club would not permit the mood.

"Momma said it." Carlino looked at his sister, who also spoke. "And Aunt Francine was there, too. They charge you double for everything. A bunch of crooks who cheat their brothers. That's what it is."

Gene called for the check and signed his name. He could not look at their faces: he had made them like the others, and they had even touched his doubts with the old stupidity said with their new tongues: it had been his belief, too; something of the lies always stuck to him.

He stood up. "Well, come on, then. No use to talk anymore."

Joanna came after him, asking about her bike. "Didn't the man say he would put the basket on by this week?"

"I'll call the man again," Gene said.

He drove them home, did not go into the house, but drove back to his office. Mary looked up from her typing reverie. "They've been calling you," she said. "They want you up there by six."

Gene went to his desk and worked at more contracts. The anonymous legal words lifted him away from the emotions of the afternoon, kept them at bay until Mary's voice came through the intercom again. "I'm going home now. And I want to remind you. It's five-thirty, and the family's expecting you."

He stood up in anger, alone in the room. He would buy an airline ticket tomorrow and have it in his pocket to prevent his begging others for release. Yet he knew it would be a sin until told.

He drove slowly, keeping the engine purposely back, and when he arrived at the door, his mother came. He had not seen her in many weeks; the castle was taking her, making another relic, to be invoked when the others shouted too many insults. *Think of Momma.*

"Is anything wrong?" he asked.

She seemed afraid to speak. "Is Poppa getting sick? Because of all this mess."

"Not sick," she said. "*He* is not sick. He has some ideas to create. And he is becoming a man alone. Alone because you did not hear him — when he came to you." She spoke in Italian, having abandoned her few American phrases, unable to use energy for the language she had found harsh and without rule or logic, a nasal ugliness better suited to animals than men.

But more than her difficulty with the sounds that never gained meaning, she used Italian now to catch her daily thoughts, some of which were shadows, increasing her timidity before the commanding children. When they had to strain to understand her, they were at least stilled for a time.

"Can I go see him and talk with him?" Gene had been noticing her reveries. "Momma. I'm here because you called. I'm always ready to do my share. Why should Poppa say things about me — like that?"

"You are like a spy." She had said it after a pause, again like something remembered, heard at another conversation. She walked before him to the study, went in and sat in a chair near the window. "He is upstairs right now. And he is coming down with the money and a surprise for all of you."

"Money? What is it? Why this way to me, Momma? Tell me yourself — what have I done to you?"

"Listen to him, Gene. Listen for one time."

"I'm getting a drink." Gene walked to the bar and poured a glass of rye and drank it as fast as he could. "Momma." He looked at her at the edge of the room. "I am asking you to say something for yourself."

156

She shook her head but smiled, then lowered her head and looked at her hands in her lap, like a member of an audience before the curtain.

Gene looked at this room around them, stiff, frightening, like an estate before an auction, the owners having died. The luxurious silence he had felt was now a silence bought with money, made of heavy rugs, walls of thick panels, tables with heavy silver vases, waxed mahogany boxes, old heavy, leather-bound books on dark tables — nothing that was theirs. It was like being camped, bewildered travelers, in a garish, unrestful hotel — for life. In response to it Anna and Angelo had tried to italianate themselves, using more Italian words in their speech, eating the old specialties that were the tastes of their early years. It was again the Naples inside their heads being invoked.

He drank again, the rye like punishment, a taste he had never liked but which he had accepted as a man's taste.

His father came in while he was leaning on the bar, facing the wall. Santoro had the suitcases. Gene watched him walk to the glass coffee table and set them down: three black leather bags, almost too heavy for the old arms. "Where is your brother and sister?" he asked Gene.

"I don't know." He did not like the clipped voice. "*You* live here."

"Go get them," Santoro said, and sat down.

Gene found Anna and Angelo in the kitchen, both standing, pacing the kitchen, Angelo with his head down, Anna holding her right index finger between her teeth.

Angelo turned to him when he heard. "Gene? Does he want us now?"

Gene had been watching both of them and remembered

them as children, on the nights when they waited for their father to return from work and give them a spanking as soon as Mrs. Santoro reported their sins. It was the same mood of waiting, as if any call from a father was a call to punishment.

"He wants us all in there," Gene said. "And he's got those black suitcases."

"See," Anna said. "It's something about them. You think he's going over? We better go in there."

She led the way to the study and sat down as soon as she reached the couch facing old Santoro, who sat in his chair, the coffee table in front of him holding the black suitcases.

Angelo stopped and stared at his father, but Anna pulled him down to the couch. He sat, suddenly feeling his neck wet, the sweat that had been coming since he entered the house. Anna watched him wipe himself and smiled.

Old Santoro looked at Gene. "Don't you sit?"

"I'm having a drink," Gene said, and went to the bar.

"Then at least stand still," Santoro said. "See what I have here." He unlatched the bags and opened them: they were filled with banded rolls of cash. "This is all my wealth now. In dollars. I sold it all. And tonight you get it."

"Just like that!" Angelo leaned forward. "No. Pop. No. That's an unwise move. You didn't sell securities?"

"All." The old man was making stacks. "You all get it now, before it's too late."

Gene poured his whiskey and drank again. This was the first time his fear was too great, as if the money in cash were proof of madness. "My head is old," he heard the old man say. "I need to give you the cares. It's too much here today. Every-one tries to get us. I don't need it. I don't want them trying to kill me, like a pack of wolves, and then make me a saint in my grave."

Gene saw him look up, the old face wrinkled as if it were surely holding back tears. "And if I give it now, it is done right. We stop fights behind my back. We keep the lawyers out of the house."

"This isn't necessary," Gene said. "You can give us instructions to follow in case anything happens. You could have signed us over the securities and we would be giving you the dividends. This way is no good for anybody."

"Don't tell me things. Don't start telling me." The old man lowered his head and finished making his stacks. "I just ask you all. I ask you only now to tell your father what your love is. How you love him."

"What a question!" Angelo stood up to put his handkerchief in his back pocket. "We're a family all together here. We don't need to inherit any money. Pop! We're all faithful to you." His eyes caught the piles, too much to estimate; he could not believe the old man had had so much.

As if responding to the thought, Santoro spoke: "It's half a million or so. It goes to you." He touched one stack. "Divided in three. Just let me hear you."

"Well, Pop, listen." Angelo took a step towards his father, then stepped back until his leg touched the couch. "You're more than any amount of money to *me*. To me, I can't find fancy words, maybe. But you're all we are. I moved here with you. You're our whole life, what you made us. I've got to thank you for it. To me, I mean, I *see* things through your eyes."

The old man looked up at Angelo's face, and more than the

words was sure he had heard the sentiment. He raised his hand. "Then here is a hundred fifty thousand. Take yours."

"No, Poppa. We'll put it in an account. A joint account if you want it like that. Right near here. The bank in the village."

"Take this. You are what I have. Take this, Angie, and remember me. Protect me better because you have it." Santoro was pushing the stacks for Angelo to the corner of the table, but Angelo did not come forward yet. "And I hope your sister and brother have the same respect," the old man said.

"Well, Pop, you must know what I did all my life," Anna said. "I took care of you, even after I got married. I was always here. And all I'm doing here today, it's for you. To satisfy you and make you feel at home. I wouldn't let a thing go wrong with you while I have any strength left. And even before, in my marriage — you must remember — we both came to you all the time. Even *him*."

"I'm satisfied with you, Anna. You're a child that kept my name right. You honored me, even in your troubles —"

"I came to you first. They wanted me to go to the cops that first day when I went to that school." Anna saw her father's face smiling at her, weak in its gratitude. "I never did a thing without your decision first. And you know that. All my life long, I was a part of you."

Santoro was nodding his head, moving the stacks for her, pushing them to another corner of the table. "I am light now. Now take this in your hands. And maybe Eugene will speak. He knows how I talked about him in his success and his honors —"

"What can I say." Gene turned to them, setting the glass back behind him.

"Say what you think." The old man sat up and looked at Gene.

"There's not much to say that hasn't been said."

"Nothing?" The old face became hard. "Say nothing? Say nothing and make nothing, then."

Gene looked away. "You gave me my life. You brought me up and you loved me. And I obey you." Gene watched the stiffened face. "I love you, then, as you loved me," Gene said. "No more, no less."

Santoro's hands went up from the table, shook in the air. "Oh no. No. Is this the way to talk? A father is giving you everything of his. How can I trust you. I'm giving, *giving* everything!"

"You were my father and I am your son. I give you back what you gave me —"

"Stop! I understand these words. *Bestia!*" Santoro made an effort to stand, but fell back on the soft chair. "Speak! *Animale!* Tell me now your fucking secrets — you kept from me. Your *hate.*"

Gene stepped back to touch the bar, placing his right hand on the whiskey bottle. "I'm telling you what you want to hear. What else do you want me to tell you?"

Santoro's face was red, as if light had come into it. "You don't want it, then? You don't want mine. You must be too smart. Stronger than all money. You *cretino!*" He raised some banded packs of the money over his head and stood up, spinning around slowly. "No, no. Then take nothing. Let it grow someplace else." He threw the contents of his hands behind the chair, towards the wall. *"Vai, vai, vai.* Go away from —" Santoro would not pronounce Gene's name or another curse if he had it.

Angelo came quickly to the table, hesitated, reached up to hold his father's arms but did not touch him. Then he ran behind the couch, collecting the money fallen on the rug and returned it to the coffee table.

Santoro had been watching and smiled at him.

"Pop, this is *money*," Angelo said, but the old man did not answer. "Pop, why don't you just keep it, like I said. Or let me open a joint —"

"Take it." Santoro leaned down to his son's face and stroked it with his hands. "This is for Angelo, too. Take it and honor me. Do what must be done for us." The old man stood erect and suddenly changed mood. "And that *maligno!* Watch him. *Attenzione! Vigliacco!*" He found another Italian word with the proper sound. "*Infamo. Infam'.*" The Italian was stronger, coming from depths, without the need to think.

Gene was becoming frightened for another reason now: something in the old man's actions was releasing him, yet at the same time his father seemed mad. "Why do you pick on me now?" Gene said. "I am your son, still."

"*I am. I yam.*" Santoro mocked. "Say what you are! Say it! A son? That I gave you all of myself and you are here to kill me."

"The same son I was. Whatever you gave, I am."

"The same son? *Animale e porcheria. Figlio di cane.* I *yam.* I *yam.* For you I sold in Union Square, on my feet eighteen hours, dollar dresses; I ate pasta fagioli every day. And took my pleasure to the bank and lock it up. For you to give me this. I *yam. I yam.*"

Santoro pressed his legs against the coffee table, leaning towards Gene. Though he let the table restrain him, Gene stepped farther back, poured another whiskey and drank it fast before speaking. "All right, then. Listen to me a minute." He placed the empty glass on the white formica bar top. "Don't you know the truth yet?"

"Shit on your truth yet. Put your truth in your bank. The others have the money. And you will get out of my house. Go. While I still speak to you."

"You want to give me money but no power in decisions. Then keep your money."

"Get out! Get out! Get out!" Santoro was pushing with his hands, sweeping out the child.

Gene walked to the door and stopped. "I am damned for having a tongue I never had."

"Die with it. Better to not be born than speak like this you have said. Get away from me I said."

Gene opened the strong door; the rest of the house was silent. He saw his mother, her fearful face on Santoro, worried about his redness. When in the silence she caught his eye, she began to raise a hand, then stopped the gesture and looked back at Santoro. Gene turned to Angelo and Anna. "I leave you his money," he said. "Take care of him. And no matter what you said, I know you."

As soon as Gene had gone, Santoro fell back on the chair and covered his face with his hands. His wife came to him and stood near him. Anna came quickly to the other side of the table. "Poppa, I know it's all right. Gene's all right."

"No, no. Don't trust him now. See what he does to me. And I am old. You don't kill the old anymore." He removed his hands, held his wife's hands. "Listen. Lock the gates. Be sure. Tell the guard to keep him out. I have my friends coming up soon to be with me."

"Friends? What friends?" Anna said.

"Julio Pirro, Cosimo, Uncle Mario —" Mrs. Santoro was answering for him. "The other friends from the Bronx. You know his friends."

"Yes. We will watch for the *scustomato.*" Santoro stood up and walked around the table, looking back to his wife, who came to him and left with him.

Angelo was about to call, but stopped. When the door was shut he walked to the table, looked down, counting piles of bills that made up the stacks. "Look at it! You can't count all the damn stuff. Look, Anna. Let's put it back in the cases for now. Boy, it *scares* me. I'll take it right down tomorrow and stick it in the bank."

"*Bank?* You going crazy, too?" Anna lifted a case, as if to pull it away from him. "Give some bank a nice record of all this. So we can give it all into taxes. We will keep this locked up right here."

"But just interest on the stuff makes it worth it —" Angelo saw her shake him off, and leaned down to collect the money.

Anna went back to lock the study door, then came back to him. "Now look. We got trouble."

Angelo paused. "Don't worry. I know Gene. He's not coming around anymore. Mark my words. He's rid of it. He's washing his hands."

"Not Gene, you stupid! *Him!* Don't you see how he's changing. That's not the same man. And just remember one thing that came to me sitting here just now. *Gene.* Gene was his *favorite.* And look what he just did. Something's wrong inside him."

"It's his age," Angelo said. "They get a little senile. You know better than me he's been acting like a hurt kid. And then all this nervousness about Carlo coming back. And when did he ever know himself? I mean, he's blown up all his life. Plenty of times he's hit me all of a sudden, a fit he gets. No good reason. Just bam. Don't you remember how he was? When we were kids. That was him, too."

"These old fathers!" Anna looked back at the door. "They're all so hotheaded. Always take extremes. And it's going to get worse now. I mean it. And *we* got to watch out. I'm telling you now. One of us could be next on his list."

"Oh, come *on*," Angelo was annoyed. He was sweating again, as if the money had been heated. He finished packing at last and closed the suitcases. "You're going too far." He stood up, brushed at his trousers, lifted the bags and shook them. "Wow. That's heavy." He looked at Anna. "But listen. I don't mind telling you, I'm mixed up. Look at what I'm holding. Is it really half a million bucks?"

"We got to make it safe," Anna said. "Put it down the cellar for now. That room we found has a thing in the wall. Come on. I'll show you."

Angelo followed her, finding the money heavier as he walked. "We got to make it safe," he said, repeating her words.

"And shut up," she said as they reached the door.

14

Angelo walked in, heaving air from his walk up the hill. Anna smiled as he came in. "You're putting on too much fat," she said. "Look at how you're huffing. You want to leave us all too soon?"

"All right, all right. Don't be funny." He walked around the shining kitchen, approached the door leading to the main part of the house and listened with his head touching the wood. Then he turned back to her. "I don't get around anymore. I'm sitting talking to lawyers every night. Wait and I tell you the latest."

"Sit down," Anna said. "Nobody's here."

He walked to the formica table and stopped, grasping the silver pipe back of a kitchen chair. "Where is he?" he said.

"Don't worry. He's down in the Bronx with the paisans today." She shook her head. "They're playing boccie. They're playing the horses. Come up here and eat like pigs and talk all afternoon, all night. Who knows what else they do; *old men.*"

"Well, get this." Angelo squeezed the cold silver pipe in his hands. "He screamed at my lawyer. Jack went to see him to sign the papers, so the money would be legally ours. And he grabbed Jack by the jacket and tried to kick him out. He *dragged* him."

"He kicked Jack Testa out by himself?"

"*No, no.* Jack walked out. But if it was somebody else, Jack said he would have boffed him a good one. Who the hell does he think he is?" Angelo released his grip and walked to the stove, touched the coffeepot, found it cold, and turned the gas jet to flame under it. "What's going on, Anna? What's Poppa trying to do?"

"Sit down," Anna said. "I'll make your coffee." She came to the stove and lowered the flame, then walked to the pantry and carried two white boxes of cookies to the table. "Sit down a minute. Eat something."

Angelo obeyed, pulling a chair out from under the table and dropping heavily into it. Anna watched him, grimacing as he struck the chair, then began to speak: "I'll tell you this much. It's getting crazier every day around here. He comes in with those old slobs. I don't know where he dragged them up from. It's like fifty years ago. They come in here smoking their guinea stinkers and play *brisk.* Always with the fedoras on, you know, with the silk band dark from years of the sweat. And just let me try to come in and clean some ashes they drop all over; he starts yelling at me like I'm some dirt under his feet. He's always screaming. The slightest thing gets him. He's on top of me with screams. And God forbid I should answer him back. God forbid."

Angelo pulled himself to the table and rested his arms on the top. "It's like now it's us instead of Marinara. Isn't that true, when you think of it."

"Sometimes, he goes off on Gene. In the night. You hear him walking through the house talking to Gene."

"To Gene in his *head?*" When Anna nodded, Angelo asked: "What does he say?"

"Say? Nothing special, really. It's like he's mad at him one minute and sad the next, all meek. A little like he's crying; sometimes you would think he's talking to a baby."

Angelo was nodding. "It's as if he's turned into an egg. You got to make nice to him all the time, or he'll break up."

Anna heard the boiling coffee and took the pot from the stove to the table. "You want to know what it is." She leaned above him, close to his face.

Angelo looked at the smoking coffee pouring into his cup, then at Anna's dark face coming down.

"You're supposed to thank him every second," she said in a near whisper, as if it were shocking. "Thank him for the money. That's what he wants."

Angelo looked down at the coffee again, and nodded. "Old age. They're like kids again."

"Kids, is it?" Anna leaned close again. "Then if kids, they get treated like kids. They get a *nice* when they're nice and a hit when they're bad. A good lesson on the behind."

"Sure, sure. We'll put him across the knees." Angelo drank his coffee, reaching for the cookies with his left hand.

Anna watched his big hands press the macaroons for softness before he bit them. They were butchers' hands, wrestlers' hands: she was satisfied he was silent and ready to listen to her.

She rested the pot on the table and stood above him, feeling disgust at his sounds: she suppressed a shout in her throat, a thought of screams and knives that was so strong it held her in shame. Carlo, who had been on her mind day and night, was blocked out, gone away. She had had the house and its silence to help her contend with the terror and satisfactions of thoughts of him; now filled with noisy old men, who opened all doors, strewed their smelly age about, brought their cheap gray-black look to the rooms, making the slum feeling again, the house becoming crowded and hunched, it was ironically free of Carlo.

Her mother had even abandoned her, staying upstairs all the time, doing crochet, rearranging clothes she no longer used, making bundles to be packed and mailed to Italy, watching TV she barely understood, never asking for food, requiring only mozzarella on bread twice a day, and nothing else.

"It's something we stop!" She let the pot strike the table hard. "When a man turns himself into a child, he pulls down his pants for you when he's acting bad. Then you got to pick up the stick and give it to him."

Angelo stopped his chewing as Anna walked away, pacing along the room, stopping to touch surfaces, the washing machine lid, sink handles (which she tightened), rags and bottles she pushed back on shelves.

"Yeah, yeah," he said. "Grab a stick. When the person is your father. You want me to grab a stick on my own father?"

"Who makes himself a *nothing*." Anna had her hands up, shaking. "*Who* does the work around here? *You* or him? Who's even paying the bills now? It's our pockets it's all coming from now. Look around here, will you. Look at the mess in this house and the way his mob walks around here and drinks and yells. *See* what they are. You don't *obey* this." She returned to the table. "You don't obey a shadow."

Angelo looked down at the table and shook his head. "Don't shake," Anna said. "Don't say no. It's your own neck, too."

"Don't talk like that." He was about to continue, but the sound of a car in the driveway made him flush.

Anna ran quickly to the windows as the steps and voices of

men came towards the door. Santoro came in first, stamping a foot. "Fix the *pranzo*. *Pronto?*"

"Ready for what? It's only afternoon." Anna stepped in front of him. "There's no supper at three o'clock."

"Cook, then. Cook it. I can't wait till nighttime." Santoro walked around her and through the kitchen, followed by his friends, five of them, each removing his hat in greeting before going by.

Angelo rose to go to the door and listen, but Santoro came back alone. "Are you getting it ready?" he asked.

"No," Anna said. "I can't get a meal down anytime you walk in. I'm no diner here, with stuff half ready all the time. Go get me some cooked foods to heat up, go ahead. And who can keep up with those mouths. You're eating me out of house and home."

"Then buy more. Here, Angelo. Take her to the store."

Angelo was surprised, suddenly noticed, but he held himself in and did not answer.

"Angelo! Take her to the A & P."

"I got work, Pa."

"You got *work!* I am asking you to do this. I who gave you a cushion you don't need to work. Just take a little ride and get my food. I ask you, I ask you, I ask you to help your father. Why do you make me yell?" He leaned against the wall and his head fell, like an exhausted dog.

"I can't serve no army every day," Anna said. "Can't you go to a diner for once?"

"This *is* my diner! My house!" Santoro raised his arms and looked up. "My house is here! This is mine. But you don't help me."

He dropped his arms against his side, loudly, as if striking himself. His head fell again. He could not control the tears; they came up almost all the time; he shut his eyes to hold them back, but finally had to touch the lids and his cheek with his hands, to rub them clean, this confession to them. "A snail has a home," he said. "A snail has his house all the time. I have your spit in my face." He opened his eyes to see the tears in his hands. "And now I hate you, you made me come to this."

Anna did not answer; Angelo looked at her, nodded, and left the house. Anna followed him to the door and shut it securely. When he had gone through the trees, she watched her father for a moment. He had not moved while his face looked to the floor, his fists clenched, almost an act, it seemed. Silently she walked past him and out of the kitchen.

15

THEY HAD been talking about vacations and had come to him to ask what he would like to do. Santoro stared at them, their lips moving like wingbeatings. *Poppa where do you want to go this year? Poppa won't you come to the hotel.*

They would leave the house, run off, smile away, crack the net that had been holding. First they had taken his wife. He had watched her luggage go into Angelo's car, some wrapped candy and food for others, and then herself; and coming back to him at the kitchen window: *Will you come with me? To my sister. Long Beach is very cool. We will sit by the water.*

"Leave," he had said. "Go see them. I stay, I stay here." And when she was in the car behind the door, had called from the window: "Leave! Leave the rag man now."

Then Mister Angelo and his family had come to stand before him. *Poppa, we are going now.* He had been stone in front of them. Anna had gone with them, placing first in his hand a card: the name, the number, the hotel.

He had watched them all from the window before he cried for himself in the silence. He walked through the rooms: they had been filling up the empty holes of thoughts, what was missing with Gene gone so long. Gene, his best Gene. Gene, who had been like himself and was a great success. Better than the others, knowing it inside, yet unable to accept the ways of everyone else, a wanderer like himself: he should have had a new country. Gene. The silence now their absence: they were like a disease in his flesh.

He sat in the kitchen when the cook they hired rang the bell and brought him to the door. He watched her prepare the food and leave. Then he went upstairs again.

He walked through the hushed rooms, this new place, world without end. *Come here,* his voice said. *Anna. Come here. Sit down. Here's the court to try you. What have you done to your father?*

He sat in a chair in her room. The thick green rug made the quiet; green shutters kept away the sound of the wind, drapes kept out the day and the light. The walls were like the vaults in the bank. The chairs were speaking at times.

I damn Anna and her stomach and her face. This prune must never live. May she dry up and her belly produce dust. Make her dust. She should be cursed.

Here she is on the bed. She changed her hair. She is new and yellow. Who made her blind? Not I made her blind. What do you say, they grew a man between her legs? I will not believe: the sun shines greater than all the little stars.

Did she give me a cup? Is this cup from my Anna? The warm soup in color? No! It is poison. Yes, I will take it. I will drink it now. You take my tears. In this cup take my voice and arms.

I waited for them. Nights. The moon was ice. I stepped alone; they came to sleep then in beds I made. Walls I covered them from all bad ways. The storm even from the libeccio. I loved them as the sun is better than all the stars.

173

You did not love me, Anna. Did not. Did not. Angelo, he did me wrong, I think. He left this house. He ran and he walked lame. And he left my house in me. The house has lost the face. My face, they took away my face from the hanging wall.

Santoro stood up and turned on the lights; he went from room to room, turning on all the lights, then downstairs for the first floor. It was hot and cold: the head burnt and the feet froze. He sat down, tired: in the kitchen he saw them again; first they were green and jelly; then stiff they rose up on him:

Gene would not laugh for me. This is a foolish old man, Gene. I am foolish. See it. I wished you at my grave when I was still here. This bad old man. Hit him, hit him. Remember the stinking wop they said I was it. The white voices they caught me. Money turned me around; my face was in my back. The sun was a cold plate here. Now will you laugh, Gene? Please laugh. For the old man. Warmth we prayed for all the time. Ripeness is —

Then give me a black box in the back of the church and the long candles. We have borne the most. You shall never see so much or live so long. But forgive it. Do not strike the old man. He is rags. Here is my prison, in my face. See. I eat the key. I am this dog behind this fence, jumping up. Touch me. Only one hand. Touch me.

When the cook came in, the lights were on, and she asked him if he were *all right*. Santoro sent her away and went upstairs. He would work.

Anna returned two weeks later and saw the pile of stones immediately. Beyond it, on a little hill that had been cleared for a garden, there was a mound of soft, tan earth, probably left by a truck. It was a project of some sort; something new her father had been doing. She felt like a fool to have left him alone the way he was, believing that he could do no harm alone.

She rushed into the house to find him, but none of his sounds were there: on the kitchen table was an open bottle of red wine, half-filled, and a large round of provolone cheese with a deep wedge cut out of it. The odor annoyed her — like dirty men's socks — and she took Saran Wrap from the pantry and covered the cheese.

Then she heard him and looked out: he was coming over the hill, dressed in strange clothes, trousers of a brittle brown-green corduroy, his shirt a thick cotton flannel in broad red checks, stained with color, the colors muted by brown earth. And somewhere he had found army-navy work shoes, the leather a cheap orange color.

Her face flushed: it was the dress of a ditchdigger and how he found it all in Westchester she could not guess. Yet it had to be madness because the whole scene was impossible.

He was wiping his neck with a dark red polka dot handkerchief as he came towards the house; but then he stopped at the pile of stones, lifted one slowly and with strain rested it on his shoulders and returned over the small hill.

It had been something unreal, the man not even her father, but some picture of nineteen-sixteen in Manhattan when all the streets were building. She rushed out and walked the hill, to get at him. Coming over the rise, she saw him leaning far over a small wall of stones, with a bricklayer's tool, fitting the new stone to the wall with wet cement.

She stepped closer, noticing the lawn grass trampled in

places and dug through: a large stretch of lawn had been ruined already. There was a new mound of dirt, about five feet high, dark and damp, dug from the hill behind the stone wall.

Then she saw the opening, about the height of an average person, dug into the side of the hill. Inside were flat stones, seats perhaps, and cement hangings, the shapes of stalactites.

Santoro sensed her presence and looked up.

"Poppa, what is this? What are you *doing?*"

He stood up and smiled. "It's a little house," he said in Italian. "The grotto. Go in, go in. It is fresh and cool."

"Poppa, what is all this? We can't have a thing like this. What is it?"

Anna's heels were sinking a bit into the damp earth and she avoided too much movement as she spoke. Her body was stiff with anger; somewhere behind that, she was preparing to run.

"Go in, Maria. It is cool. Very nice." Santoro moved towards the entrance; his eyes were alive: he touched the entrance, pointed inside. "Look, look."

Anna turned from the dark opening to his face: she saw the mask on it, the smile of an idiot, angelic in madness. She turned and walked as quickly as she could back to the kitchen to call the family doctor.

"What can I do," Monachino said when he had heard the story. "You *could* have him committed if you insisted. But not without tests, of course. Not till they check him out." Monachino's busy breath came panting over the wires. "He's *old,* Annie. Old people, you don't like to put them away, you know what I mean. Unless it's awful bad. Because once you do, it's hopeless. You understand. The minute they go in, it's like the end —"

"Then what am I supposed to do here? Wait until he hits

me with a shovel. I told you, he didn't even know my *name* anymore."

"Well, you'll have to get him downtown, then." The doctor waited for Anna's voice. "For the tests I mentioned. Those people are all downtown. But listen, what's it hurting? Could be you should just let him build it all. I see old people all the time and they've got nothing left to do. Nobody even lets them take care of the kids — housework — anything. They vegetate. So maybe your father's got something —"

"That's just what I need. A house where every day he's got a new project with mud pies. Look, Vince, I'll call you back. Let me think."

Anna put the phone down, then struck it with her right hand: Monachino was the man who told sick housewives with five kids to rest in bed for a week. Just take it easy.

She went into the study and removed her hat and coat. Alone, she could do nothing: she telephoned Angelo and ordered him up to the house.

Angelo saw his father, then came into the house. "Is he building to China?" He smiled, watching her giant's look take him over. "It's funny," he said. "Come on, admit it."

"It's a big joke. Just laugh. Sure. And just wait until it gets worse and he starts pissing in the house. You stupid fuck! It's not funny!"

Angelo was thrown back by her words, worse because she rarely spoke this way. It was almost not Annie anymore: in the kitchen, week after week, she was turning into a new, hard thing, her nose, eyes, staring unchanging, like the statues in church shrouded on the death holidays.

(And in the mountains people at the hotel had either spoken to her in quiet tones of respect or been afraid to approach her, as if she were a celebrity or a witch. One man asked if she were running the family business these days, unaware that old Santoro had sold it.)

"What do we do, then?" he said. "You want to be the one who puts him away? You want that on your soul?" He walked back and forth, his movements working with the anger he had left in him. "Tell me," he said to her. "Go ahead and tell me."

"We both do this," Annie said. "I call the doctor downtown, and you go take him in."

"I get it. I lay my hands on him. I get *that* job."

"All right." Anna turned her face away from him. "Just go up there and see it. Over the hill. See what he went and made up there. And talk to him. And then you come back here." She went to the window and looked at the hill. "Go ahead. Over the rise there. He's up there knocking rocks together."

Angelo went out, and she followed his walk with her eyes. As she stared at the hill, he came back over the rise, running. She went to the door and opened it. "Anna, Pop's hiding in there. He took one look at me and ran into that cave."

"All right, you see something now."

"He thought I was some kind of police. When he got inside, he started calling me *marshal. Maresciallo.* Talking Italian all the time. Then his hand came out slow, and he offered me some cheese if I'd go away."

"Now what do you call that? That's the answer you want."

"All right. Then call the doctors while I go back and get ready. And phone me when I should come up." He left quickly, rushing away from his own words. Running to his car, he drove out, not certain where he was going, but by habit went to his lawyer, Jack, to ask about the legal aspects of commitment.

Jack filled his head with alternatives, making him uncertain of any action. He left the office and drove to a nearby bar, called his wife to tell her, then called Anna. "I had to go out. What happened?"

"This kind of doctor will definitely not come up here. They don't make house calls." Anna spoke very fast. "I spoke to him already and you got to take him downtown and that's it. And they charge, let me tell you, they really charge."

Angelo heard the exasperation: it was the same tone in his wife's voice when he had told her, and in Jack's. They did not want Angelo to come with this extra, useless pain, and their irritation accused him of being responsible in some way. "Look," he said to the sounds. "You got to give me a few days. I'm going to find a way to handle it."

"The appointment's set for next week, on Monday at eleven o'clock in the morning. We get him there."

Angelo did not say good-bye, but backed away as he placed the phone receiver on its hook, walked into the bar room where the odor killed his wish for a drink. Instead, he drove his car to the Kensico Reservoir and sat in the sun at the base of the great rock wall, fishing for thoughts. They came up in moments, three or four tangled together, next to a fund of anger like a big, clumsy hand ready to crush them.

He sat in the driver's seat, his door opened so that he could lean out, his right hand on the steering wheel. He hung over, almost panting, the anger becoming a lump in his throat, his voice uttering groans to clear the lump, a sound like crying.

When he straightened up, sat back on the hot vinyl of the seat, he felt he had been sitting for most of the day. They would all be calling for him. He drove back and went right to his rooms, without stopping at the main house.

Emma came to the door. "Oh, I was a little worried where you were. I thought you got hurt or something."

"No such luck," he said, and went into his bedroom and shut the door. All the hatred collected towards Emma; if she walked in and spoke, he would smash her head in with both fists.

He sat on the bed, panting again, his neck sweating for the sin against Emma. The room was dark in dusk, but the darkness was no help: darkness was where his father walked.

16

GOING ROUND the house, through the air of the rooms, frightening when they were silent (as if something were growing, a black shape with the face and energy of her own rage) Anna's thoughts ran, and looked for the others not present — Carlo and Gene.

They had left her. Yet abandoned she was superior to them now; she was on top, not the dark Anna who had to be shown how to start things, who had to be led to an airport, shaking.

But that was not love. Could she love them in every way. Must she love them, again and again and again. She had no way to run free. (Like being on a road, she ran until clear of everything and everyone, but then their essence came through the air itself and entered her and she must love them and do what they wanted her to do, and be the Anna they wanted of her.) Even serving was a crime now, putting a plate before a man's fingers.

She had the house and held the keys, yet she still heard the barking of the beasts of her mind in her ears. Because here in the hill, behind the trees, inside the high wide electric fence, guarded by a gunman, she was still penetrated by someone without a face and could only fight by becoming a beast among beasts.

Unconsciously, she was talking to Gene; she had dialed the number without knowing: "Gene, I'm scared and I don't mind telling you. I know I shouldn't bother you. I know how you feel. You washed your hands of it, I think. You signed it away, and I don't blame you, me here in this thing I got on my hands. But you want to know. Poppa's going crazy and here with his friends first, these damn spaghetti benders, and then digging ditches and caves in the backyard garden and bringing up cement like they were still working for City Hall. I tell you oh it's a crazy house around here. And then he's got his private war on me, dropping rocks and glass in my machines in the kitchen and so much more crap I don't know where to start. Who would make a grotto in Westchester —"

"It sounds pretty. A grotto. I mean, it sounds like it might be something nice in a garden."

"Oh stop it, Gene. Not you too. Don't talk like that. It is definitely not fun time up here!" Earlier her mind had wanted to say that she would not take that crap, would kill the old bastards; now she heard Gene, like Dr. Monachino, men talking for men, men who never cleaned up. Men who could walk away from home. "This is an old man!" she screamed. "Who's going to piss on my floors, in my bureau drawers, on top of my hankies. You got to know this. You have got to help, now. This is not a joke, my brother."

Whether it was danger or a worm in Annie's head, Gene still came to the desperation, drove to the house from his office, met her at the kitchen door and sat down, first to answer her litany on how everything was, from business to family.

"Francine was relieved because I didn't come up here anymore." Gene thought of her. "But then, she started to worry. About Pop. Probably because she couldn't see him and couldn't talk to him. *Where is he? What is he doing: you think he could be sick.* Sometimes she got very jumpy about it. *Something's wrong with Pop. I know it. Why don't you go up.* I told her many times, *Call. You* call. It's less embarrassing because Pop might not want to talk to me. I kept telling her, Annie knows you, Pop and Mom know you. But it's something that scares her, a feeling that flies around inside her, like a moth. Sometimes one person's father is like everybody's. Francine has a row of old men lining up in her head. Sicilians. Lining up. I told her one day, don't suffer, you didn't kick anyone out into the street. Don't cringe."

Anna began slapping the kitchen table. "She's right, she's absolutely right. I know it's something coming. Some damn thing is rotting on us. Something's going to get us. I don't want to talk about it and say the words some more. Just help me, Gene. Please help me."

"How can I help you?" Gene sat, as Angelo had, and received coffee and watched as Anna walked the kitchen, serving, talking, preparing, cleaning surfaces, as if she were running a house for hundreds, something in her blood.

She came and went; she stared at him. "Help Poppa," she said. "That's what help means. Get him to a home. Or get him to live decent here. And talk to me like a human being and not some filth he just found under his feet. I just won't take that. You hear me, Gene. I'm not the same anymore either. I'll do something to him if he keeps up."

Gene was blocked with thoughts, with ways of saying what had gone on since he had left. He sat holding a coffee cup: he drank coffee, lit cigarettes, stared at the enameled walls. "I left this place, Annie." He heard her voice stifle a *no*. "I left this place the day of the money. You *take* the money and you *take* the storms."

"You mean it's all in my lap. That's all that says."

"I mean, when you took the money on that day, you took what was going to happen after that." Gene had a realization, words that had been unable to come up before this: "That's what I was trying to explain to Francine when she kept bringing up Poppa night after night. It's an old story. You get what you pay for. But Francine, she really wanted to come up here and get her share of the money and fall in the soup, too —"

"Go ahead! Say it all!" Anna looked at his disclosure, dropping Francine along the way. "And also tell me, what about your father. *Your* father."

"All right. That's where you get me. That's where I can't disappear."

"Then you'll help us, and go to him." Anna was standing across the table from him, gripping her chair rungs.

"No," Gene said.

"No? You just said yes. What the hell is this, Gene? Are you getting nuts, too?"

Gene was up, to get away from the house again, like a stranger's dwelling so quickly, the sense of imprisonment lying about its grayish walls. Anna came after him, unwilling to let him go. "But *I* can be shit on," she said. "That will be OK."

Gene stopped. "Not by me, Anna. I took nothing that's yours, and I made none of your problems —"

He stopped himself; Gene had caught his own glibness; since Anna was on the spot and asking for help, it had been easy for him to hit her with smug, blameless phrases. But now he also thought that he had helped hurt her in bringing back the children, taking them from the sunny mess of Amalfi to the air-conditioned funeral of Korvette's.

He was guilty again, and softened by it. "Look, Anna. We say too much, don't we. All of us. I'm not letting you down. Just do this first. You and Angie try to handle it your way. If it doesn't go well or you need any kind of help, *then* call me up. *Then* I'll step in."

Anna walked with him to the door, silent, shaking her head. "I don't know. I don't know." Her voice was small, deep inside her, behind barriers. She looked up when she felt Gene's arm across her shoulders, met his embrace, his face on hers, his moustache touching her cheek, his brother's kiss.

She felt her tears as if she were going to fall, weak as she was not weak. It was the first touch in months; even the kids did not embrace her anymore nor kiss her goodnight. "Everybody tells me the same thing, Gene. YOU DO IT. They think I can handle it all. But I don't know, Gene. I'm still a woman."

"Just call me. And mention my name to Poppa. Find out if he'll talk to me. Make up something; ask him if he ever sees me anymore. If he'd like to see me now. Get his reactions."

Gene was out and gone into his car and down the hill. She had time before the afternoon raid of her father and the paisans. She was unable to act, even though her hatred was almost into her hands: she had once been on the verge of slamming the kitchen door shut and locking the whole house of doors. But her father's face at night, his presence, made her realize that the house without him was more dangerous, yet he, stalking through it alone, frightened her beyond reason.

Gene she knew would stay gone. He would not be back because he had shaken their dirt from his shoulders, whatever that dirt was — being with each other, being too close to one another all the time. That thought came to her, first as merely a part of her desperation, then slowly as reality: she was chained to her father whatever he did, stuck to him, as if the years made the air they lived in like a clear glue; they took it wherever they went or could go; but really they did not go because they were caught in the stickiness; they could not jump up; they descended into the stuck moment day after day, a time ended only by death, if death ended it.

But Gene had cut his way out; Gene was moving away and though he said it had been the money he gave up, it was something else, some control he had over his heart, over the moods that drove you back into the house with your parents, that kept them in the house of your mind wherever you were.

She was pacing as she thought, and found the emptiness of the rooms like the days that were draining her: she would call Angelo, but not tell him she had spoken to Gene and asked his help.

Gene had stopped after going through the gate and looked back at the hill, up at the grove of trees where the house was hidden. He had held himself in, had swallowed the rotting words he could have said to Anna and her money; he had held in the anger of being kicked out by his father and the nights of sadness and fury when he almost drove back, almost called to ask.

His own nights of sweat were peeling from his mind, but he had not forgotten what he had sat through alone, waiting for any of them to come out of their pot and call him; if Anna had only told him what had been going on, how everyone was.

They had not looked for him, the silence their agreement that he could leave their world. And now the desperation of Anna was like her own separate pain, like a growth under her

186

skin; he could only see it and tell her to get it fixed, cut away by someone else.

His father lived up there, but it was as if the old man had been cut into pieces and transplanted into the others. Anna yelled about him but sounded more like him, had his accent, the same wildness in the eyes, the blackness, the unexpected temper — it was coming through her even as she complained that he was growing in rage.

Gene knew he was not separated from them, and that any stupid way they fought to get rid of each other, he would be affected.

But not as much, not as much now; having held his own anger for all this time, he had also lost being dependent on theirs. His nights of sweat had set some pieces of him loose, but like a single man on a raft into darkness. The silence of not knowing about them had been frightening; now he would like to try more of it, to die alone, in his head, without a family, and then come alive again in some way, because of it.

17

LATE SUNDAY afternoon Angelo heard the phone, which Emma answered. "Annie says go up right away. It's important. Hurry up, Angie. She's alone up there."

Angelo walked out silently and went up the hill to the kitchen. Anna was standing near the sink, looking into the open hole of the washing machine. "Look at this. Just look down there."

He came to her and looked into the opening. "Looks like glass," he said. "Broken glass. What is it? What's broken glass mean?"

"It's *him*. It's got to be him. Nobody else is here. Glass doesn't walk in." Anna slammed the top shut. "And I found dirt in the dishwasher. Real earth and small stones in it; it all fell down and clogged my motor up. The damn thing almost burned out."

She wiped her hands on a dish towel hanging on the wall. "It's got to be him. He's trying to destroy my machines. You understand?" She threw the towel on the sink top. "He throws glass in my washer and rocks in my dishwasher. There's no doctor going to help that."

Angelo leaned against the sink. "Well, *what* the *hell* am I supposed to do!" He went to the washing machine, opened it again, reached in and removed a piece of glass. "Yeah, yeah. What do you do for this? You can't stick him in jail now, can you?"

"I don't want to stick him in jail!" Anna shook her head slowly and walked to the table. Her soft slippers made her walk a shuffle. She sat down in a white chair and sighed. Her face was dark again, the morning face before makeup. "Listen to me," she said. "I thought and thought about it. Here with my hands freezing in summer and my head spinning, ready to explode. First I filled up — I wanted to go after him, get him. Hit him. Hurt him good. Then I almost went crazy, yelling at him alone in my bed up there. Do you know I kept thinking he might come after me."

She was eased by the words coming out and placed her hands on the table top and looked at them. "But now. Look. I don't want to hurt him no more. I just want him to be safe. I want somebody to take care of him, make him feel peaceful. I can't do it. I can't be with him. Get him the right medicine. Somebody. I don't know how. Oh, those damn doctors. Throw their physics in the wind, they're no goddamn good. I just want something — pour it in him and make him OK again." She folded her hands on the table. "Whatever's right, Angelo. Please. Let's get him wherever they can help him. And before Momma comes back. And let this house *rest*."

"I never liked this house." Angelo looked at her for a reaction, but she did not respond. "All right," he said. "Now let's try with that doctor tomorrow. I'll get him to go." He carried the piece of glass with him to the door. "I'm going for a little walk now."

"Angie!" Anna came to the door and met him on the steps.

"Angie, listen to me. Did you ever want to kill him?" Her voice was hollow, the small voice of the past, the abandoned Anna. He reached up and took her hands. "Maybe I'm doing it tomorrow. That's what gets me."

"It all started because of me, you know. I'm the fault. I broke up everybody's house. I destroyed —" She stopped as Angelo released his grip and stepped back. "Stop it now," he said. "Just stop it. Do what you have to do."

He left her on the steps and went home. Emma was especially silent and stayed waiting whenever she could, in case he might call. After walking, Angelo came in and asked for food. The children came in from play while he was eating, and he peeled fruit for them and gave them bits of buttered bread and parts of his meat. He continued to eat after they left, chewing silently, hunched over the food as if it were healing medicine.

Emma wanted to warn him, stop him, but the eating obviously refreshed him, even if it made him sweat. Finally, he stood up with the iced tea pitcher and carried it to the small TV room, and Emma followed. "At least we kept our kids out of it completely," he said. "They don't even know what exists up there; even those damn kids." He sat down. "I just want to watch a little and go to sleep. Boy, I am really exhausted. Every which way. You know what I mean."

"Every which way," Emma repeated. "It's not fair to you. Angie, it's all on your back now. Can't you call Gene?"

He looked at her but did not answer. Ready to come out were the words *tomorrow it will be all over*, but he swallowed them quickly, sat down in his big chair that faced the receiver. "Any special channel?" Emma said.

"Anything, anything. My mind'll be a million miles away, anyway." He saw Emma's small worried face and smiled at

her. He couldn't say the things aloud; they would be im-
proper, but he wished to say that he was doing it now, he was
not waiting for others; *he* was doing the actions.

He watched until he fell asleep and remembered Emma
helping him to bed. In the morning he went directly to the
house and up to his father's room. "Well, Pop. How are you?
It's a nice day, isn't it? Did they tell you I was coming over this
morning?"

Santoro was lying in bed and smiled at his son. "Why do
you come?" He was happy; his eyes filled with tears. "Do they
come? Do they call me?"

Angelo walked to the bed, took his father's hands, then
leaned down and kissed the warm face. "Poppa. Today we're
going downtown to speak to a man. A friend of mine. I want
you to meet him."

"The friend?" Santoro said. "The friend with peace? The
friend with a knife." He continued to smile. "A *padrone?*"

"No. This is my own friend. An American man, and you're
going to like him."

The old man was pleased. "I put on my dress," he said.

Angelo released the hands. "Want me to get out a nice
suit?" He walked to the closet. "Here's your nice brown gabar-
dine. Wear this. And a white shirt with a tie. You want me to
help you?" He turned from the closet and saw the old man,
out of bed already, immensely pleased with something. "I
will shave myself," he said. "And then come down."

"Then I'll wait downstairs." Angelo left the room and went
down to the kitchen; Anna was preparing breakfast. He sat
down while she served him coffee. As he drank, he felt the
rosary beads in his jacket pocket and removed them. "Look,"
he said to Anna. "I just remembered. I tried to say a rosary last

191

night. But I never could finish. Why do you think a thing like that would happen? I couldn't pray when I needed to."

Anna's face was turned away from him; she faced the stove, watching the boiling eggs and the toaster behind it. Angelo waited for an answer, but she did not speak, either lost in reveries or uninterested in his question.

"That's the kind of shape I'm in," he said.

She turned to him. "Don't talk that way, Angie," she said in a low voice, as if someone might be listening. "We'll all go nuts talking like this."

They heard Santoro, who came in and sat down and was served his boiled egg and toast. Anna served him and walked quickly away. Santoro did not notice her face and gestures, but looked at Angelo and smiled. "Take more coffee," he said at one point. "Maria. Here," he called to Anna. "Get the coffee. And get the bottles out. Be ready when they come tonight. Twelve o'clock they all start coming."

Anna tried to smile, but turned away at the words, their very gentleness, his belief in the fantasy disturbing, as if her father saw the real scene he was talking about, saying something to his wife and the past.

Angelo, who was not afraid, began to remember. The *bottles* were homemade liqueurs — Anisetta, Coffee Sport, Rock and Rye, Mandarino — all placed on the kitchen table on New Year's Eve in the Bronx, when the whole neighborhood went from house to house for drinks and greetings. It was a time when they were together, the family and the neighborhood families; though they were all poor then, there were more days like vacations, more times to wait for and celebrate.

Driving downtown he asked his father if he remembered

the old celebrations, mentioning some feast days and some of the people who were most pleasant, like Tommy Rizzo, who laughed like a donkey at midnight and woke up the little children. The old man smiled and answered *yes* while he stared at the sunny windshield, but Angelo did not think he was remembering.

The doctor's office was full of old rugs and magazines, and the doctor was a small, gray man with a soft voice, whose inner office had a desk, a couch, a few leather chairs, a painting of a cow at a river on the wall in a gold frame, but no medical equipment, nothing white. The doctor asked Angelo to wait and escorted Santoro inside, calling him *signor* instead of Mister: the use of the Italian word embarrassed Angelo, who sat in the waiting room deciding the doctor was a fool.

When Santoro came out, he was nodding; they were finishing a conversation. The doctor shook hands and bowed, like a servant instead of a doctor. He escorted them to the door, but said nothing.

Angelo drove uptown, becoming increasingly angry that he had received no diagnosis. He parked the car near a stationery store and told his father he had to buy cigarettes.

Inside, he went to the phone booth and called the doctor, who said he would phone his report to Monachino. "But let me say to you that I found him a bit senile yet otherwise a very pleasant person. I'll write up the whole report for you and send it to Dr. Monachino. But you know, there are very nice *homes,* if you would like to do that. Not hospitals, but places where old people have a little society."

Angelo could not listen anymore and hung up. He walked out to the car and found it empty. The streets were fairly clear: he looked into a few shops, then went back to the store to call the doctor, who had not seen Santoro again, then Anna, who had heard nothing. "I'll start to look around this neighborhood and call back," Angelo said. "That stupid fucking doctor said he's all right. Now what the hell does he say to this. The old man might be walking towards the river. Look. You wait before you call the cops. Let me look around first."

Angelo went back to his car and began driving through the streets, making his way towards the river, cursing his father, caught in his own failure: the old man was not to be seen. Finally stuck in traffic between trucks that rose around him, he damned the old man and turned north when he finally reached intersecting streets.

But on the highway he thought of his father walking Manhattan alone, blind, without money, with no memory, perhaps even his own name lost to him by now. Angelo parked in one of the emergency parking lots and watched boats on the Hudson before deciding to go back. He could not guess the pattern of the old man's wandering but decided to start at Union Square, the neighborhood of the family factory near Houston Street, the places his father had known and walked.

18

SANTORO HAD seen a subway entrance while he was waiting, and remembering home, had gone down and taken a subway to Grand Central Station, then a local to Tuckahoe, and walked to Gene's office not far from the station.

Gene was about to leave for lunch when Mary told him his father was waiting. He went to the door and welcomed the old man with an embrace. "Come on inside, Pop. I'm so glad to see you. And *you* are looking good." His father walked in, and Gene shut the door behind him. "Did you need some legal advice?" Gene said, and came to embrace him again. "How are you? How are you? Sit down, sit down. Have a cigar."

He was enjoying the smiling face, with peace in it. "I haven't seen you in so long. It's like years, Pop. You know, I wanted to come up. I was hoping you'd call. Just this morning I was thinking about you. I'm going away for a trip and I wanted to come up and say good-bye."

"Bringing more in," Santoro said, and winked. He walked to a leather chair near the desk and sat down.

Gene smiled. "You mean more stolen kids. No, no. No more of that. My snatching days are over. I'm just going over for myself this time. For myself. I want to see what happens."

The old man was nodding his head; his hair was pleasantly silver again, the lines in his face a pleasant design: it was age, but like peace, features you knew would never change again and so were more compelling because they were complete, the heat of emotions gone from them.

"Why do you smile?" Gene said. "You think I'm going on a hayride? Right? Well, maybe a little bit of fun too. That's not so bad."

"Bring them in because they deserve," the old man said. "They are good people. Just like us. They make Americans."

"Who is *this* we're speaking about?" Gene wanted to laugh: his father's seriousness was like a gentle joke.

"But watch the *ladri*," the old man said. "And *padroni* on the dock. Always there to steal them all. *Zitto, zitto.*" The old man put his right index finger to his lips. "These don't hurt anybody. Some maybe become bad. The bad apple in the barrel. But you good, Gene. You do good."

Gene was beginning to catch the sadness behind this talk without meaning: his father knew the substance of his words, but Gene did not, and the disparity was enough to make the world hollow, a world in the old head, alone there.

Still, whatever it was he was saying, it pleased the old man and part of it seemed to be praise for Gene. "What have I done so good?" Gene said.

The old man winked again and made his gesture for quiet. "Do it, Gene. Bring them from the misery. And I can help, too. Let some come to me and sleep in my place."

"All right, Pop. I'll help everybody I can. OK? And a little bit for me, too. A little trip to bring me back to life."

Santoro stood up and walked to Gene, kissed him on the face and began to walk to the door.

"Pop? What is it? Where you going? Are you feeling OK?" Gene came after him. "How is Mom? And the house? And money? Do you have enough these days for yourself? Do you need anything?"

The old man had reached the door, his back towards Gene. "I need the sun now," he said.

"Sure, sure. It's such a nice day. I was just going out myself. You want a ride home?"

"I go now to play boccie with my partners." He opened the door and walked through the outer office, and Gene followed him to the street. "Can I give you that ride?" Gene said.

The old man nodded and smiled. Gene took his arm and walked with him to the car, waiting for him to speak what seemed to be at the tip of his tongue. But Santoro simply allowed himself to be helped and sat staring ahead into the glare of sunlight on the hood.

As they drove towards the city, Gene tried to get an answer, asking about recent days at the fort, but the old man had little to say: everything was fine. Apparently, the specter of Marinara was disappearing in some way.

"Did you go away?" Gene asked.

"Yes," the old man said.

"Good. And you had a nice vacation?"

"Very nice."

They reached Arthur Avenue and parked near the boccie alley, behind a row of two-family wooden houses. Just before his father walked away, Gene asked again: "Tell me. What do you think of my going over there? What do you say?"

The old man looked directly into his eyes, coming down from his stare aloft. "Go, go," he said, with a bit of irritation. "I told you to go. Enjoy it. Enjoy it."

Gene drove away, along the street of stores, and stopped to buy fresh cheese and a loaf of bread. Whenever the Westchester Italians were down here they felt compelled to stock up with food from the source, as if this neighborhood had inherited the totem of purity from Naples. But after buying, Gene decided to have lunch along the river, the spot he had shown to the children.

He drove to the Parkway and parked again near the river, walking to the slight hill where the river turned and where crayfish used to be. The cheese was watery and soft and he held it in his left hand, the loaf of bread in his right. He sat down, hearing the cars behind him and a slight sound of water below, rushing to the bend, then slowing down.

His father's mood had closed his decision finally; Francine would have to cry a little more. She was his wife but not his arms, eyes and legs, not a shareholder in his mind. It was the hardest fact to believe, and he had said it to himself too many times because whatever she did affected his heart: he was hurt or sad or happy. Now his father's detachment, like a man walking in air, was like permission. The loosened mind had spoken behind his scattered words and made Gene's direction correct.

The kids had found their pleasures in bikes and things made in plastic factories; Gene accepted what they had become. Later in their lives, if there was anything left for them to look for, they could start again.

But having lost a father and part of a mother, they probably would always live for *things*. The lack of voices to soothe and hands to touch you, in any way, made it necessary to have rugs in the house, cameras and power motors in the cellar, archery kits, dryers, TV sets in every room, whatever new machines came out. Francine was getting it, and it was his fault. And the more you had, the easier it was to lose. There were always others coming to take it away, new people, darker people, yellow people, rowing towards our shores, hungry for our cellars, our kitchens and garages.

Gene looked at the slow river now that he had finished eating and was feeling good inside. When he had walked in that water, his sneakers tied around his neck, the summers had promised nothing. (The books he had been reading lately, discovered at the drugstore paperback stand, novels that began with the impatient mood he understood, all ended by saying that going back to the innocence of the river was the best way. They wrote nothing about the days after mid-life when the fear of your own death walks into your nice bedroom at night. But the books were not lies, were only inadequate, written by men who were boys.)

He remembered the days after law school when he was studying for the bar exams, and his mother was there to chat at lunches, joking with him, calling him names in Neapolitan: *Strampalato.* That was the most frequent: the confused, messy, but enjoyable fool. He did not care how he looked or if there was a car or what was on at the local movie or even when meals began.

He rose and saw a hard tip of his loaf on the grass and threw it into the water, hoping fish might rise for it.

Then he went back to his car, to drive home to Francine and tell her he was leaving in three days.

PART THREE

19

Waiting for the plane he had decided to have a drink at the Alitalia bar. A young woman — perhaps she was middle-aged — dressed in a white suit with a very short skirt over shining legs — had looked at him along the bar and smiled a few times. He had smiled in return but could not get free from the thoughts of Larry Spina's words when he had said good-bye at the terminal entrance, minutes before.

On the way out, perhaps in the murky emotion that always accompanies leaving, Gene had tried to confide the whole mess in his mind, explaining that the trip might be like a search.

"I know what you're getting at," Larry had said. "Last year, when I had those migraines, I took off to Jamaica. Did you ever stay at Round Hill? And I just laid there for two weeks and ate fresh fruit and drank Myer's Rum. It changed me. Completely."

"It changed you completely. Bless you. Like my mother used to say, *Beata te.*"

Gene saw Larry's face hurt and did not go on. As they were parting at the door, Larry had grasped Gene's hand. "Get some rest, Boss," he had said very loud, then realized it was not his real thought. "Come back. Come back soon. What do you think we're all here for? We'll help you work it out." Gene had stared at him, beyond understanding. "What the hell are you doing this for?" Larry had shouted. "Gene! Gene? What's wrong? Tell me what's wrong." Larry had waited, then turned to look at his steering wheel. "All right. Take care, then. Take care." He seemed to be holding back a strong emotion. "And don't worry about the office. I'll do everything." He pulled the door shut and drove away, angry, or to avoid the show of other feelings.

Gene had carried his bags to the door, where a porter took them and walked to the weighing desk.

Now he was caught in that departure of Larry, different from Francine's, which he had understood. Larry should not have thought that Gene was doing anything against him, yet Larry resented him, too.

When they announced his plane's departure, Gene had time to notice the families saying good-bye, the noise of Italian families, embarrassing and comforting at the same time. He followed the main crowd to the plane, and walked through the hatchway and along the aisle. The noises were gone; the rows of faces were silent and expectant, looking from the small windows to have a last contact with the outside.

When the stewardess came through, everyone sat obediently awaiting the starting of the engines. Quickly, the plane began to taxi and he lost the thought of the crowds and the terminal, finding his own fear in the force of the plane that rocked along the runway, stopped to increase engine power and shake the plane, which felt too thin to hold together. Then it released itself, the passengers blind to the movement.

He turned to the window, saw the passing of lights and then darkness, as if the sky had been blotted out. The night had been clear on the ground; in the air it was a black fog until he saw stars above that seemed only dim spots.

His thoughts began to cover his eyes: of his father, who had been the easiest to leave, then Francine, who gave him her tears and her anger, her last curses for his betrayal: he was a man of filth because he had left her: there was no other way she could see the trip.

He had believed it again and become frightened. His head ached, and he felt the dizziness that he had been thinking was heart trouble but told no one about. Francine had had no pity; instead she insisted that *she* would get ill. But she *had* been ill, tired, most of her life, part of every month they had lived together, losing her temper a little more noisily every day, to the peak of exhaustion, the last day of her period when she would clean the house from morning until night, then fall asleep at seven, to awake, replenished next morning, explaining that it had not been her fault but nature's, craving forgiveness from Gene for what had attacked her from another source.

Gene's mind did not go on: he was bored with the battles of his head: fighting her, condemning her at the end of it. What he had tripped upon in Naples, then Amalfi, unexpectedly, was something else, like a void or a black crater.

When he reached Rome and his hotel room, lying on his bed while the traffic below sounded like Manhattan, he began to think of his money. It had taken him here a second time and could take him again. He had had no real knowledge of it until he took planes, rented hotel rooms and cars. Money had been something with which to collect stocks and property, which were money again. Money was a daily re-created net to throw out and catch more things that in time would become more money.

The first trip had turned it into the power to move and even hurt others, to have strangers quickly his employees. In the lost suitcase he discovered that he could quickly replace anything that was gone, and not be weaker: once he had shaved with an old rusted razor for two months because his electric razor had burned out and something inside him had not realized he could buy another in a moment, without affecting his wealth. Here, now, he had no more need to subordinate himself to hotel clerks or salesmen of all kinds, to solicit their lowest prices with jokes.

Thinking of all this, he went for his traveler's checks and lay back on his bed to count them, stopping after eight thousand. And it had not dented his account back home. It was a surprise to him on the day he withdrew the money (worried about Francine's safety) to see how much remained. It proved Francine wrong once and for all. At home that night he had sat in his room, locked the door, afraid that people outside might guess that all this time he had been richer than anyone expected and had more money than their Bronx minds, still stuck in kitchens and thinking like the black alleys of Santa Lucia, could ever conceive.

His first thought here was to buy Marinara a present that would astound his belief, then give enough to Elena to free her from work.

He fell asleep and awoke a few hours later to call the desk for a hired car. In the morning he came downstairs at seven and the desk clerk raised his brows when Gene asked for the car. Nothing began until nine.

Gene went out to walk, finding the river and then the narrow streets of the old city. He did not feel furtive as he had with the children, and walked through piazzas he tried to remember, all vaguely familiar but unknown.

He had breakfast at a bar near a heavy, dark building, with an enormous columned portico and a swollen back, staring at it while he drank his coffee, finally asking the bartender what it was, and receiving, after a pause, the name: the Pantheon.

Gene smiled at himself, his ignorance beyond belief, as if he had come from another planet.

"The Trevi fountain is just nearby," the bartender said to him. "Where they throw the coins."

Gene accepted the directions silently, left a tip and walked out, finding at last a large wide street, which led him to the Colosseum standing red and quiet in the morning light. After the steps and an hour of staring into the silent bowl, he left and went across the street for more ruins and found himself exhausted. He returned to the street for a cab to the hotel and found the car ready. His bags were packed in the trunk, his map on the seat beside him; he drove to the autostrada and the two and a half hours to Naples. Then, without stopping, he continued to the Pompeii-Salerno autostrada and went to Salerno for the road to Amalfi. There was much more traffic now; it seemed that everyone in Italy had come to the Amalfi drive, and the towns were vibrating with the crowds.

In Amalfi he found the house and parked around the corner in the piazza where he had hidden the first car on the day he left with the children.

The streets were different, alive with faces from everywhere but Amalfi: at the door he stopped before ringing the bell and prepared his face for Elena. But a girl of about fourteen, with dark eyes and pale skin, came to answer, looked at him and smiled as she noticed his foreign clothes. Gene told her he was a relative from America; the girl let him in and called into the house, receiving no answer.

Gene followed her along the hall and up the familiar stone staircase. A woman came out to greet him. "I am the sister of Carla Gennatasio," she said. Her lips were thick, shapely and red, and she was heavy and bulging in a tight skirt and sweater. "We are preparing the wedding."

"That's why I came. Carlo invited me."

"From America? Actually?" The woman could not believe that a wedding, no matter how important, could generate that expense. "All this way?"

"Yes," Gene said. "Let me see Carlo and tell him I have come."

"He will be ready in a minute. There is a tailor with him now." She was looking at Gene and stepped back to allow him to precede her to the living room, which housed the same round wood table, high chairs, the giant sideboard, the couch in the corner. "Please be at home. I will get something to drink."

Gene sat down and noticed the young girl he had seen first, staring at him. "Is this your daughter?" he said.

She had opened the cabinet doors and removed two bottles of vermouth and some small glasses. "Eva? She works for the house." She had stopped to speak, then came to the table to pour.

Gene smiled at the girl, took a glass of red vermouth and held it up to the lady, who began to observe him.

"Are you here on your vacation?" she said.

"I hope so," Gene said. "After the wedding."

"Alone?"

"Just myself and a car." Gene saw that her face found this exciting.

"Good!" Marinara's voice came up behind him. "Eugenio! *Porco?*" He held out his arms. "You have come!"

Gene stood, as Carlo came to embrace him, and felt the strong arms. "Don't crush me. I have to see you get married."

Marinara stepped back, then sat down. He saw the forgotten sin of his marriage in Gene's presence. "You are here alone?" he said.

"Only me. As I told this lady." Gene saw the woman smiling, unaware of the tension between Carlo and himself. She took Gene's glass as he placed it down, smiled at him, and began to pour again.

"Would you excuse us, Violetta?" Marinara's voice stopped her. She rested the bottle on the table and stepped back. "*Sì,* Carlo," she said, and left the room, followed by the young girl.

"Eugenio." Carlo stood up. "Why did you come now? Unless to do me harm." He clasped his hands together. "How have you planned to destroy me?"

"No —" Gene jumped up quickly and touched Carlo's arm. "Carlo. Don't think such things. I came to wish you good luck — a happy life."

"If I am in your prayers, I am happy." Carlo reached for his glass, to turn away from Gene. "And I know too I am in your debt. And you know that."

"Let's drink to the wedding." Gene held his glass up. "Carlo."

Marinara touched glasses and drank. He believed the sentiment, then could not understand Gene's purpose here: no one came merely for a wedding, all that distance, though he had been taught to believe such ceremonies were the most important events in life. His emotions went hunting Gene's motivations in what he knew of his past life. He found nothing to explain Gene's presence: he had more than enough money, and position, two grown children succeeding on their own, a pretty wife, a large home. "Is everything well at home?" he said.

He sat down and stretched out his hand for Gene to sit. "Yes," Gene said. "Everything is all right there. Poppa is getting old, though. Forgetting things, names of people. Getting old, I'm sorry to say."

"He was such a good man," Marinara said, and felt the emotions he had had with old Santoro, his sight at the table, a father always in the same correct position, someone to respect: it had been Carlo's protection and relief when newly arrived he tried to be like the others without understanding Westchester, his own head filled with the pictures of America he had constructed in Amalfi. "He never failed to help me," Carlo said. "He approved of that loan. Wasn't it him?"

"Yes. He did it."

"And he was always at the table on the hour. Remember that. Always his dinner had to be ready on the stroke. Never a minute late." Marinara was invoking one side of the feeling for fathers, whose love he felt by listing their moments of protective power.

"He is always doing something new," Gene said, and Carlo smiled.

It was not the father. "How is your wife?" Carlo asked.

"Still dashing around. Still looking fine. Even if she doesn't think so. She didn't want me to come."

Carlo was not sure how to proceed. Was it possible that

Gene had run, like himself. Could their women be that powerful, to chase men from their own bank accounts, where they had their power. "I am sorry, then," he said. "But nothing painful happened?"

Gene drank another vermouth. "Nothing happened. Nothing really bad. And nothing wrong." He looked at Marinara to smile, but shook his head, caught in the question of it. "I had to make this trip." He turned the glass. "Can you tell me why?"

To beg my forgiveness, Marinara said to himself. *For being a beast. A thief.* Then he smiled. "Why? To come to my wedding. To be my guest of honor. That's why."

Gene stood up. "It must be that." He pushed at his chair. "I'm going to get my room. I rented in the same hotel, the Suisse —"

"On the water. Yes. And then come back here. We are going to start festa."

He walked with Gene to the hallway and down the steps. "That girl who was here," Gene said at the outer door. "Elena? I would like to say hello."

"We sent an invitation and hope she comes. She is married now. To a Calabrian up in the mountains. Near the Sila. Or in Aspromonte. I shall ask my mother."

Gene turned and walked out, then drove to the hotel parking lot on the sea road. He had supper sent to his room; the summer traffic was continuous and intense, as if more and more people kept entering the town in the middle of a party: the sound of engines, wooden clogs and laughing voices was too much to hear yet. He shut the doors to the terrace and went to sleep.

In the morning he found a garage that had a car for sale.

It was a yellow Fiat 850 that had been repainted and was ready to sell. He arranged to have the papers drawn up and the car delivered, then took the bill of sale with him for Carlo.

When he reached Marinara's he found Violetta sewing. "A last part of the veil," she said, and began to speak out of her thoughts — of the church service in the main cathedral, the reception, the cake everyone was talking about, a surprise from Carlo and his father, some monster they had concocted. Carlo called as Gene was listening, and he walked to the door to answer. "Gene? You have your car?"

"Yes. I am here by Hertz."

"Your Hertz. Come out." Gene met him in the hall. "I have just talked with my cousins in Ravello. There are some people who must come down right away — they are helping for to-morrow. And listen. My cousin Bianca is back from Rome. I want you to have a guide here. A *guide*."

"Your eyes say I better meet her."

"Come and see. She is *ottima*." Marinara led the way out, and they drove towards the town up high beyond Amalfi. All the way Marinara talked, looking at nothing. He told Gene of meeting this woman with children, Carla, discovering her out of memory and going into the blank silence of Atrani to find her, as if it had all been planned.

Then he tried to explain what there was — enough love, a woman already a companion, something that became *dolce* in his eye, not keeper of the keys. Neither were young, of course. But she was attractive, very much so. He held back some descriptive words out of respect to Carla: it was a conflict between this respect and his bulging pleasure at what he had, especially before Gene, to show what he had been able to win after having been cut down in America. Large in body, shapely, gentle in nature, proper — a lady — subservient and yet independent. Intelligent in her work, strong in human affairs, though deferring to him, meek when necessary (an exciting trait), yet also cold, efficient, even hostile to the outside world.

Marinara described her as if he were constructing her there, helped by his hands: as they rode along Gene watched the hands' reflection in the front glass of the car. Carlo enjoyed it as it came out, though he had projected more than one woman by now.

"Don't ever give her too much money," Gene interrupted.

"What? Never give her money?"

"I mean, keep her in Amalfi. Don't let a woman like that get out."

"Yes, yes! Keep her upstairs. Keep her in the house. Keep her fat. And waiting." Marinara was exultant as they reached Ravello's first streets. "Never let her get cold."

He guided Gene to his cousins' house. Four women were waiting, three of them in black dresses, but the cousin who had been in Rome, the *guide,* was clearly different already, her tan skirt very short, her posture loose, legs spread apart.

Marinara was pleased with her and ran to embrace her. He took her to the car, sat her next to Gene, then squeezed into the back with the other women.

They returned to Amalfi, the women at the door, but Marinara stopped Bianca. "Go with Gene to park his car and show him the way back."

Bianca looked at Gene and smiled. "He is a complete stranger?"

"Yes," Gene said. "Complete."

Bianca waved to Carlo and went with Gene to the

parking lot. She waited for him to set the subject, but having heard about American men, she expected anything.

"That is the restaurant of my hotel," Gene said. "Will you have lunch with me?"

"Yes," she said. "If we don't talk, we might as well eat."

"What do you mean?" Gene said. He looked at her young face, which seemed to have no thoughts in it.

She took his hand and walked to the restaurant. When they were inside and had sat down on the porch over the water, Bianca spoke. "First tell me what you do in America?"

"I'm a lawyer. And I sell houses."

"Selling houses? Is that a profession?"

"Yes. People always move around."

"In Italy we will have to build on the water to build anything more. We are stuffed in. Or we might start in America."

Gene looked at her; she was turned to the water and the bright light fell on her face, which shone with the youth he no longer had and thought a sin to watch. "Would *you* really think of going to America?" he said.

"Yes, I would like to try it." She spoke as if she were tired and the statement a defeat she had already had. "What is there for me in Rome? I have no profession. No money. Though I like it."

"But would you leave your family, your country and all your —"

"Don't make sad songs," she said, and turned to look at his eyes. "I know what I would leave. And I know what you are over there."

"What is that?"

"You are killers," she said.

"Killers? You mean people like me? Do I look like one? What paper have you been reading in Rome?"

"You buy or you kill everything. We are all yours now, and you know it. Don't act as if you don't see it. Did you see Rome? Did you see whose ships are in the water of Naples?" A waiter brought bread and wine and took their order and Bianca lowered her head until he had gone. "But I would be ready to try it," she said.

"I don't know why. If you feel that." Gene saw the waiter coming with bowls of soup and sat back until he placed them. He watched her take up her spoon and finally look at him. "Because the place is full of things I want to buy. And that is all there is for some of us." She began to eat.

Gene continued to look at her; he had thought that conversations here would go away from the office, and from money, but it had come back again, right to the door of his office, where everybody came. "I really could get you a job, if you came."

By now he knew the lie was like the fantasy he had had about Elena. Bianca would not be admitted for ten years; her youth would wait for the quota call, the list already miles long with sick grandmothers, infant nephews, pining husbands, jobless cousins of those already waiting.

But he had held it out to her, the picture it always returned to, the candy America, the great store, the dollar shower; it was what he had to boast about instead of monuments and towns like Amalfi.

When the meal was completed, Bianca had been affected by the silence, certain that she had caused it. "I am sorry," she said. "We hardly know each other and we fight."

"It's a good sign. Like being married. But I caused it —"

"Caused it? My life? For bringing up *my* life. You didn't cause that." She placed a hand on his jacket sleeve. "I think about it too much when I come back home here. Everything turns into that. There are those you go from and take with you inside. You know all that — I am sure. But when you come back, it is like a flood. With hate. You cannot hold it back."

"Let's walk a bit." Gene stood up. "I wanted to hire a boat and see that grotto."

She nodded and smiled. "A good tourist. Then go to the paper mills. See Ravello. Better than this."

Gene helped move her chair; she stood up close to him. "You are much taller than me," she said, then quickly walked out to the street entrance.

When Gene had paid the check and walked to her, she took his hand and led him along the street. "I think I should go back to the house and help. It is tomorrow and they are not yet ready."

As they walked, she looked at him. "Don't be melancholy," she said. "It isn't your life that makes the misery."

"Tonight we can talk about my life, then. And really get depressed."

She took his arm and walked faster. "Good. I can discover why Americans get sad with all that money."

When they reached the house, the young girl, Eva, came to the door and stood looking at them as she held the knob. Gene stared at the child face caught half in sunlight, half in shade, then turned and went back to the piazza, driving the car to the restaurant parking lot. He was caught in the drowsy feeling of the afternoon, the heat stopping everything, and he went to his room, which was cool but too silent because Bianca had gone. He thought he had hurt her, and it opened the lid of his own sadness again.

He slept until it was dark. Once again he had dreams and awoke, seeing the body of the new maid, the young child of fourteen, nude, standing before him.

When the dream image left, he thought of Elena, the crude dress she wore, the tight feel of her body underneath the aprons.

He washed his face and went out for a walk in the darkness, unable to go to Carlo's and get Bianca, embarrassed at what they would think of him.

Along the shore the night was quiet, and he walked to the rocks at the end of the shore road, where the street ended. He stared into the sky above the water, seeing the lights of an island he had not noticed before, probably Capri in the darkness. Something stirred the water and made small waves that came in among the stones at the edge; he watched them breaking with a hidden speed of their own until he was aware of the wind that must be moving them, which now came onshore and shook the flowers behind him in a small square garden, moving them in the same rhythm.

The flowers, the waves, the stars were one, as he sat, all joined in the same movement: he had never seen the stars move before, had rarely seen the night, finding it from the recent airplane windows, bleak and black, like a fiber to be torn through.

Amalfi came together for the first time, and he no longer needed to go to the next unfinished minute; all the moments were in this one that held all together. There was no need to get up, none to remain. But he could not have come back to find merely this. Yet it seemed that he could never know more of satisfaction than this.

When he felt the cold, he stood up and walked away, to his hotel phone and a call to Bianca. "It is very late now," she said. "And I have been helping them all night. Could we start tomorrow?"

"Yes." Gene did not know what else to say for a few moments.

"Gene?" Her voice was concerned. "Will you be here tomorrow? Are you going?"

"Of course I'll be here. I want to start tomorrow. Just as you do."

20

GENE'S EYES had been reacting to his staring at the two un-moving figures facing the altar, the lights of banks of burning candles catching his eyes, making point after point, like waves of water. His eyes were filling with tears, and the sound of the organ from the rear of the church to announce the end of the ceremony brought up a strong emotion to fit the tears: he was moved without sense, as if he had been witnessing a tragic play, but there was no reason for the intense reaction other than the sight of the ceremony.

He saw Carlo and his wife coming closer, treading the aisle slowly, relatives and friends turning to them, coming to the end of the pews to touch them. A few women held back and looked down and seemed angry; some older men looked only at the bride. Behind him, as he moved along, he heard a conver-sation and turned to see three young men near the graying stone holy water fount, ignoring the energy of the ceremony completely.

It was like all weddings he had known in the Bronx, in black and shining white, with candles like daylight, festive and holy at the same time, the white soaring altar rising in light as if it could leave the ground, take the two ordinary neighbors, one stiff in black rented clothes, the other in the heavy, impractical gown used only for one day. (He had always stared at the windows of bridal shops, at the gowns that made no thoughts but made names disappear, disguising the ordinary face of neighbors, creating something holy without fear and dark kneeling, without punishment: it was the holiness that came with laughter, an elegant shining but not on the priest, reserved instead for the ordinary girl who could become as special as priest and altar.)

Carlo's suit was as stiff as all the others, his special white shirt shining as if it had been polished or lighted from within. As he passed, Gene knew he had forgotten that one detail again: that Carlo was still married to Anna. The fact was also unreal now in the two faces in the aisle, beyond themselves in some way.

The crowds in the pews followed the couple and surrounded them on the steps. Gene stayed behind in the church silence, an altar boy behind him already capping the candles.

He moved to the door, where Bianca came out of the crowd to him. "Now you should be ready to celebrate," she said, and smiled, looking into his eyes.

"Yes, I know. *Don't* I look ready. With this face."

"At weddings, the faces change so much." Bianca looked to see who was near her. "You never know what is happening. Some seem to be watching a death." She took Gene's arm and began to walk after the crowd moving down the long steps.

"I was sitting there and my feelings came up like a flood." Gene had to make it lighter, less like an embarrassing secret. "I was like a sink, a stuck-up sink, suddenly disgorging — not very nice. Not very jolly."

"I know the fault." Bianca looked at Gene, who had stopped to rub at his eyes. "Are we thinking why are we not happy right now? As full as they are with it?"

"Yes!" Gene looked at her. "Like a pig. I want what they have."

Bianca shook her head. "We think, what must one do, get married *every* year to be happy in this way. Especially if you see the happy ones after a few years."

"But do you think it's only *us?*" Gene began to walk again.

"Us? What is *us?*" Bianca pushed his side with a hand.

"Did you feel any muscle there?" Gene looked at her face, but Bianca looked ahead, following the crowd reaching the piazza below. "What I mean. I mean this," Gene said. "Is this the way *we* see it? But the truth is not this at all; we are only putting our thoughts into them, whoever they are. And they are like dolls. *We* make up the game."

"Like the little bride and groom of sugar on the cake." Bianca looked at him. "Do you know we give that stupid thing too much respect?"

They reached the piazza and walked along the narrow, shaded street to the house. People watched them, smiling, recognizing them in the wedding party. At the door, Bianca began to remove her hand, but Gene held her. "I need somebody today."

"Stop it!" Her voice was angry, but she squeezed Gene's hand. "Let them all go inside first."

They watched until the others were all in the house. Gene saw that her hair had been dyed a lighter color. "Your hair is really brown," he said.

"Yes, brown," she said, and seemed angry again. "I haven't called you by your name yet. Is it *Gene?*"

"You know it's Gene."

"I have not said it yet." She stepped into the darkness of the entrance. "I try to stop myself on days like this. Gene? Do you know what I'm saying? This is my town. My family is here."

Gene walked in behind her. "I'm sorry," he said. "I get here in Amalfi and I become different."

Bianca took his arm, but he did not move. "I asked Carlo about you last night," she said. As he looked at her, she smiled. "He said he could not guess what went on inside you. You are a mystery. But you are an honest man. Is that it? Are you an honest man?"

Gene walked up the steps; the cousins and friends were moving towards the back of the house, down to the backyard piazza. Some carried boxes, which they placed on a hall table, and Gene remembered the car he had bought for Carlo, thinking of the extravagance as stupid now.

Bianca went to a bedroom to remove her hat and brush her hair. Gene walked downstairs and saw Carlo busy with guests. His orchestra, four guitarists and two grizzled old men with mandolins, began to play, and the crowd became louder.

Carlo saw him and rushed across the yard to embrace him. Then he took his arm and led him along to new faces, introducing him each time they stopped. "We are reaching Carla," Carlo said.

When they stood before her, she was flushed and hot, lipstick stains on her smooth cheeks. She looked young, though her body was thick against the gown, bulging in the manner Carlo had talked about, her movements slow. Gene thought of Bianca's nervous walk, the long, impulsive strides, the doubt in her movements.

Carla greeted Gene shyly, accepted his kiss and held her

arms around him. Gene removed the envelope in his pocket and showed the car papers to Carlo. "I wanted you to move around," he said. "I bought you some wheels."

Carlo read the papers slowly, then passed them to his wife. "Gene? Is this true? Is it a car?"

"Not a new one. But pretty enough."

Carlo embraced him again and spoke to his wife. "What did I say about this man? This man is the best material made." He looked at Gene. "You know how much you gave me? A life again. After I had died here." He was unable to control himself and brought both hands to his eyes to stop their flow; then he rubbed his hands against his jacket and took Gene's hands. "What do you say to a man —" He nodded as his voice stopped. "A man. Why don't you stay here? Can't you just live here? Live here, Gene! Where is Bianca now? Is Bianca here?"

"She's coming down," Gene said.

"Get her, get her. This is a day for eating —" Carlo looked beyond Gene. "Look!" He stepped back. "They are bringing it from the bakery. The cake we made. Just look at it."

Two men had carried in the large cake his father and he had baked as a surprise, and the guests were beginning to applaud as they saw it, rising taller than the men carrying it. The band played louder, and Carlo took his wife's arms. "I am going to show her the size of it," he said to Gene.

Carlo smiled and placed the car papers in his inside jacket pocket, finding another envelope. "Look at this, Gene. They gave me this letter for you. It is *my* wedding, but they send *auguri* to you."

Gene took the envelope, which had been sent from somewhere in Italy, but did not open it in the confusion of the cake. Bianca was coming down the steps and moving towards the crowd.

Gene walked back to her, and she took his hand while people began to dance, as if the presence of the cake were a signal. Bianca led him out too quickly for him to refuse; though he did not know the dance, he did it with her.

When the music stopped, they were sweating. Bianca looked down at herself: there were droplets of perspiration in the V of her dress. "Shall I remove that?" Gene said.

"But not here." She rubbed herself with her fingers while Gene watched her hand against her breasts. "Let's drink something," he said, and took her arm, leading her to the table inside where food and bottles of wine were lined up. There was an old man Gene had not met, but he recognized Gene and called him by name, then gave him a bottle of wine. "Try this. It is our own."

Gene took the flask and drank from it before giving it to Bianca. "No glasses today," he said, and saw the old man smile. "It will make a climate inside," the old man said of the wine. "And very healthful for today."

Gene watched him shake his hand, suggesting the excesses of energy in the wine. "Did you hear that?" he said to Bianca. He watched her drink and pass the bottle back to him. They continued to drink until the bottle was empty. The old man had been smiling and nodding and had another bottle ready. "There is more here than you can accomplish," he said.

"Did you hear him?" Gene asked.

Bianca moved off, to the corner of the square, and began to drink from the new bottle, slowly, assuaging her thirst in the heat. The piazza was in steady movement, the dancers jumping in the steps of a local tarantella, and Bianca lost her attention watching. Gene could not read her expression, but she did not seem pleased. "Is your family in the crowd?" he said. "Your mother and father?"

She looked at him, at the bottle in his hand. "Can we go out and cool off? Away from here?"

"Would you like to ride?"

"Yes. Let's take the car somewhere. Is it near the house?"

Gene nodded. "Outside. Very near." He led her to the steps into the house, carrying the bottle. "Wait." Bianca held back. "I must get my purse."

"I'll bring the car to the door," he said. Bianca brought her hands to his face, held him, then went towards the bedroom. Gene went out; on the street he stopped in the coolness, then found the car and drove back to the entrance. As he waited, he felt his shirt wet and removed his jacket, hearing the sound of paper and remembering the letter.

The handwriting was not familiar, the postmark unreadable. He tore open the envelope and found a single sheet, with the lines of careful Italian calligraphy. *Dear signor Eugenio: I am living in San Nicola, province of Calabria. My dear husband Amaro, who is a good Christian, has permitted me to write. He works as a stonemason and thank God there is work. I must inform you that I have a child, who was fathered by you because of its time. My husband accepts this, and the child is given his name. However, I must inform you out of concern so that you will know you have a child in the world. With greetings, Elena (Mancuso).*

Bianca had come out; he saw her body through the door window and placed the letter in his pocket. Then he leaned over and opened the door; she sat down and leaned across the seat to kiss him, her lips moist with fresh lipstick. "Where are we going?" she said.

"Where do you want to go?"

Bianca felt the change in mood. "Don't *you* want to go? I could go as far as Rome."

Gene looked ahead. "Yes, we could make Rome tonight."

"I am going back tomorrow," she said. "My job. Or they hire another. Have you seen Rome?"

Gene turned to her. "Yes, let's go to Rome tomorrow." He started the car and drove to the shore road towards Atrani and Minori.

Bianca sat back. "It's perfect to escape a thing like that. Just sneak out and never come back."

"What about your family?"

Bianca leaned forward and looked at him until he caught her eye. "I am not coming back here. I know that. I'll stay in Rome for my life. Whatever —"

They drove in silence as far as Vietri, where the summer crowds were coming out for the night, parked near the beach for a few minutes, then started off again, back the same way. "What is it? You don't speak." Bianca said. "Do I annoy you now?"

"Let's go back to my hotel." Gene drove fast along the mountain roads. "You have to see something."

Bianca waited until they reached his room. As they entered, she stood next to him in the darkness and placed her head against his chest. Gene kissed her cheek, too gently, and walked to the light switch of the small lamp near his bed. "I just received this. While I was waiting for you in the car."

Bianca took the letter and read it, then turned to him. "Is that why you stop?"

"I just read that. How would you feel?"

"Then it changes you. You must still love this woman."

"No," Gene said. "I didn't even know her. Two or three days —"

"Two days. If you loved her, then two days." Bianca sat down on the bed. "Do you have to cry for it now?"

"No, no. It was only a passion. One time. I don't even believe her. You can't have a child like that. It's impossible."

"So what. It is always a passion." Bianca stood up. "The child has a mother and father. You don't enter anymore." She saw Gene holding the letter like a telegram of grief. "Do you have a hairbrush?" she asked. "The wind blew my hair."

Gene pointed to the bath and she left him standing in the silence. When she returned he was looking at her, almost in fear. "You have this baby caught in your head," she said. "You must want it. So I will leave you with it."

"No. Don't go away!" Gene followed her slow steps to the door. She was sixteen or seventeen. A girl.

Bianca reached the door. "Tell yourself whatever you want. But don't tell me about it." She turned the knob, went out and shut the door softly.

Gene stood at the door for a while, then went out to the street. He saw her along the shore road and ran to her, taking her arm to stop her. "You can't run away," he said. "That's not right. Let me get over this. I showed you the letter —"

"I'm going home," she said. "I go back tomorrow. I work."

He let her shake out of his grip, then followed the movement of her walk, her body under the light yellow dress, hips rising as she stepped along, moving with her nervous strides.

He ran to her and took her arms again. "I had to show you the letter. To be honest with you."

"It is not necessary to be honest," she said, and shook herself free again, but Gene grasped her tighter, turned her towards him and embraced her, bringing his lips down to her face.

She moved her face away. "Stupid. How could you kiss now?" Her eyes were wet. "I was going to Rome with you. And now I am not."

Gene held her; her eyes were black and her hair moved in the sea wind, turning in waves to cover her face. "Look. Don't worry about your job. Whatever money you need, I'll pay it. Let's go. Tonight. Can you go tonight?" His eyes were excited, and she was pleased. "We'll drive down there and then up to Rome. We'll have time in Rome."

"Down there?"

"Calabria. I must see this child. Ride with me. Come with me down there."

"*I? I* should go down there?" Bianca did not pull against his grip. "You want a nurse. Or a nun. A nun to go with you and hold your hand."

Gene was smiling. "You would be a good nun," he said. "A great nun. You could lead men back to the church." He rubbed her sleeve. "In this habit."

"No. Gene. Let's say goodnight here." She was looking at him and knew his excitement, his idea that would take her eventually. "But I don't want to get into your troubles."

"Get your bags. What do you have in Ravello? What is it, dresses, some shoes, a coat or two? The hell with it. We'll get you all new things. Just say a nice good-bye to them and we'll go."

She did not answer, but looked at his face: the power made it older, the age in the slightly gray hair, the moustache of an owner of things, the suggestion of fathers.

"Say yes. We'll cable your office and get back to Rome a few days late. Can you leave tonight?"

"They know I'm leaving tomorrow. I can go back and tell them I have a ride with you in the early morning, to save train fare. They understand that." Bianca was free of his grip and she began to walk. "Do you want my thoughts?"

"Go ahead. Go ahead." Gene was smiling at her.

"Don't see that child. Go the other way. They want your money."

"Then let them have money." Gene took her hand and led her along. "I will pack as soon as I get back. I'll be at your house before seven."

Bianca stopped and touched his face. "Who are you, Gene?" She shook her head. "That I am going with you to some disappointment. They are waiting to get you. With their hands out."

"All right. Then I'll expect you to protect me." Gene led her along the piazza, lit up and filled with walkers, then back to Carlo's. "I am going in to say good-bye to Carlo right now," Gene said.

They went into the house and down to the reception. Gene found Carlo sitting on a wooden chair, his jacket off, his stiff shirt gray with his sweat. When he heard Gene's good-bye, he sat back and shook his head. "Stay with me. You should not go. What is it?"

"It's business again." Gene took Carlo's hand. "Was I really here, Carlo? Did I see all this?"

Carlo stood up and walked with Gene to the door. "Perhaps

what happened here can't exist over there. Is that not wise to say?"

Gene embraced him. "Nothing happened here," he said. "It all happened in my head. It's one of my dreams."

Carlo watched him run off, as if he were a young man chasing a new girl. He was happy to see Gene this kind of man, sure also that his excitement meant a new woman in Rome, and if it were Bianca, Carlo already envied him.

21

BIANCA WAS different in the morning, tired, reluctant to move, embarrassed to see her suitcase placed in Gene's car, irritated with her mother's hard stare every time she left for Rome.

When they were on the road south, she removed her kerchief and began to brush her hair. "It's a long trip. Did you know that?"

"We can stop at Reggio tonight," Gene said. "And get up to the mountains tomorrow."

The Sunday morning roads were clear, and they were able to make good speeds, reaching Reggio in the late afternoon. When Gene asked about Elena's town, he found that it was closer than he had thought. Bianca was willing to do what he liked, and they started into the mountains, arriving at San Nicola just before dark. The house was pointed out to them by a barman. "I'm going to wait here near the lights," Bianca said. "You will have to see this alone."

Gene left the car next to the bar and walked up narrow, walled streets to the house. When Elena stood at the door, she did not recognize him.

"I am Gene. Eugenio Santoro. *Gene.* I have your letter. The letter you sent to me at Carlo's. The wedding. Carlo was married."

She opened the door wide and let him in. "How did you get here?" Elena was frightened with him in the house. "What do you want? What do you want of me?"

Gene stepped back towards the door again as he saw her eyes. "No. Don't. I only want to see him — or her."

She had walked to the other end of the room, behind a table, what must have been the kitchen table. Gene looked at it, then her face, then the room around her. She had become a woman, thick, heavy in the hips, her hair dry and her skin beginning to wrinkle about the eyes from the weather or the darkness of the house. She had become a mountain woman, and he would have passed her on the road, never noticing her.

"You will not try something bad. You have not come to take."

"I want to leave you something," he said. "That's all." He reached for his checkbook, then put it back and took out his Italian money. "This is for the child."

"You have nothing to pay." The money was on the table; she looked at it, became embarrassed at the room.

"You can't deny me leaving something for a child that's mine." His face felt hot, knowing only after he had said it that he had insulted her again, taken away something.

When she did not answer, he wanted to run out of the house. She was standing with her head bowed, like a slave, and he knew that he could take the child now, or, if he wished, order her to do something else, even go to the piazza and be disgraced publicly.

"Elena. I am going away from here in five minutes. And

you will never see me. I have a car in the piazza and I'm driving to Rome. Just let me see the child."

She turned and walked to a door behind her, then stopped, and without looking at him, spoke: "This is my child. I have little else. Do you understand what I say."

She waited until Gene said yes, then led him into a room lit by a small plastic wall lamp. Gene approached the bed slowly; the child was just falling asleep and turned, surprised, to see his mother and Gene.

Gene looked down in silence. The face was small and round, resembling no one he knew, completely unlike himself or his family.

"That is my husband," Elena said, and Gene saw her pointing to a photograph on a high chest of drawers.

"The baby looks like that," Gene said.

"Yes. Both are dark. With that curly, tight hair that his family has. They say because it is close to Africa here." Elena was smiling. "He is an image of Amaro."

Gene reached a finger down to the child, but there was no response. The child had closed his eyes and was asleep. Gene studied the small, curled fingers and the body. There was simply no resemblance. He turned and walked back to the kitchen, seeing that he had left four ten thousand lira notes, unable for a moment to estimate the amount in dollars.

"Get the child some nice things. Or use it — any way. Any way you need." Gene did not turn. "Good luck to you and your husband. Where is he?"

"They reach home much after dark."

Gene was at the entrance and turned. "Do you hate me?" He held up his hands to stop her from answering. "I mean, for *using* you."

233

"Did you use me?" Elena stood near the bedroom door, which she had closed.

"No!" He opened the door. "Good night. Take care of the child."

He waited for her to speak, but she did not. He went out and returned to the car, where a small crowd of men were staring at Bianca. "I am popular here," she said. "Can you see my club?"

Gene drove off quickly, down towards Reggio. "We'll get some food and rooms and start early tomorrow. All right?"

"Food. *Please.*" Bianca was watching him.

"It's not mine," he said.

"What?"

"You know *what*. That child is not mine."

Bianca leaned across the seat. "Did they ask you to support the child? Money?"

"No," Gene said. "She didn't want money."

"Then you gave her no money. And he wasn't home."

Gene looked at her. "*I* decided to leave something. As you would for any child."

"Yes, yes. A christening gift. A birthday present. A name day. What is it called?"

"It isn't mine. I know that." Gene was caught in the firmness of it. "It's exactly like the father. Her husband. Exactly him in every way."

Bianca took his right hand in hers. It was shaking, and she kissed it. "Worse things have been done, you know. Things done in hate."

Gene did not answer, but brought her hand to his mouth and bit it gently. "Ah, you bite," she said. "I did not see the wild man, too."

At the entrance to a hotel, Gene stopped the car and looked at her. "I know this much," he said. "It can't be mine. It really can't. It's something I feel. I sense it. That is not my child, and I know it."

Bianca listened patiently, knowing he was serious and hounded by the thought. "I can go back with a free conscience," he said. "Knowing that I did not leave a child. I know that."

Bianca did not speak, but waited until Gene left the car and followed him. They went directly to the hotel restaurant. "Would you like to leave after we eat?" Bianca asked. "I'm ready."

"No, that isn't necessary." Gene looked at her. "You are staring at me. Did you know that? And you hear all the echoes, don't you?"

"It isn't hard," she said. "You are loud enough."

They sat at a table in the cold dining room of the hotel; the few diners in the room seemed tired, uninterested in them. Gene ate silently, leaning down, keeping his face away from Bianca's eyes, ordering his food in anger. There was noise in his head, growing, forcing his thoughts away from the present: only the anger kept him in control.

To Bianca he was changing, becoming powerful, his mood preparing him to give orders, a man of property and money again. She decided she would sleep with him, here or in Rome, wherever he chose to start. With him, she was free from the stares of women in black dresses, those who held the keys and stood on doorsteps and said good-bye.

After dinner, he rose from the table and stretched. "I'm going for a little air," he said. "But first I'll rent rooms. Should it be two or one?"

"Whatever you say." She was afraid for a moment because she was alone, could be abandoned by him; she was not sure if her purse held enough money for a train to Rome.

"*You say.*" Gene looked at her. "It's the same to me. Whatever you think is best. Whatever you feel able to do."

"What do you think is best?"

Gene sat down and leaned towards her. "Bianca. Look at me. See this face." She was uncomfortable, as though being called on for punishment. "Is this a young man's face?"

"It's a man's face, I hope."

"Yes, and you know something to watch out for —"

"What is that?" She smiled at the mood.

"You know I am still fertile." Gene touched her lips with the fingers of his right hand.

"Thank you, then. I will remember that for a long time."

He stood up. "All right, then. Tonight you'll have a man." Bianca smiled, thinking that he was still talking in the mood of his joke, but he was serious, the last statement said with much belief, yet to her like an intense actor saying strong lines.

He was smiling again. "Pick up the keys at the desk," he said. "I need a walk, a little walk alone."

She watched him leave, walk through the lobby and stop at the desk to register. He looked tall there and was a face and body she would gladly share a home with, for a life, for a time.

He walked through the lobby and into the streets until he found a lighted piazza, with bars at the outer edges and a central square under rows of plane trees. The cathedral face behind was lit and silent, the stone figure of the patron saint at the foot of the steps, half in shadow, half light-sketched. Gene walked past the tables, the hunched men in serious conversation, talking in their moments.

He walked out of the piazza lights, along a way that was unlit but clear enough for walking. At the edges of the walk was a stone wall, a few feet high, and Gene sat down and looked back at the piazza, lighted, coming to more life as it got later.

Nothing had been settled; he was in another town, another new place, thinking of documents, gas coupons, hot water, eating new foods and running out of clean shirts. But there was payment to the eyes, the sight along the road to Reggio, the barely known Calabrian shore, broken castles, ruins of newly found towns, partly dug. It *was* what he had come for — to travel in it and be a stranger. The wandering was good, washed the mind, removed the film, the cast of sameness from the eye's view, erased the drugstore sandwich of his lunch hours, his desk, the telephone like a wire leash from home to office.

In the cool air of Reggio, the breeze blowing from water (the straits of Messina he had seen as he approached Reggio), his mind felt the presence of sky and water again, the odor of earth and flowering trees. Tonight he would gladly sleep alone in a forest: he was ready for a cold blanket and a place under a tree, with nothing but the stars and the words that roamed his mind, becoming fewer as his thoughts gave way.

But he did not believe this wish to be alone, as if it made you larger or cleaner to go off somewhere and give up everything. It was the nice, clean dream to hide the fact of your money, if you had it, or your rags if you had none. Sit under a tree and let your feelings go through you like the gas through swiss cheese. It was something to do if you could not go back to a room, with someone like Bianca waiting: there were few better actions than returning, going back, up into rooms.

The thoughts, the mind-sight of the silent child in the bed, was suddenly across the face of his mind. He stepped off the wall and walked quickly towards the hotel, as if to outrace the thoughts. But they were at his side like the streets and people of Reggio, demanding something without looking, watching him as long as he felt watched.

The child was his own seed, but not his own, and that was what the girl (he was already honestly forgetting her name) wanted to show him. Still he had the planted repetition of himself, the copy if he wanted it to be. But only a buffoon would recognize one child as different from the rest, as if he needed to make a shrine of it, come down here to make it special.

Caught like a fool in a web of his own choosing he walked to the hotel and upstairs. As he stepped inside, he was excited at the presence of Bianca, in a nightgown, reading in a chair, like someone who had awaited his thoughts.

"What did you do?" Bianca rested the magazine in her lap. "Look for the father?"

Gene removed his jacket and shirt. "I was trying to find somebody —"

"The father?"

"No. Not the stupid father. The child, maybe. One part of me wants to see the child walk up to me, then go away." Gene saw his suitcase opened, his pajamas on a pillow. He took the pajama jacket in his hands. "I am anxious to get back home sometimes. Like dope addiction. I want to run sometimes. Run right back home —"

Gene walked to her and held her hands, then embraced her. "Can you understand that?"

Bianca was amazed by his troubles: their wandering interfered with the pleasure of the room, the good supper they had had, the day's ride in the open car. What could he want beyond these things; what chased him or did he chase. She decided it could be only the guilt dropped on his head because of the child.

She stepped back. "What's wrong?" he said, but she looked at his eyes and saw that he had expected she would back away from his mood. "Then think!" she said. "And decide what to do with the child?"

Gene began to laugh. "Your magic Neapolitan mind," he said. "That *is* my problem, isn't it?"

"I am ready to do what you wish. Do you want to go now, to go and take — it?"

Gene remembered Tubino the lawyer, his eyes when he made the snatching gesture, wide open for a moment, like an actor registering surprise. Tubino and Bianca were shocked to hear themselves say what they had been thinking, as if the disobedience of their voices set them in a decision they could no longer refute: to take what you want, even the infant in the crib. "You're willing to share the bond of blood with me," Gene said.

"What blood?"

"Committing the ultimate sin. Stealing the bambino from the crib. The sacred thing down here. The million bambinos in Naples, *presepio* everywhere, even a museum full of bambino scenes —"

Bianca knew his intentions were to lighten the mood, but

she did not like what was in it, more than disrespect, which she could accept; rather, Gene was shifting the work to her. "Wait. It is *your* child," she said. "It is your sins we commit."

Gene left her and walked to the window: there was a view of small, lighted streets, a whiteness that characterized Reggio in its slow-moving silence. It was too much silence for him. And Naples had been like a cauldron of screaming people, smiling as they were strangled by the cars, the crowds of people, too many of them struggling (just as in Tuckahoe too few did). Rome had the balance from what he had seen. "Let's go," he said, thinking of Rome.

"I am ready to go with you." Bianca's voice was tight, the sound of the brave and foolish temperament he had seen here: it was inside of Carlo and Elena, like a medieval warrior still alive today, swearing allegiance, giving word and hand, ready to sacrifice name and reputation for any desire that someone could not do without.

But it was dead; it was a joke; it was the sweet unreal of Naples and the south, having too little to eat and so feeding off their grandfathers' dreams. It was the habit of people before credit buying took hold and the discount house became the shrine.

"I don't want anybody's child." Gene left the window, came and sat on the bed. "Nobody's child and nobody's house. Nobody's bills. Nobody's fight. No prisons I can avoid —"

Bianca came and sat down stiffly at the other side of the bed. Gene saw that she was affected by his forgetting her, being alone in a room with her, and what it meant she gave him; he had lost sight of her attraction, her lithe girl's body, the black eyes, the memory of her movements when he had followed her in Amalfi. He wanted to reach for her hand, but the mood was still incorrect; he would be doing it as a corrective, not a feeling.

"*I* went to Rome to leave a prison," she said.

They were like words of his own thoughts; he was going to Rome, to live years or months there: it was out of the prison to him, what his thoughts had brushed against but not made words.

He lay back on the bed, letting his head relax on the pillow; it was the first time he had released the tight guards inside, curled and knotted and prepared for a pursuer. "Rome," he said. "Rome and no work. I'll do anything but work. Shit on money."

He looked at Bianca for her reaction; she was nodding, with her face in a twist of sarcasm. "God bless those who need not work. The cardinals with their soft white hands. Will you paint pictures?"

She was cut off by Gene's hand, grasping her shoulder and pulling her harshly to the bed, even a little painfully. Yet she preferred this in him, when he struck like this, with words or a movement, and as her face was drawn close to his, she caught her first glimpse of his face at very close range, like a person of a different race.

AFTER TWO WEEKS in Rome, Gene left his hotel room on Via Portoghesi for an apartment he had rented nearby, still in the ancient quarter. He had asked Bianca to live there with him, but she had refused, following an instinct she would not explain, something stronger than the assumption he would go away.

At night, after meeting her at the bus that brought her back from work, they would go to the nearby restaurant, Orsetto, where the owners, a family, already greeted them as neighbors, as if they represented some unity with love in it.

And at a table, night after night, Bianca would refuse. "What should we call this, then," Gene said. "Friendship. Are we cousins?" Bianca would shake her head, knowing the mood should be kept cloudy.

"I had thought we left Amalfi understanding," Gene said. "Which was clear in Reggio."

"It is enough to know. We do what we do."

"You know what we do," he said. "And I think you like it —"

"You know that." She felt held down, ordered to sit and

reply; and she wished to get away from the desperation coming from Gene. "What do you want me to say. Gene, I am
twenty-six. With no education. They are not crowding to meet
me on the Corso."

"That's money again. I told you I can take care of that."
The tone that had erupted in Reggio was still with him, but
Bianca was not the same.

She did not answer, and soon they finished and were walking along the Via Portoghesi to the apartment.

As Gene opened the door and switched on the hall light,
Bianca saw the letters on the small table near the entrance.
They had rested there more than a week, letters to America.
She felt Gene's hands on her shoulders, then his helping with
her light coat, taking it to the closet while she walked into the
living room. "You need some good chairs here," she said, to
forget the letters.

"And good beds," Gene said.

Bianca turned to look at him. "I have seen American beds in
the films. Very large and round. Do you have one like that,
with motors and buttons?"

"No. Only two singles — ordinary beds." He turned in a
sudden memory of his room and walked to the kitchen for the
bottles of vermouth and whiskey.

"You have not mailed them yet," Bianca called out to him.

He came back with the bottles and glasses and set them on
the floor near the couch and sat down. Bianca was standing
and pacing, awaiting an answer, but Gene poured whiskey for
himself and vermouth for her.

"Don't answer me," she said. "You don't have to answer.
Because I don't wish to be explained. And I don't wish to ex-

243

plain. Just remember what you have. Rome for yourself, and money, and even someone here who loves you. And you can go away when you like."

"I am not going away."

"That is what your feelings tell you now. And that may be true for now. You don't tell me nice stories like an Italian. You don't insult me with lies I have to believe." She came up to take her glass, then walked to the end of the room and a darkened window. "Only look over here and see me. You met me down there. There are no lies about what I am and what I do not have."

Gene drank fast, then made a gesture for her to come back to him; she came and sat next to him. "I can tell you the truth," he said. "Seeing people look at us when we walk. Hearing the thought in their heads: look at the old man with his young girl. When will she run away from him."

Bianca kissed his cheek and kept her face against him, but Gene pulled back. "You *will* go," he said. "But I am asking about now. Not now."

Bianca had been hurt by his movement and the need to press for an answer when she had none. She stood up to talk. "Let us say I am not sure of anything — with you." She walked away. "Americans." She turned to face him from the center of the room. "You are the Arabs. You come and go. Pitch your tent here. Sell us something. And then go back there. Where the money grows for you."

"How much money do you want?"

"I don't want your money." She came to the couch again and stood with her legs against his. "Though I like it, I like it very much. I like eating beef at Orsetto instead of cooking my plate of spaghetti."

Gene embraced her legs, and she sat down again. "But I see you only spending money here. There is an end to it, isn't there?"

"I may do a little work right away. Tomorrow I have an appointment at the embassy."

"Really? Is this true?"

"There are two or three jobs with American firms." Gene was annoyed. "Doing law work. A friend in Washington is helping me."

Gene stood up suddenly and took the whiskey bottle in his hand and walked away. "Do you want all my credit references?"

"What do you mean?"

He poured whiskey. "I think you have the woman's disease. Once you get a man, it makes you paralyzed. You will never be able to go out and work again if you make the deal."

She sat silently for a few moments, while Gene drank and kept his eyes away from her. "Listen. Once I get a man I want to make love." She had cut off the vulgar word for it, looking at him.

Gene came towards her, still holding the bottle and his glass. "What is this?" he asked. "I am only saying I don't want to be alone. What is it?"

Before she could answer, there was a knock at the door, sounds of voices outside. Bianca stood up and took a step towards the bedroom. "My God! If it is my father —"

Gene turned towards the door and walked to the hallway to listen as the knocking continued. He was silent, and eventually the footsteps moved away.

Bianca came to him. "I must go to my place. If it is my family, they will keep looking for me."

Gene placed the glass and bottle on the table with the letters, then took her hand. "Tell me. Why would they come here?"

"I don't know. Except that they knew when we left together. Saw my face when I was with you. I don't know."

Gene took her coat from the closet and walked downstairs with her to the street and watched her leave. A guilt he had not imagined was striking his body, his neck and shoulders stiff and aching, bringing back the illicit feeling he had had walking with Bianca on the streets, adding now the eyes of home, people too far away for judgment.

Turning to go upstairs he heard the *portiere* call him. "We were knocking," the old man said. "A relative of yours with important news."

Gene saw faces. "What was he like? Did he seem American?"

The man smiled and pressed on his beret. "Oh no. This was a southerner. With a Naples accent."

Gene thanked him and went upstairs. The family of Bianca had sent someone to do something about honor, with a gun or a knife. He locked the door carefully, held in this Italian mood: yet his fear was worth the strength he was getting, ready to defend himself as a man, with his own body, for what he had done.

He did not know what they would demand, and he walked to the bedroom removing his clothes, flexing his arm muscles, stopping in front of the small bedroom mirror to inflate his chest and look at himself.

He did some exercises before getting into bed, then slept soundly. In the morning he was up early and went out for milk and fresh bread.

The neighborhood had at first seemed dirty, like Naples, until he saw the working of its streets, heard the sounds of carriage wheels on the gray-black cobblestones, market women, first their voices, then their hands and arms against the background of the fruit and vegetable stands. Coming back he passed the carpenter and his sanding machine starting up, a boy apprentice outside on a chair sanding wooden arches for new chairs. Through the open door of the restaurant he saw the family, the mother making the daily noodles, other women preparing vegetables, the men in their white shirts, without their jackets and ties, sitting at tables drinking coffee.

He became lost in it, as if its picture was something to learn and the people who nodded or smiled a welcome ready to tell him something. He walked slowly until he was near his door, not noticing the man staring at him.

First he did not recognize Carlo, in a dark suit, looking tired and confused, his hair uncombed. And before he could speak Carlo shouted his name and ran towards him.

Gene stepped back, ready to defend himself, but Carlo quickly sensed the strange response and stopped. "Gene. Gene. What is it?"

"What do you want with me?"

"Your father. Don Francesco." He had used the honorific name calling Gene's father, then reached into his pocket for the yellow cable.

Gene took the paper, still looking at Carlo, ready for something else, then began to read the words of his father's dying.

"I came for you," Carlo said. "And I went all over this damned city. Bianca was never home. The embassy said you lived at the hotel. Only a man said he thought you were living

247

in this street. Gene. I am so sorry." He went to embrace Gene and clumsily held his arms down. "When did this come?" Gene said.

"Two days. This is the third day. What have I done!"

"What do you mean?" Gene saw Carlo take his hands and pull them through his hair.

"I brought you this horror."

"You didn't make it. Come on." Gene took Carlo's arm and led him upstairs, into the kitchen. "Let's make some coffee," Gene said. "Then I will telephone."

"Go," Carlo said. "Go today." He watched Gene take a pan, pour water, fill the coffee cylinder. "There is no time. Just go now. I can sense it. A little time to see him. To say good-bye. To say a prayer with him."

Carlo was pacing back and forth, the repository of a knowledge he was sure of, something he was never told but knew, which existed in the air of everywhere he stood.

He kept talking, and after coffee walked with Gene to a telephone office to try a transatlantic call. When they were told the wait would be six hours, Carlo began again, telling Gene not to delay.

Now Gene was affected by the desperation, and called airlines until he found a place on an evening flight. Carlo escorted him to the office, where he bought his ticket, and then home to pack.

Gene would not let Carlo come to the airport. "I need you to help me here," he said, and Carlo nodded. "Tell the *portiere* I will be back. And I am meeting Bianca tonight. I want you to tell her two things — that I am coming back and that I would like her to stay in my apartment. To watch it."

Caught in the power of death, Carlo listened carefully and

agreed, had none of the suspicion Bianca suggested would come from home. Gene showed Carlo where her bus would stop, then left him and went to the terminal.

When his plane was in the air, he saw reddish light still on the city (though the field had been dark on takeoff), but his thoughts of it were pulled away from him as the ship moved towards his father's dying, as yet an empty fact, though his feelings, still wordless, were already on him.

He felt hot and turned the air conditioner tube directly on his face, but it did little to hold back the sweat that came from inside him. He was concerned with the embarrassment of the dripping on his face, what odors would come, and he noticed a stewardess too solicitous, trying to divert him with newspapers, a pillow and then, ridiculously, a lap robe. But he saw that he was the picture of a man in fear, his hands tight around the chair rests, his face staring straight and stiff, tightening with each slight dip of the plane in air.

Each hour was more frightening, and he shut his eyes time after time but found no sleep coming, only the darkness his lids made, and the increased sense of his body, the perspiring, his breathing in change, a thought like an eyeless worm, curling and burrowing when he tried to reach it, then surfacing again to announce itself into his panic: he was dying, he would crash, he would fall from the heights and break up in the sea, he would explode with the engine that was about to catch fire.

No one met him at the landing; the day was clear and sunny, already fall in New York. He went from customs to the taxi ramp and found a cab to take him over the Whitestone Bridge and up along the highway into Westchester; he had decided to go directly to the castle, as if a few extra minutes spent going to his own house would make him too late to see his father alive.

The guard stopped him at the gate and told him that no one was at the house, and as soon as Gene explained himself, the man said his father had died a few days before and was at a funeral home in the Bronx.

Looking at the strange face, the uniform resembling a milkman's more than a cop's, Gene nodded as if hearing a simple direction; his throat burned (as if cut), and he was unable to say anything more to the man.

The cab took him to his own house, which was dark in the growing quick dusk. He went up to his bedroom for his car keys. On his bed was a large garment bag, of green plastic, stuffed with his clothes.

The night table contained his keys and credit cards and the plaque from the community group, department store receipts, two cigarette lighters that no longer worked, fountain pens that had already picked up a layer of dust, and many slips of paper with phone numbers and messages he no longer understood. He sat with the sight of it, picked up items and dropped them. But they held him, the dead objects, like nail parings saved because they were part of the body.

Then he walked down in darkness to the garage and his car. It had been closed up, and as he warmed the engine, the odor of the seats made him remember pleasantly days he drove out, nights that he went along the highway as the crowning pleasure of a day. (And even that had stopped when he became too busy and had time to get home, eat quickly, then fall asleep with the lights on and the night just begun.)

As he drove towards the Bronx, he recognized it better than he ever had, reaching the city line at last after the blank

edges of Mount Vernon, like a temporary outpost of people
who had planned to build a city there in some future. And the
stores along White Plains Road, the old neighborhood, which
always had reminded him of the facade rows in frontier towns
of cowboy movies, also seemed temporary, like a way station
on the road to a settled place. The black tracks of the elevated
trains over his head were silent, cutting out noise now as they
cut out seeing.

The funeral home was where it always had been along the
street, but it had a new facade, a Colonial brick front, with
white wooden doors and brass lamps jutting out. In front,
against the brick, were faces he knew without names, twice
removed cousins, others who had called themselves cousins
after the button business grew enormous, friends from the old
neighborhood, with less hair and more skin, church friends,
mostly women, neatly dressed and obedient, waiting like patients in an anteroom. The signal lights above, along the edge
of the elevated tracks, threw shades of red and green on faces
and hands, making movements upon the standing crowd.

The first greetings were handshakes, old friends who came
towards him worried about their lives, asking how he was, adding a few words on Santoro and the good he represented, giving their sorrow in a few words.

Gene had not yet gone inside and seen the reality. Not facing the truth of his father's dead presence, he felt this prema-
ture end in the street, a solemn moment of people struggling to
express the right emotion for him, like practice for another
occasion. No one had the words that prepared him for what
was inside and since none of the others had a father in there,
they could only placate Gene in a way they hoped they had
learned.

He went into the lobby, pink rugs and pink walls, air being blown through the room heavy with perfume. As he stopped to read the black announcement board, which listed the rooms of the different dead, a man — it was Angelo — came out of the crowd and threw his arms about Gene, crying in the same way he shouted and laughed, letting all of himself fall into it.

"I thought you were gone, too." Angelo stiffened his body, wiped his eyes with a handkerchief from his jacket pocket. "I'm so stupid. I started thinking you were in trouble. And then, with Pop going, that something happened to you, too."

"I just got off the plane," Gene said. "Tell me what it was. How did it happen?"

Angelo took his arm and led him through talking crowds, strangers who had left the inner rooms where the dead and their close relatives waited together. "A stroke, I think it was finally." Angelo held an arm on Gene's shoulders as they walked. "He wasn't exactly paralyzed. But he was gone. A week or so he was going like that. You could see it and you had no hope. But I don't think he was suffering."

"Did he talk to you?"

Angelo stopped, held Gene by the arm and looked at him. "No. He never said anything to me. He was in death but still breathing."

"Did he know I was still away? Did he ever say anything?"

Angelo did not answer. "Well. Let's say we still don't know. You're supposed to be on business. Gene. What happened?"

"I'm going to live there."

"Is that all?" Angelo patted his back. "Well, Poppa never knew one thing or the other. I talked to him the last weeks.

252

Before he went. He never had no hate for you. Nothing like the night of the money. He could forgive, you know."

"Forgive what? I never did anything to forgive. I didn't even take his money."

Angelo was silent, shaking his head slightly, embarrassed at the suggestion that the dead had anything less than perfect, saintly emotions. He began walking again, holding Gene's arm.

At the end of the carpeted hall, a gray curtain covered an entrance, but from inside the heavy sound of many conversations came through like the moaning of animals locked in night barns. Angelo pulled the curtain aside and stopped to look at the casket, supported and placed high on a carpet-covered platform, with rows of kneeling pews beside it and wreaths of flowers surrounding it all and hiding the neon light strips but not their blue light that ran along the ceilings and walls.

Angelo did not point, but it was clear that he wanted Gene to look, perhaps admire, the sight of their father, his rich casket, the many flowers. He took Gene's arm and brought him to face the casket and kneel.

Gene saw the face covered in powdery cosmetics, hair sprayed or lacquered, eyes swollen in some way. There was enough suggestion of his father in it, but the figure seemed wood more than flesh, and the body under the good gray suit was smaller and thinner than Santoro, like a wire outline of the man he had been.

When Gene finally saw the stubby hands, entwined with rosary beads, the stuck stiff moment of these hands, unable to embrace the beads, stiff as the glass of the beads themselves, his tears broke on him and he lowered his head to cry. The scraping at his throat — his resistance to the tears — hurt like a knife, but he continued and lost the sense of time. When he was finished, he was embarrassed to turn, expecting to find all the others watching him. But only Angelo was looking, and at the edge of the front row of chairs, in black, Francine was smiling.

He went to her and leaned down to embrace her, seeing her face without makeup, as if called suddenly out into the streets in morning. She did not speak, but pointed to Anna and his mother, sitting along the row of chairs near the center of the room and closest to the casket.

Gene went to them. His mother waited for his kiss, his embrace, then smiled and asked him to look at Santoro. "Doesn't he look good?" she said in Italian, and Gene nodded as his eyes filled with tears, and he looked up to see other women in the next row nodding with him.

"Where did you go?" he heard his mother say.

"To a good place," he said. "Your country."

His mother did not answer, but Anna reached up and took his hands. "Gene. He died in my arms," she said. "*Me* he called. He called my name, and I went up and held him while it happened."

Gene nodded, knowing that he must help in her forgiveness, and he held her hands tightly. "Sit with us," she said, and moved aside so that Gene could sit between her and their mother, who looked steadily at her husband.

After a long while, Gene saw Angelo near the curtains waving to him, and he stood up quickly and went to him, going along the hallway again. "Come out here," Angelo said. "I just been making lists for the funeral cars and collecting from people who are giving. What should I put you down for?"

"As much as you want," Gene said.

Angelo smiled at him and touched him with a hand again, caressing his shoulder. He had been worried that Gene away, Gene who had refused the money, thought nothing of this rite; now he was relieved and happy, as if Gene had said something flattering about his own life.

"Let's go outside a minute," he said to Gene. "I just want to show you something." He led Gene to the double doors and the street. "Look down this block," he said. "You remember this neighborhood? Remember when we were kids here? You could go up for an ice cream, a Pepsi, a pizza on Sunday night, and that was before everybody discovered it. Or we'd buy the dough and Momma would make it home and we could eat outside under the grapes and there was no soot and shit on top of everything. You know the grapes die now. From the air! And the ones that come out, they got skins like leather, just to live. That's what it is. It's hell now. A kid can't even walk here. A girl they'll pull her into doorways and give it to her right away. There's people from jungles here. Kids in their own cars, dropping beer cans on the sidewalks. Motorcycle men. And not just blacks, you know. Our own people. And all of them. They're like dogs in the night. The more they got, the more they shit on their neighborhood. The fucks! I could kill them all."

Gene looked but did not see the change. Angelo was venting himself of emotions that had been locked in the funeral parlor, where they had been stirred into being and held in.

"And you want to get out of it altogether," Angelo said. "Is that what you're telling me?"

"I'm running, that's what I said." As Gene spoke, an elevated train passed and covered him with noise. "But in my mind, I didn't think I was running from this. Is it different?"

"Just come down and talk to people." Angelo held his hand to Gene's arm again. "But listen, let me ask you. You're not going to leave a family back here for others. I got enough on my back."

"Don't worry." Gene saw the big face trying to be firm when it was only able to be sad, ill with guilt from the living as well as the dead, in war with indignation and pity. "Angelo. Listen. I never leave my debts for others."

"Thanks." Angelo moved his arms around Gene's shoulders again; since he had been leading people to the casket his movements in touching others had increased. "Now tell me one last thing," he said, leaning close to Gene's face. "Are you splitting up? Is that why Italy?"

"If you mean getting married again or thinking about it, then no. A man in Naples told me he couldn't understand the way we divorce over here. Why exchange the disease of marriage for another form of it." Gene was looking at the traffic, the horror Angelo described, but it was tawdry as it had always been. "Yet there is one thing," he said. "If Francine will not come. Then I'm going anyway. Phil Di Maris already helped me get some work there."

Angelo rubbed his hands together. "There's a lot of importing going on. Macaroni, oil, new things. Shoes, they say, and even peppers, eggplants, flowers. Maybe we can get into something. I got the money."

Gene did not answer, but turned to the entrance where the lights had become dim. "That's the signal," Angelo said. "They close at ten. Let's go inside and see him again."

256

The various families came out silently as the two men walked in. Meeting Francine and Anna with Mrs. Santoro in the hallway, they went to the street, to the noise again, night walkers passing unaware of them.

Gene walked to his car with Francine, after saying good-night to the family. It was as if time had crossed out the weeks he was gone. She took his hand as they walked, and he felt her familiar touch, the knowledge of it like the grasp of a friend, the touch of the few who knew him, who accepted him at all hours.

They drove in silence, the movement beginning to stir the dizziness in Gene from his flight. "I thought you were dead," Francine said finally.

"That's what Angelo said. I'm sorry now, the way I did it all. You either stay away, or you don't —"

"Well, if you want to leave a wife, it's better just to tell her."

"No, no." Gene could not say more.

"Yes," she said. "It's true. But maybe it doesn't mean so much anymore."

He did not answer, and they continued to the house, Francine waiting for the car to stop in the garage before speaking again. "Well, do you want one now? And your kids? They're inside there, sleeping. They're here for the funeral."

"I'll tell you what I want, tomorrow," Gene said, but when they reached the bedroom and were ready for bed, Francine began to talk about his luggage. "Do I unpack? What do I do with it?"

"You leave it. And if you want, you pack, too."

Her face that had taken death was calmer than it had ever

been and beautiful to him; for a while it did not gyrate in movement, like a secretary chewing gum. "Do I understand you correctly?" she said. "I am to pack my bags. Leave everything as it is. My home and my friends, maybe even my kids. Just say good-bye all and go live somewhere I don't know at all."

Gene was seated at the foot of the bed, looking at her, the standing figure, erect, pretty in the stiff pose she assumed when she was angry or shaken. "Angelo was talking about the old neighborhood down there to me. The filth. The madness. This is really some paradise you hate to leave —"

"Oh stop it, Gene. I told you so many times. And what the hell is over there but starvation. Where the lights go out and the water doesn't run and they strike every week. That paradise you want me to go into. That home of nothing works."

She turned and walked into the bathroom before he could answer. Gene lay back on his pillow, the vertigo from flying spinning inside. He shut his eyes until he heard her in the room again. "Only the people work," he said.

"What? Two hours a day before they take a nap." She made sounds at her dressing table, bottles tinkling, jars lifted and put down.

"The people are the thing that works. Like human *feelings*, like seeing one another — I don't know if I make myself clear. The difference between flesh and blood and ants."

"Like I said before, you must have felt a lot of feelings over there —"

"And like *I* said, you think it's a cathouse whenever I tell you there's decent human feeling over there. Even strangers. Oh, the hell with it. Say I went crazy like you always say and

258

the rest of them must be saying now. Because I found out I never really even liked living here. Even at its best. Maybe that's how you and I are different. I never knew it until I got there, though. You might see it, too. But the Bronx — when I grew up, I loved it. It was my childhood; why not. What did I know. Your childhood is like a dream right away and you love it in your stupid stuffed head, as fast as you forget it. But it was *always* rotten fucking apartment houses, with fathers who came home seven o'clock half dead — thank God, Pop fought his way out of it. And we had cement streets to play stickball on and the ugly trains overhead. And my museums were stores and more stores. What a great sight. But. But then we got the dream; we got Westchester. And I ought to know it. I helped build this living cemetery myself. I don't think *any* of us ever liked it here, this dead place with empty streets. And people around here who never liked us — we were too *dark* for them."

He opened his eyes and sat up. Francine had turned around and was listening. "I want to go," he said. "It's the only thing I ever wanted for myself. All the rest, I did it the way you were supposed to do it. Schools, and the shingle, and business. For those who quit school, you went right away into the electricians or to learn the stone work from an uncle. If you work your ass off long enough, you get to build a house. America has to make a statue for us — we were the uncomplaining drones, the donkeys. Let them make a statue of a smiling jackass — the wop who works. Who smiles from the shoestand, who takes any shit, who lets them call him anything. Do you understand that just the way we look is something to laugh at here? So stick around for that. I told you I'm going. I ask you once more if you want to come."

259

"Yes, you *are* crazy. And *no,* I don't want to come, and if I did, I wouldn't want to come like this — the way you just said it."

"What I just said? It's the way I feel. I'm not crazy. I found something I like. Do you want to see it?"

Francine put up her hands, wet with cold cream. "No."

"You're not chained here," Gene said. "Why do you do this to me?"

"*Do* to you? You make me leave my home and family. And now, right *now* when a father's gone —"

"*Now* is the time. Now is the sanction to go. Don't you get that?"

Her face was suddenly shocked, as if Gene had negated the grief she believed he felt. She turned her back to him and slowly rubbed the cream on her face. "The things I like. My friends. For all time." Her voice was low, as if talking to herself. "Is it so nice to be *alone,* even in Rome?"

"I never said it was nice to be alone. It's hard to get used to not having the world you know. The things you know by habit, without looking." He stood up, about to go to her, but stopped to give more attention to his thoughts. "But I don't have to tell you how alone inside a person can be here." He saw her smiling and went to her, touched her face with his hands, put his lips against her cheek.

"I can hide here." Francine said it softly, against his face.

Gene stood up and smiled. "Wait till you see it. You'll get feelings you never knew. That make you like other ways. And you'll even feel it's not so bad being Italian. You might even feel some pride."

"What the hell does that mean. I don't need no Rome to feel pride —"

Gene walked back and sat down, shaking his head. "You know what I know, even if you can't say it. We're second-rate around here. Too short and too dark and we got too much black hair and we're too heavy-set — what about the money you and Anna spend just to get blonde every week."

"That's only style. Blonde happens to be in style right now; that's all."

"All right, then what's in style over there is *me*. Everything likes me there. I match."

Francine was embarrassed with the strength rising in Gene's voice, a disgrace to death, which requires at least doubt in selfish plans: he was running from the place his father now would never leave, abandoning the network that they must keep together, that death demands — loyalty to the cemetery plot they had just bought, large enough for all of them; Angelo had spoken about it this morning, defining each person's space in the plot and the charges.

Gene had seen her shocked face and stopped himself, turning around and resting his head on his pillow.

She switched off the small lamp and came to her bed and lay down. "Are you asleep, Gene?"

"Yes," he said.

"Put some cover over you."

"Yes."

"Gene? Would it be possible to try it out?"

"Try what out?"

"Rome."

"You'd have the right to leave when you wanted. It isn't a criminal sentence."

"And the house?"

"Rent the house. Sell the business or have Larry run it for

us. The kids could even stay here in school. I'll explain it to-morrow."

Gene turned the switch of his lamp, moved his body under the covers. The total darkness reminded Francine that she had been sleeping with lights on, and the dark brought the rage that eluded her, Gene's running away. After the first moods, alone and desperate, she had found calm, night after night without the demands in his presence, his schedule. But now he was no longer the man who came to breakfast clean-shaven and silently ready, expecting her to be ready each day but never expressing pleasure in what she had waiting.

So much of what he had said had disgraced her: that they should change their lives, at their age, and be what they never were. Rome itself she had seen as a dream world, more the stuff of TV than life, fit to imagine but not to live in and certainly not for her lifetime: it would be like suspension in air. And if something happened in this world of daily wars, they would be the first sacrifice, the first to be refused food.

In the darkness Gene found the steps of his emotions walking to death and saw his father as he had seen him tonight, the powdered replica, and then as he had known him years before, now never to be either young or dead father; it was the worst part of Santoro's present death that he could never be alive as the early father of Gene's mind, the father remembered, the loud, ambitious, spirited man he saw come off the train each night, leading all the neighborhood men from the station, his good suit looking still pressed, unaffected by work, a father whose arrivals gave him relief as he ran through the house and called to his mother of the coming.

That that father, who had been gone for thirty years, was gone again as Gene's thoughts received him in many ways and times, tore at Gene's throat continuously and filled up in him with tears and cries, almost choking him in the effort to erupt in enough sound for the grief that came. He felt Francine's hands softly on his shoulders, but could not turn or stop. She spoke to him but he could not make out the words because of his own sounds escaping without control.

When his voice subsided, he heard only the occasional sounds of passing cars on the nearby street and then was quickly asleep as the release removed his tension and permitted the exhaustion in him to fill him again.

23

In the morning his face felt bruised, as if he had been hit during the night; and his features seemed small, almost shriveled in his hands as he touched himself while shaving, tracing his facial lines.

While he dressed, his muscles moved stiffly, his thighs tight with the strain of long running. He went slowly to breakfast, enjoying the sight of the house, then drove off to see Larry Spina at the office.

Gene found him in the inner room, which had been Gene's private office. Larry was overdressed, clearly prepared for the funeral; still the glimpse of him among the memos was enough for Gene to see the daily breaking up of the man: Larry was signing papers, starting to dial numbers, rummaging through desk drawers. The rush of it informed itself to Gene: Larry was trying to rid himself of the work quickly: the point was to get it done in flurries before you might notice your revulsion. But the more you did fast, the more came to you and you were left with the satisfaction of the avalanche, and the money piling up beyond counting, and everything outside within reach of your wallet, though you had only a few weekend hours to grab for it all.

Larry was startled by the sight of Gene, hidden at the half-open door. "Who is it? What do you want?" Larry had screamed it, and his hands began scrambling for a weapon as Gene came the rest of the way. "Oh Christ! Gene. Gene. You're here!" Larry rushed to him, stumbling across the placement of chairs he had not yet memorized. He embraced Gene, squeezing him almost as if in fury, driven by the shock, the embarrassment of Gene with death, the guilt of his being in Gene's office and beginning to take over.

This mood made Larry anxious to work out an arrangement. "I'll even come over to you and make the reports," he said. "All by my lonesome."

"You really *could* take a vacation there, you know," Gene said.

"Sure, sure. I'd like to meet some nice Sofia. How about that."

Gene could not penetrate the dream pictures that Larry kept around him like a fog which prevented his movement out of the little squares of home.

Larry insisted on being driver for the day, giving his service as driver to keep the respect of his position next to Gene. "It's not necessary," Gene said. "The hired cars will be taking us."

"I know, I know. But I can drive you to the parlor and back home. Your mind won't be on driving."

They went out to the car and drove to Gene's house, where Larry parked in front, like a taxi. "I'll be a little while," Gene said. "I haven't seen the boys yet."

"Then I'll wait here," Larry said, and Gene left him, sitting straight, his eyes facing front, acting as a chauffeur with an unconscious humiliation Gene did not like.

The boys were waiting, sitting on the living room couch like guests, but rushed to Gene with the embraces they had had as children before they left.

Gene junior, who had inherited his father's seriousness and conscience, asked about his plans, facing him quickly with the embarrassing situation of the present, jumping over death with the ruthlessness of the young. "And Mother has been telling us — well, that things are also not so good between you. So you might be taking off on us."

Gene was so startled he sat down. *His* child as arbiter, the eighteen-year-old voice working itself into the right counseling tone, forced Gene to suppress a smile while he felt the irritation. "Just what did your mother tell you?" he said.

"When we got in the other day. About your wanting to stay abroad. And perhaps, alone. Because I gather she is not anxious to go." Gene junior looked at Frank, who nodded with the agonized feeling of sixteen years, his skin irritated already by the subject. "I didn't hear it all," Frank said, and coughed. "She doesn't always make too much sense." He saw his father's face reacting. "I mean, Dad. I mean in her order of logic. In that sense."

"Oh, I see. Her logic." In a few minutes he was enjoying them.

But they stood too respectfully, faced him as if he were lawyer for another cause. "I have to ask you, then, what would you think of a person who abandons his own country, to live in another place. Is this wrong?"

He looked at Gene junior, knowing him spokesman, and the boy seemed to chew the words. "Do you mean *Rome?* Yourself?"

"I mean me or anyone?"

"Could you make a living in this place?"

266

Gene began to laugh. "Yes, yes. I'll give you an audit of my books. Business is great. Phil Di Maris is stirring the pot. All the American hands are grabbing the Italian pie. And they need crooked Yankee lawyers to write contracts and such."

Frank was smiling. "You're OK, Pop," he said slowly, with a little of the heaviness of Angelo.

"Thank you. At least, when *you* think I'm crazy, you like it. All right, then. Come to crazy land with me. There's good schools. And I'll tell you a little about the land."

"It's great!" Gene junior lightened with an association. "I know it. Buddies of mine went there last summer on student trips. Oh, it's great." He was excited. "Be great to have a place to go. But I want to finish up here. And I think Frank —"

Frank was nodding. "I see," Gene said. "You can come for vacation."

"Yes, that's right." Gene junior turned to Frank. "That's great, isn't it. Flying over after school."

"You don't have to worry about us here," Frank said, and now Gene saw that they were appealing for a continuation of their lives.

They had become young men of the world he had sent them to in order to become better than himself and Francine. And that success seemed clear: except for Frank's family resemblances, both boys were taller, lighter than the family; they moved with the grace of American athleticism and spoke the Eastern prep dialect that Gene had heard for the first time at thirty, when he began to fight the old Connecticut landowners and their tyranny over property.

"I don't know how it's going to work," Gene said to their faces. "I can't tell you what money will be left in three more years. I don't really care, either. I can't starve." They were looking at him with the worry of old men. "Suppose I just quit work?"

"Why would you want to quit?" Frank said.

"Not to work anymore," Gene said. "And learn to get a little less grabby. All my friends, my age, we learned to grab too much. We've got to have things. You know, we're shit collectors." He saw Frank smiling again. "It's too much; we got too happy making piles."

Frank came to him and shook his hand. "You're OK," he said.

"Why do you keep saying that?" Gene rose, seeing Francine at the entrance to the room.

Frank turned to see his mother, but stood next to Gene. "I don't know. I think you're saying something right. But it's a little freaky."

"Freaky?" Gene took the new word. "Crazy, freaky. Well, come on."

They walked outside together, stopping at the car. "This is going to be very hard," Gene said. "I'll be holding my mother and Anna. I want you to stay together."

They nodded and moved into the car and the silence of their fear, and Larry drove down into the Bronx again. They were led through the funeral, driven in the black limousines, to Mass and its music and chanting, taming the sound of grief, then in lines behind the casket, walking in rows, up steps, driven in slow procession through the streets of the old neighborhood, in lines along the Thruway, in file and column at the cemetery, finally dismissed quickly after the burial. Gene had waited to watch the workmen around the grave, with a concern about the completion of the burial, but his driver honked a horn gently to speed him up.

Friends and cousins came to the castle, many with food and all with memories to fill in the years they had not met. The guard opened both gates and left them open. When Gene left, passing with the boys and Francine, he saw that the gate had remained open.

At home, Francine went upstairs, but the boys stopped Gene, asking him to sit and talk in the living room they hardly knew. "Frank and I were talking up at the big house. About what you said. How do you know you want to live over there forever?"

"I didn't say I know." He saw Gene junior with either fear or demands. "I'm only trying to get there. And maybe find out."

"Then why go! If you don't know." Frank had spoken up, perhaps in anger, too. "Isn't everything here?"

"I know what you mean. And I think it shakes you to get pulled away. But don't look at me like old men, like I'm the child." Gene had been on the couch, and now stood up. "I just don't want to go the rest of my life on the head of a pin, buying and selling. Like a human cash register." Gene passed before them, the ragged edges of conscience making them judges. "I can't explain it right. I tried to show your mother. Maybe you'd get it in ten years. If you had a life on a pin. When the big thing in life is to get home to your favorite Friday night TV show. Chewing on TV for the night. With the shades down so you can't think about the invaders. Oh, I suppose Rome has it, too. People stuck in their holes. But not for me there. It's new for me. I *see* everything. And I like the mess there. The chaos in the final analysis. It's good. The less the better. Inefficiency is better. I want to learn how to do one thing at a time. And not in the same rut. Your rut is your grave. It's the first cut in it." He looked down as his words had shaken up emotions and made him forget the boys as audience. "I can't talk anymore."

He left them, without their answer, and in the next days finished the arrangements with Larry Spina, going to the office a few hours each day, finding Larry anxious to prove himself and filling with the pleasure of being boss. The boys did not wait, asking to go back as soon as possible to school. Driving back with Gene, they began to ask about Italy as if the plan had now been made for years, accomplished and working. When he left them he thought they were changed. "Is it just me?" he asked. "Do I see you're both more in it now."

"Well, write us," Gene junior said, and turned to Frank, who smiled. "We'll want to hear how you're doing."

Frank kissed his cheek. "It's not such a big thing, is it?"

"Only a bad one," Gene said, and Frank smiled again.

When he came back he went to see his mother and Anna, both of whom had retired permanently into black, with faces that seemed to ask for a seat in shadows. They asked Gene to sell the castle and find a smaller house and were happy when Gene told them they could live in his house.

Neither Anna nor his mother seemed very interested in his leaving, as if it were unreal or beyond concern. Anna said she regretted that her children would not see as much of him, but her tone did not sound convincing. Anna's calm made her losses complete, and she was prepared to live in a small room again, with a window and a sewing machine, her money sleeping peacefully and having no more anger.

His mother told him she was afraid of airplanes and too tired for an ocean voyage; he must promise to visit her, speaking as if he were a few counties away. But she wanted him to go, her mind completely Italian again, cleansed of the broken English and its years, smiling into a vision and perhaps aware of a continuity with what she understood of Gene's talk. One day she would remember an old church in a part of Naples and remind him to go there; another, her memory would find a name, a cousin who had been in one of the towns along the Amalfi drive. "See Concetta Reparata in Massa." It pleased Gene, constructions which may have concerned people no longer there, yet making Italy a home.

He would return from the visits to find Francine in the middle of preparing, filling boxes from the accumulations of closets. She would ask him to help decide on clothes she had not worn in years. "Let's leave it for Anna," Gene said. "She can throw it away with less conscience. I'm terrible at it. My damn bureau drawers are full of little notes I can't even throw away. I saved my own crap too long. Just leave it or take it all."

"We'll get it done." Francine saw his face, crushed by the days, all the leaving, all the waste, pointing towards him. "You think of something else."

She was working on forgiveness, seeing more clearly that the stranger Gene had become was the cruelty of all other things not herself. First she had thought her decision was to be made to go, but in the packing days and watching Gene with everyone else, she was deciding to go along with him; and the place — Rome — was not on her mind. Even when they had made love and she thought Gene had learned something else from someone, she found herself pleased, as if she were not the only one who was needed to think him attractive.

But the packing was change, and it came with exhaustion, almost like illness. She was too tired to sit with Gene at night, to come down when Phil Di Maris came to talk with Gene, finally being called down by Phil, who told her Gene would be back in a year because he couldn't leave his home *turf*. "You'll get sick of it," Phil said. "I've done business with them. And they'll drive you nuts."

He left his addresses and deals to come, dismissing Gene's assurances that he would not cooperate. "Just don't expect any action from me," Gene said at his door, as Phil was leaving. "Get that straight."

"All right, all right. Go ahead. Go fuck around." Phil squeezed his hand, then struck his shoulder, and walked away.

Gene left a few days later, another plane, going to find another apartment, larger and permanent. Bianca was to have the one he had left, and she was waiting there.

But the apartment had been changed by her, with curtains she had made and a cloth on the table and flowers in vases. "You're making it a home, and you should have it," he said.

"No. It cannot be my home, I think."

Gene believed it was the coming of his family she sensed and what it was in him. "I understand. You see how I am. I hope I didn't lie too much to you."

"No." Bianca shook her head. "I told you I was getting old. Twenty-six. But I met another person. He is from Portici."

They had been facing the curtains. Gene smiled at her. "I don't know why that suddenly shocks me," he said. "As if I found you here, and you were supposed to be my possession."

"Yes, I know it. But it was good to be with you and feel that."

"Shall we meet at family reunions?" Gene sat down, looking at her. "Come sit on the couch. Tell me what we do."

She smiled and shook her head. "If people did what they

wanted, we would do what we want." She took a few steps back and Gene noticed her legs. She smiled at his look and came to sit down. "It is a very confusing net. Too many people want each other."

Gene sat back. "Well, at least I got away easy this time. I got back. And I saw the Pantheon walking over here. And you're here."

"And you are not the same."

"No. Of course not."

She took his face in her hands, tracing the lines of his face with her fingers. She had fallen in love with him in Amalfi, and in another way in Reggio; it was like the love for a father, though she would not explain that now and bring on his worry of age. And he was at the age that events make quickly change, looking much older than he had been before he left. "You were my first American," she said.

"And what does that mean? A list?"

"No, no list. I mean, we all are attacked by Americans. I know them. But you were the first I thought was human."

She stood up and started for the bedroom.

"Will you explain that?" Gene asked.

"No," she said, and walked inside.

Gene sat alone, his thoughts losing Bianca until her voice, singing as she prepared for bed, came to him, a sound separated from her, the song alone in the room.

Now she would drift into Rome, and the streets would become alive for himself.

And what he had already done here was not piled up like acts that had to be paid for by justifying days. They had happened; they were *there*, like pages in a book, a story he understood. He could see it because he did not lose it in forgetting.

273

Forgetting nothing. A thought as thin as a wisp of smoke had everyone in it, from children to fathers, past to present. The whiskey he poured was an inch or two of gold, at one with the Pantheon that held still, a picture in his mind from passing it an hour ago.

Did Rome hold it in its own air, as if magic were true, the continuum unpolluted here in a place or here in him? He knew what he could not tell, and could not tell what he knew.